Ludwika

by

Christoph Fischer

First published in Great Britain in 2015

This book is a work of fiction and any similarities with real people and events are unintentional. Although some elements of the book are inspired by true events and real people that I have encountered during my life, this book does not contain their stories. Their lives have nothing to do with the characters and the story I have told.

Create Space ISBN – 13978 - 1519539113

Create Space ISBN – 1519539118

Cover design by Daz Smith of nethed.com

Over the years chance has moved many great friends out of my life. This is dedicated to two who were found again:

Ofer Hamburger and Anni Kunzmann,

With gratitude and best wishes to Andy, Maxine, Christina, Lisa and the extended Gierz and Florko family.

www.christophfischerbooks.com

Table of Contents

Part 1

Chapter 1

October 1939

There was a loaded silence over Przedborów. On a sunny October's afternoon the Polish village and its surroundings should have been heaving with harvesting activities and Ludwika Gierz should have been looking after the livestock, followed closely around by her five-year-old daughter Irena and maybe some other kids whose parents couldn't look after them during the busy season.

Children liked Ludwika for her cheerful attitude, the many songs she knew and the enthusiastic way she would sing them. She didn't need to 'look after' the little ones to keep them under control like other parents did. She could keep doing her chores and often even found a voluntary helping hand from her following, which made her the perfect nanny.

She was 22, playful and always in good spirits. Her infectious mood made her the pied piper of the village and commanded children's attention effortlessly. Other parents were in awe and frequently took advantage of this talent.

Today, the streets of the sleepy border village were almost deserted. Many had fled from the area during the recent German invasion and had tried their luck further east, only to witness the entire country fall into the hands of the aggressors a few weeks later.

This being harvest time, farmers couldn't as easily abandon their homes to seek safety with relatives in houses away from the border, and so many stayed. They thought the country would only need to defend its borders for a short time until the allied powers, who had guaranteed to protect it, could mobilise their troops and counter attack the German army. A multi-fronted war and foreign troops on its own soil invading from France would soon make Hitler see sense and withdraw. That had been the hope.

Initial Polish resilience faltered with the border regions being overrun. Ludwika's father had disappeared with the retreating troops and she hadn't heard a word from him since. The Germans had annexed large parts of the country and behaved every bit as barbaric as had been feared. Civilians were shot on even the suspicion of resistance and many were arrested, never to be seen again. The hopes for a British bombardment of German cities and an attack by the

French turned out to be false and when Russia began to invade Poland from the East, the fate of the nation seemed sealed.

By now, the entire Polish Army had been defeated and disarmed, yet, Ludwika had no way of knowing whether her father had been killed, interned or deported. There were rumours that some soldiers had escaped and were part of a resistance movement. Few of those who had left for safety at the beginning of the war had managed to return to Przedborów since; the Germans wouldn't allow them enter what was now part of the Reich. The villagers who had stayed behind had to endure random acts of violence by their occupiers, many were evicted from their homes to make space for the occupying forces, and the rest had to try and keep the farms going with the severely reduced manpower.

Not knowing about their father was torturous and were it not for her daughter Irena, Ludwika would have broken down a long time ago.

Ludwika felt young but she had replaced her mother as the leader of the female pack. The Gierz women were attractive and three of her sisters had married and left the home already.

Ludwika, her youngest sister Stasia and her mother Agnieska had to work the farm on their own for now, which they did with dedication and a sense of duty for the family and the country.

Without her father or other helpers it was impossible to do everything; the women had to make tough decisions. The most important thing had been to keep the animals alive. Theoretically, her father could defeat the pessimists by returning any day and it might not be too late then to borrow farm machinery and empty some of the fields. However, as more time passed without word from him or the other men of the village, and with no sign of political improvement, the pressure mounted to rescue as much of the crop as they could.

Ludwika and her sister began harvesting the wheat. It was exhausting having to do such a big field with only scythes but it was the best that they could do. Ludwika had seen Karol Wojick, one of the neighbouring farmers hide parts of his machinery in a shed in the woods before he had joined the defence. Many of those who had decided to flee the invasion had taken as much of their valuables with them as possible and hidden the rest in the hope of retrieving them later. This had created a shortage of material and, coupled with the reduced manpower, made the farming work so much harder.

"We'll never get it all to safety like this," Stasia said, looking with frustration at her scythe and throwing it on the ground. "If the rain comes it will all go to waste."

Ludwika understood.

"Keep your heart up," she said. "Look what we've managed already. We can be proud."

She pointed at the wheat they had cut.

"We need to get it off the field, too," Stasia added, close to tears.

"Don't worry," Ludwika said, trying to stay optimistic. Her sister was right, though. Something needed to be done soon. Yet, as much as she tried, she couldn't come up with any good solution. Then it hit her – the farm equipment Wojick had hidden in the woods.

"I've got an idea," she said and told her sister about the shed.

"You're crossing a line," Stasia warned her when she heard the plan. Her voice, however, carried more admiration for Ludwika's audacity than it did gloom or worry.

"Sooner or later the 'szkopy' will find the shed and take away what's in it," Ludwika replied defiant.

Stasia giggled at her sister using such a bad word for the Germans. Even though they were alone, she looked carefully around to see if any of the 'castrated rams' could hear them.

"Better it got some use before then," Ludwika said, serious despite the joke.

"We promised mother not to take any risks," Stasia said, although her warning sounded half-hearted.

"You know I have to do it," Ludwika said and Stasia nodded. "There is so much wheat," Ludwika pointed out. "We can't let it go to waste. We've got no alternative. Collecting it by hand would take too long; and you said yourself that the next rain will ruin it all. We have no choice and the Wojicks aren't using it, are they?"

Stasia grabbed the scythe and bent down to cut more wheat.

"I'll be waiting for you with the bushels," she said.

Stasia was always so full of energy and optimism and Ludwika was grateful that the brief moment of weakness had been overcome.

"Be careful," her sister added without turning around. "We all need you."

"I will," Ludwika replied, although she didn't know if being careful was going to be enough.

It hadn't been difficult to break the lock of Wojick's shed and even less difficult to get the old tractor going that she found there. Her brother Franz had borrowed it often in the past. He had drowned in the river two years ago. The memory of his passing still stung Ludwika; she missed him more than ever. But thanks to watching him closely when he used the tractor, she would be able to bring the bushels off the field and into the safety of their family farm.

Ludwika's dark curly hair kept falling into her face as she steered the tractor out of the woods and onto the open road. She had lost her hair band somewhere on the way and was struggling to keep a clear vision. For her, this was a welcome distraction from the dangers that were looming and were foremost in her mind. That engine made a terrible noise; she worried over the attention it could bring. Would the 'szkopy' allow her drive on the road, she wondered? Would they confiscate the tractor if they saw her? Would they beat her as they had done with so many others for no good reason? Anything a Pole could do was automatically 'verboten', it seemed. If she was found, the Germans would understand, surely - the crop had to come in. It was already late in the season, since the war had delayed the harvest. What did the invaders intend to do, let the harvest go to waste? Didn't they need provisions, too?

She kept her eyes steadily on the road and tried not to think about the dangers.

The Germans had not been seen around their tiny village for a few days, which had been one reason why Ludwika went ahead with this risky enterprise on her own.

At a height of 4 foot 10, with piercing blue eyes, an attractive bone structure and a curvy figure, Ludwika turned many a head. Her beauty, once an asset, had attracted the wrong kind of attention from the brutish soldiers. She wished for her hair band now to help distract from her features.

The roads into the village were deserted, only some women were digging for potatoes in the neighbouring field. The tiled roofs of Przedborów's stone farmhouses nestled into the woodland, surrounded by sheds, stalls and orchards. It was difficult to know what was going on behind the next farm. What was a quiet and peaceful atmosphere in the days before the invasion, now felt eerie. The women in the field were visibly relieved when they realised that the engine noise they heard was coming from Ludwika's tractor and not a German tank. Soon she would join Stasia on the wheat field. Ludwika hadn't felt comfortable leaving her sister alone but today it was unavoidable. For a 17-year-old, Stasia was mature in looks, and very pretty. She was also overconfident and loud and likely to do something hasty. Ludwika feared this would make her a target for passing soldiers; it was a constant worry for her family.

Still, Ludwika wouldn't know what she would do without her little sister. They supported each other in this frightening time and kept each other's spirit up. They refused to believe the rumours that all Polish people would be deported from their properties and that their land and livestock be given to German settlers. With so many empty houses and farms around, the Germans couldn't possibly have enough workers to take them all over? Surely the Poles who had stayed behind and hadn't been deported would be left their possessions. Ludwika couldn't imagine this 'cleansing' to happen as many feared. Regardless of how shockingly violent the force used by the occupiers had been so far, things had to calm down and sense had to prevail. All bad things would come to pass and might even return near to normal, she told herself. Whenever their mother believed those rumours and got herself worked up, the sisters had each other to put things into perspective and keep calm.

Today's desertion of the village was due to another one of those rumours. Further north, Germans were said to be clearing entire villages and forcing the inhabitants to march east. The more hysterical reports even claimed that people were being led into the woods and killed by machine-gun fire. Others told stories of children being taken from their parents, to be given to childless couples in Germany. Who had heard of such cruelty?

Seeing other Polish farmers showed Ludwika that she was not the only one who believed the stories to be exaggerations and scare mongering.

She was almost at her field and could see Stasia waving at her when she heard the sound of a motorbike behind her. On it sat a German soldier who waved at her to get out of his way. She pulled over, expecting him to step down and talk but he gestured her to get off the road altogether. She only had a few yards to the next crossing, behind which lay the exit to her field. When she tried driving on the man blocked her way and pulled out a gun. She ducked and lost control of the vehicle, which now swerved into the ditch by the road. The soldier put the gun away and mounted the tractor, pulling her roughly from the seat. She pointed at her field repeatedly, hoping he would understand. She didn't speak any German. She pointed at herself and said "Ludwika" and then pointed at the field and said "Ludwika." He finally got it and drove the tractor out of the ditch for her and onto the field as she had intended to do herself. She ran after him and managed to catch up with the tractor as he stepped down. He pointed at himself and said "Manfred"; he bowed, then did the Hitler salute and went quickly back to his motorbike. Not a minute too soon as it turned out. He only had got back on the bike and started driving when a convoy of army vehicles came up behind him and rolled past the field into the village.

Their sudden appearance was a worry. On the other hand, Ludwika told herself, Manfred the soldier had been very kind, which he wouldn't have been if the Germans were up to something terrible. She even found him rather handsome: about her age, broad but also tall and quite strong. She had noticed his dark hair and skin; she reckoned he was probably Austrian or Bavarian, like her school friend Lena's cousin.

She gave a little smile at the thought of the handsome German and then climbed back onto the tractor and drove to the end of the field

Stasia made a suggestive face when Ludwika pulled up next to her. It was so typical of her to try and lighten an otherwise tense situation. The sisters laughed and began filling the tractor's trailer with the bushels. Some of them had already gone off: the field should have been harvested weeks ago. When they couldn't fit any more wheat on, they drove towards their farm. German troops could be seen at several of the houses that they passed. Was this a routinely check or could this be the 'cleansing' that rumours had warned them about?

Ludwika's felt nervous but she drove on. She had to. She was glad that she had made Stasia hide within the wheat Her sister wouldn't see what she witnessed: she watched as the Melniks, an elderly couple, were dragged from their home, the harsh barking commands of a German soldier ringing in the air, mingling with the fearful screams of Mrs Melnik as she was dragged towards a waiting truck. Ludwika kept going, glad that nobody seemed to pay her any attention. She worried what she might find at her home.

They reached the Gierz farm safely: it wasn't large but, unlike many others, the main building was made of stone, which was a big advantage in the winter and it had a good-sized barn with stalls. Her father had always taken pride in appearances and had maintained everything well. Ludwika immediately drove the tractor into the barn, hidden from the street behind the house. Once Stasia had come out of the wheat they locked the door. Nobody needed to see the tractor. They rushed to reunite with their mother Agnieska and Ludwika's daughter Irena and were relieved to find the two of them unharmed in the cow shed. Neither sister mentioned what was going on in the village. Their mother was worried enough when Stasia told her about the poor state of the harvest. Irena was over the moon to see her mother and after she had fussed enough about Ludwika, the girl asked for all four women to sing her favourite tune about the goose, the fox and the hunter.

Their rendition got interrupted by the sound of gun shots and machine-gun fire coming from the village.

"Oh my God…" Agnieska started to panic, but Ludwika gave her a warning look, nodding towards Irena.

"How funny," Ludwika said quickly to her daughter, who seemed more curious than frightened, judging from her expression. "They must be having fireworks again."

"The Germans always have fireworks," Stasia said and forced a laugh.

"How silly of them," Irena said and laughed, too.

Ludwika smiled back and said: "Yes, how silly indeed."

Agnieska shook her head in disapproval; she had long given up persuading Ludwika to be truthful with the child. Agnieska made no secret of her feelings that such cushioning could only harm Irena. In her opinion, the child needed to know what the Germans were really like, or else she could run into serious danger. Ludwika disagreed.

There were more 'fireworks' and Agnieska's eyes went wide with terror. She clung to her youngest daughter. Her panic showed and began to infect Stasia, whose lower lip quivered as fear began to take hold of her. Ludwika acted fast.

"We're going to play a game now," she said and winked at Irena. "We're going to sneak back to the main house without letting the Germans or anyone else sees us. I'm going to show you: I'll crawl behind the pig sty on all fours, I'll look if anyone can see and then I'll quickly run the remaining metre to the back door. Then you'll do the same and then Stasia and then grandmother. How do you like that?"

Irena smiled and nodded.

When Ludwika got to the edge of the pig sty she could see that no Germans had come to their farm yet. Irena, Stasia and Agnieska got safely into the main house and began to prepare dinner. Frightened and tense they went about their business, subdued as they waited for the soldiers to knock on their door. When the knock came, Agnieska insisted on opening the door and told the others to quickly hide. An old and grim-looking German police officer, two young assistants without uniform and a Polish translator forced their way into the house and searched the premises. Irena's giggling gave the women away and the Germans ordered them out of their hiding in the loft and brought them downstairs where the officer took a look at the official papers for all of the family. Compared to what Ludwika had witnessed happening to the Melniks this was incredibly respectful and surprising.

The man slowly wrote down all details, while conferring with the translator. Irena smiled all the time and hid her face in her mother's cooking apron, still treating this like a game.

When the policeman saw Ludwika's name he grinned. He said something in German and showed the document to the translator, who nodded knowingly. Ludwika was sure she had heard the name 'Manfred'.

"It is my pleasure to inform you that you have been selected for the process of Germanisation and are permitted to stay here," the translator said. "We hope you'll appreciate this great honour bestowed upon you. You will hear from the new administration soon."

"Germanisation?" Stasia asked. Agnieska looked at her daughter, worried that the question was seen as a provocation. Fortunately, the man didn't seem to mind.

"You're part of the Reich now," he explained and smiled warmly. "All Polish citizens will vacate the village and move to the southeast of the country, now called the General Government."

The assistants returned from their tour of the farm and gave the officer the all clear.

"Heil Hitler!" the policeman said and extended his arm to the salute.

He looked expectantly at the women in front of him.

The translator also said "Heil Hitler" and gestured for everyone to do the same with a strong sense of urgency. Ludwika was the first to understand and comply, the others followed suit.

After the intruders had left the farm the woman looked at each other, astonished by what had happened.

"Allowed to stay?" Agnieska asked. "How mighty of them."

"I wonder how many in the village were selected," Stasia said. "So the rumours were true and the Germans are making people leave."

"That would be silly," Ludwika said and nodded meaningful at Irena, who was blissfully playing with her food, "with all the work that needs to be done. Don't be so pessimistic. It probably means they know we are no Jews. They're the ones the Germans are after and since we're not Jewish we're safe. That's what Germanisation must mean."

"Oh dear," Agnieska said. "The Melniks are Jewish. God help them."

She buried her head in her apron. "And we'll see what will become of us, too," she added.

Chapter 2

The next day, Ludwika and Stasia tried to rescue as much of the wheat as they could while leaving Agnieska and Irena at home to take care of the animals. The village had become very quiet and in the evening, when the sisters came home from the field, their mother told them that most people had been evacuated, exactly as the rumours had predicted. The luckier ones of the exiled villagers had been granted a few minutes to collect their belongings; the majority were simply forced onto trucks and taken to a transition camp in Torun without such privileges.

"Who's going to buy our wheat now?" Agnieska asked. "How are we going to run the farm without petrol and men to do the hard work?"

Irena looked with concern at her grandmother's stern face.

"Don't listen to her," Ludwika said and put Irena on her lap. "We're going to be fine."

She started singing the song about the goose, the fox and the hunter and Irena quickly joined in.

The next day Ludwika and Stasia continued with their harvest. They could see people in the potato field next to them but they were strangers. As it turned out, the Germans had already brought their first settlers to the village.

Over the next week more arrived from all parts of Germany. Some who had been allowed to stay, such as Ludwika and her family, had their farms taken over by those hated 'szkopy' and were being reduced to the state of servants in their own homes, made to sleep in sheds and barns, and surrendering their living quarters to the imperious intruders. Their status and treatment, from what Ludwika and Stasia could see in the potato field, was more that of slaves than of employees.

It could only be a matter of time before the same fate would befall the Gierz farm, Agnieska warned her daughters.

The three women were scared of making contact with their new neighbours, who had an air of gloating self-satisfaction about them. Some seemed friendlier than others but, as Agnieska warned, how could you trust people who had simply stolen the land they now lived on. Ludwika was the only one who managed to walk through the village smiling. Not because she felt like it but because she knew better than to provoke the wrath of the 'szkopy'. Thus far, her family was one of very few who still had control of their own farm and she hoped this would continue until the political circumstances stabilised. The Wagner family, Polish citizens of German descent, were now fully accepted members of the Third Reich and were quick to rub necks with the newcomers. Ludwika guessed that would come to haunt them when Poland was rescued.

A few days later, quite late in the evening, the German soldier Manfred came to visit her. He was driving a small truck this time and brought two men with him. They were Poles. One of them spoke German and related what Manfred had to say.

"Herr Tischler is pleased that you were allowed to stay," the Pole said with a distinct mocking tone in his Polish. "This fellow promises to keep an eye on you to make sure you will be treated as best as possible. He has sent us here to help you with the farm and has arranged that the wheat be collected. Mister Big-Shot here has written a personal recommendation for you that you are to keep and show in case of any trouble with the authorities or fellow German citizens. He is giving you this German dictionary so that you can all learn the language as soon as possible. He hopes you will take advantage of it so when he comes to visit you next he can speak to you. That is his only request."

The Polish man sounded tired and bored with his task and did not put any emphasis on the words he spoke; unlike Manfred whose enthusiasm oozed from every word, even though the women couldn't understand them. During the entire conversation Manfred could not take his eyes of Ludwika, and he had a smile that could not be wiped off his face. Ludwika returned his smile, more shy and reserved, to express her gratitude and humbleness. She understood and agreed with the translator's sarcasm. Unlike him, though, she was not willing to risk showing even the slightest bit of resistance.

Ludwika thanked the German on behalf of the family and promised to try her best to get to grips with the new language.

"If you need help, he advises to ask the 'boys'," the translator said with obvious disapproval and reluctance. "That means me," he added.

"Thank you again," Ludwika said. Although she appreciated the effect of his grand gesture, she was outraged at his presumption and felt very uneasy about the translator hearing her every word. She knew that by accepting gifts and preferential treatment it was only a small step to collaboration with the enemy – or accusations to that effect. If she said too much, the Polish people would hate her, if she said too little, Manfred might feel rejected and her family might suffer in return. The German was only a boy himself. The way he had pulled out his gun on the road, only to immediately turn into a helpful and kind gentleman. . . there was a lack of experience and established routine in his mannerisms, yet he had to have some influence to save the Gierz family. If only she knew more about military ranks to grasp how influential an Untersturmführer actually was. His three silver pip collar patch looked mighty but he seemed too young for such a mighty position.

Manfred didn't stay long, saving her the awkward toeing of the line between gratitude and reserve that was needed. He excitedly shook her hand with both of his, saluted her with "Heil Hitler!" and then disappeared into the night.

The room turned quiet for a few minutes afterwards while everyone digested the news.

"I'm Michal," the translator broke the silence and shook hands with everyone. He was strong, maybe 30, with pale skin and blond hair, tall and lanky and looked permanently angry and dissatisfied.

"This is Piotr," he said, pointing at his comrade. Piotr was the same age but smaller and stocky.

Michal then told them their story. . .

The two men were from eastern Poland, which by now had been entirely annexed by Russia. They had been part of the Polish army units that surrendered in Radom early on in the war. While many of their colleagues had been shot or kept in prisoner camps, Michal and Piotr had been amongst those selected for farm work.

"We are lucky to be with a Polish family," Piotr said. "Everyone else has come to work for German settlers," he told Ludwika. He was more optimistic and at ease with his lot than Michal.

"I hope the German keeps his infatuation for you," Michal said suggestively to Ludwika, "or we'll all suffer. You better start learning German quick."

Ludwika ignored him. She took Irena by the hand and brought her to bed, while Agnieska offered the men shots of Slivovitz and pickled eggs. Irena was excited and wouldn't fall asleep easily.

Ludwika had to read her several stories before her daughter drifted off. When she got downstairs, the men had already gone to bed, exhausted from their travels. Agnieska had made up beds for them in Franz's empty room.

"I hope your father is safe somewhere like this," she said and kneeled down in the corner to pray.

"Ludwika Tischler," Stasia said playfully, again trying to make light of the tense situation. "That has got a good ring to it."

"Are you completely mad?" Ludwika hissed at her. "You mustn't joke about me and that man. People might think that I have feelings for him and that our privileges are all my doing. We'll forever be branded as Nazis. You can't be too careful."

Stasia waved her hand dismissively, stood up and began doing the dishes.

The next day Michal and Piotr continued the harvest of the wheat field, leaving Ludwika and Stasia safely at home and free to clean the animal sheds that had been neglected over the last week. Late afternoon, Agnieska returned from the village shop with tears in her eyes. To be able to talk freely to her mother, Ludwika sent Irena to pick some wildflowers for the house as decorations.

"Maybe there are still some cornflowers left," she said and Irena went excitedly on her way.

"Those shots we heard the other day," Agnieska said under tears, "that was the Germans killing the Baniks. Someone said it was because they were old. The Melniks and the Maksimovs, the Jews, were allowed to live and were taken away with the rest of the village. I tell you, there is no rhyme nor reason to it."

She dried her tears with her apron. "They were good people the Baniks," she continued. "Everything you said that were only rumours has come true. They shot the Stokowskis and the Kubicas and took their children. What is to become of our village?" she asked and cried again.

Ludwika took her mother into her arms.

"There's nothing we can do about that now," she said and stroked Agnieska's back to console her. "You need to stop crying, or Irena will grow up to think there is no good in the world. Whatever happens, we need to keep our spirits alive. When the Germans are defeated and Poland is a free country again we will see what we can rebuild from the ruins. Don't give anyone the satisfaction of breaking down. We owe it to Irena and to Poland," she said firmly. "Now pull yourself together before she comes back and sees you like this."

Agnieska smiled. "I wish I had your strength, Ludwika. You're right, of course. You're right."

The next day a large truck arrived to collect the crop and wheat from the barn. The family was surprised as they had not arranged for this. The German man who took the harvest from them didn't pay much but Ludwika thanked him enthusiastically all the same.

In the evening she had her first language lesson from Michal. Irena sat with them. Although the little girl had yet to learn to write and read, she picked up the words much faster than her mother did and over the next few days kept repeating them all day long, which was a great help for Ludwika, who knew she had to demonstrate her eagerness to Manfred somehow.

"I hate to think what is happening to the people the Germans took away," Agnieska said one evening after they had all finished their dinner. "We're lucky to have been spared their lot, but I feel ashamed for it."

"Your shame or guilt aren't going to help them," Piotr pointed out. "Feel how you want, it's not going to change a thing."

"That's right," Stasia agreed. "Let's just be grateful for every day that our luck lasts and not spoil it with guilt for something that isn't our fault."

"I wish it were that simple," Agnieska said and went to pray in a corner of the room where she had put a statue of the Mother Mary and lit candles every day for her husband. There still hadn't been word from him but the women kept the pain of their absence to themselves.

Manfred came to visit the farm a week later. He was impressed with how much Ludwika could say in German already, even though it was only phrases and singular words that she had learnt by heart. She knew nothing much of the grammar, yet.

"Sie sind sehr nett ('You're very kind.')," she said, hoping she got the rehearsed sentence right.

"Wie bitte ('Pardon')?" he asked, not having understood her.

She said it again, trying harder to get the pronunciation right this time.

"Aha," he said. "Sehr gut. Danke. Es ist mir ein Vergnuegen."

She didn't catch all of it, only 'good', 'thanks' and 'pleasure'. She was encouraged.

"Danke fuer Ihre Hilfe ('Thanks for your help')," she said, articulating as best she could.

Manfred soon lost his patience with the slow progress of their conversation and her frequent referrals to the dictionary. He demanded that Michal attend and translate for them.

"Next time I come here I will bring you a book for the grammar," Manfred promised her and reprimanded Michal for not teaching her more.

"Can you find out what happened to my father?" Ludwika asked him.

Manfred frowned. "You poor thing," he said. "Of course I can try and find out. You must worry about him; it's only naturally. It will be very difficult, though. You see, there is so much going on in Poland and the desk pushers and stenographers have a hard time keeping the records up to date. I should know. I am one of them, haha."

He kissed her hand and looked in her eyes. "For you, of course, no trouble is too much."

Ludwika was terrified of his physical advance, more so as Michal was standing right next to her, watching. The Pole's face was one of unconcealed contempt. For that moment only she hoped that Manfred would not take his eyes off her so he wouldn't be able to see the hostility. How dare Michal let his feelings show so openly?

"Danke," Ludwika said and smiled as radiantly as she could muster.

"I have good news," Manfred said full of excitement. "My wish to remain in Poland has been granted. I will be able to visit you regularly here on your farm."

"Wunderbar," Ludwika said when Michal had translated.

"Yes, it is," Manfred said and kissed her hand again. She looked away, hoping the soldier would see it as embarrassment and shyness rather than rejection. Manfred indeed pulled away from her, crossed his hands behind his back and kicked his heels together.

"Fräulein Gierz, I better go now," he said and saluted her. "Heil Hitler."

"Heil Hitler," she said, without the hand movement.

"Nein," he said. "Do it right."

He took her arm and straightened it for her. "That way!"

"Danke," she said and curtseyed.

"That's better," he said and smiled again.

After he had gone Ludwika went to Michal and slapped him hard on the cheek.

"You idiot," she shouted. "You were the one who told me to keep him keen and what do you do? You grimace right where he could have seen it. What do you think would have happened? Don't you see that our luck hangs by a very thin thread? Last week you sounded like you were happy to sell my body to the Germans and today, you're being like this? You are mad!"

Michal held his cheek and looked stunned at her. Piotr burst into laughter.

"She's got a fiery temper," he said. "Who would have thought?"

"Shut up or you'll be next," Stasia warned him, joking.

"I'm sorry," Michal said. "I can't help myself. I can't stand that slimy guy. Knowing what the Germans do all over the country it's ridiculous the way he plays the benefactor for us. Everything we get comes at the expense of other people. Your mother is right. This is a shameful existence."

"We're lucky to exist at all," Ludwika said. "And even luckier that all of this is not coming at a price for us," she paused, "or for me," she added with emphasis. "I don't want to pay it."

"If it wasn't us, it would be a family from Germany," Stasia said. "It wouldn't be someone Polish missing out."

"You're right," Michal admitted and walked away, his head bowed low.

"I think he might be jealous," Piotr suggested.

"Then I hope he can keep his feelings under better control next time," Stasia said, without sounding too surprised over Piotr's comment.

Ludwika looked much more concerned.

"You'll have to talk to him and tell him that he and I have no future," she said. "Even if I wanted to, we can't afford even the slightest suspicion, do you understand? This is serious!"

"I understand alright," Piotr said.

"Then make him understand it, too," Stasia said.

"It's not as if the German settlers are pleased to have us as their neighbours," Ludwika said, "and the Polish workers either envy us or think we're up to no good with the 'szkopy'."

"The Poles know," Piotr reassured her. "I got to talk to some of them and they don't blame you."

"For now," Ludwika said. "We need to keep it that way."

"Enough of your fighting," Stasia interrupted them.

"Yes," Ludwika agreed. "All that doom and gloom is not helping us."

She left and went looking for Irena. As she did so, she saw Stasia go after Michal. She prayed that her sister could make Michael see sense and get him to behave.

Chapter 3

As winter approached, the fields had been ploughed, thanks to the 'borrowed' Wojick tractor and petrol rations, courtesy of Manfred. The mood on the farm seemed to sink all the same. Manfred hadn't come for a while, which was good in some ways and bad in others. It meant that Ludwika was spared awkward moments but they still had no further news about her father. Agnieska began to fear the worst and every day saw her pray more desperately and express her worries more loudly.

Michal became really moody, too.

"You're not the only one who has these fears," he would tell Agnieska. "I don't know the first thing about my family, either. Who knows how bad the Russian are going to treat our people?"

"It's not a competition," Ludwika pointed out. Stasia had tried hard to take the man under her wing and cheer him up, but Michal was stubborn and never missed an opportunity to moan.

"Yes, but your mother's constant whining gets me down," he said. "I'm having a hard enough time to keep going as it is. If I were somewhere else, maybe I could join the partisans or do something to get rid of the Nazis. This existence only to survive is not for me."

"Surviving is the first thing we need to do," Ludwika said. "With how things stand, we can't do anything else but that. You should be grateful. Don't you dare do something stupid."

"You don't have to worry," Michal said. "There are too many 'szkopy' keeping a tight leash and a close watch on their servants. You never get to speak with another Pole for longer than a few minutes and they come running and shooing us apart. It's too hard, or else I would have done it. I'm not suicidal."

"I'm glad we got that straightened out," Ludwika said.

Christmas came and went with no news. The evenings were often awkward, as nobody wanted to speak about the worries on their minds. Michal was a skilled storyteller and entertained them all – especially Irena – with his tales, but it was never quite enough to cover up the tension and sadness.

"Don't scare her," Ludwika would reprimand him sometimes, but Irena loved even the stories about dangerous bears and ghosts. It pleased Ludwika to see her daughter so confident and shielded.

Despite promises to the contrary, there was no visit from the German admirer all winter. Ludwika continued to study the language all the same. It would come in handy now that the Germans were ruling Poland.

Manfred sent her a few postcards, which arrived at the farm in February, one of which he had sent from Bavaria, where he had spent time with his parents. He was urging her to learn German and wished her well, promising to see her soon. He finally came to the farm in March, on a Sunday afternoon when nobody expected him.

The women were gathered in the kitchen, baking. Stasia ran to get Michal from the wood shed so he could translate for them. Manfred tried some of their pastries and was delighted.

"Göttlich!" he said and pointed at the sweets. "Did you make them?" he asked Ludwika.

"Ja, Ludwika," Agnieska said and pointed proudly at her daughter.

"Divine!" Michal translated. "He thinks you're very talented."

Manfred took Ludwika outside and walked with her to a bench by the barn. It was a private place. It turned out that Manfred had no news about her father and he was seriously taken aback that she had asked him about him so soon after their initial greeting.

"My dear Fräulein Gierz," he said, sounding wounded. "I had hoped you would be a little happier to see me."

She understood too little of what he tried to explain to her about the reasons for not knowing and about his work for the administration, so Manfred asked Michal to join them to translate.

"Mr Big Shot says he is an architect of the new Europe," Michal summed up and turned away.

"Of course I'm happy to see you," Ludwika said and articulated as much in German: "Ich freue mich sehr." Manfred beamed. "That's better," he said.

He put his hand on top of hers.

"One day I would like to show you my home town in Bavaria," he said. "We have big mountains there and many lakes. I think you would like it."

Michal translated, but Manfred sent him away.

"I would like that," Ludwika replied, unsure how to encourage Manfred a little but at the same time not go too far.

"May I kiss you, Fräulein Gierz?" he asked. She understood what he meant but pretended not to. She looked confused at the soldier. Manfred got up and called Michal back to translate the question. He didn't seem to mind at all that there was a witness to his courting.

"Maybe next time," Ludwika replied and looked away. She was shocked when Michal said "Go ahead," to Manfred. She couldn't have said it herself but she understood the meaning of those German words very well.

"I'm leaving you two lovebirds to it," Michal said to her and walked back to the house.

Manfred nodded appreciatively at Michal and then leaned in and kissed Ludwika. With Michal gone this was a little easier for her, although not without complications and possible repercussions. Manfred fortunately didn't do anything beyond what he had asked. She was glad nobody could see her. He was skilled at this and it was not as bad as she had feared it would be.

It had been years since Ludwika had kissed anyone. She remembered that fateful night at the fun fare where she had kissed Milosz, the boy with the stall that sold sweets to children. He had been so lovely and she had melted in his hands. By the time she had discovered her pregnancy the fun fair people had moved on. Milosz had mentioned the name of his village by the Ukrainian border but when she made enquiries, nobody knew of him there. He never returned with the group in the years that followed. They said he had met a girl and followed her to Hungary.

Nine months later Irena was born. The shame of Ludwika's fall had attracted a lot of mean-spirited comments at first and she was treated with contempt and hate. Fortunately, her father had stood by her through the difficult period and the family answered all unkindness and judgement with a wall of unified and dignified silence. It was a tough time but she endured it patiently. Ludwika didn't mind being called nasty names by the other villagers; she was only concerned for Irena. Luckily, because of Ludwika's popularity with all the children in the village, the hateful comments ebbed away soon and they didn't give Irena too much grief for being born out of wedlock. Nobody called her daughter a bastard or worse, only a few hardliners shunned the Gierz family for their disgrace.

Since Irena's birth, there hadn't been any more kissing for Ludwika. She knew her chances of getting married to a respectable man were slim, so she'd devoted her life to the farm and to raising her daughter. She wanted to be as productive a member of her family and society as possible.

The situation with Manfred was promising. He would have seen her papers and known that she had a child out of wedlock. With the language barrier, it was difficult to raise that subject in conversation. The way he behaved with her was so respectful for a man who could probably easily take whatever he wanted by force. She trusted him to be a gentleman who would take good care of her and Irena. She asked herself: could she see a life ahead with this man? If the Germans lost the war eventually, would he want to take her back to Bavaria with him as his bride? If Poland was lost, would he consider her good enough? The way he kissed her showed great affection and admiration, his touch, after years of loneliness, was making her weak. He became more passionate, yet, it was he who eventually pulled away.

Manfred indicated his wristwatch and made a sad face. He had to go. He took her by the hand and led her to the main house to find Michal to translate his goodbyes. He found him with everyone else in the living room.

"I have to hurry now but I will be back soon," Manfred said. "I look forward to speaking with you about the future then," he added. He radiated happiness with a face that would not stop smiling. The room fell into a pregnant silence when he left. In her confused state Ludwika didn't want to be around anyone. She didn't want to talk about her feelings, which she couldn't find a name for yet and she didn't want to endure lectures, sarcasm and ridicule, which she expected. She grabbed Irena and took her to feed the chickens, avoiding the family until she had a better idea of how she felt herself. She loved her daughter over everything and that was a huge part of her decision about how to respond to what could be a proposal from Manfred. Then again, would a German be allowed to marry a Polish girl?

Was she foolish in believing that the man had honourable intentions and was fully able to see them through? She didn't love the man but she didn't hate him as she did with other Germans.

What was she to make of Michal's deliberate error of translation which had led to all the kissing? Did he think she was a commodity that could be traded? Was that what she was doing, too: trading?

When she returned to the farm house nobody commented or asked her about Manfred. Either Michal had told them about the kissing and they all made their own assumptions about it, or they didn't know at all and were upset that the German had been unable to tell them more about the fate of her father.

Nobody could give her advice. Nobody knew how she felt. Not even she did. Ludwika would have to find out what Manfred's intentions were first anyway and then make a decision – if she was given a choice.

Although the world was at war, there was an atmosphere of oppressive but endurable tranquillity in the village. The German settlers didn't mingle with the Gierz family but didn't bother them either. After the period of war destruction and the waves of deportations, the political dust was settling and life on the farm was getting very busy and distracted them from their worries. The fields needed to be prepared for a new crop; it was lambing season and spring created a sensation of hope and looking forward. The days until Manfred's next visit seemed to rush by, long before Ludwika had had enough time to think through all the possible scenarios that he might propose for the future. She had no idea what to make of a man who could be so kind and yet be involved in such a terrible occupation of her country. There were only a few outcomes for her dilemma she could think of but there might be quite different scenarios on the cards for her. She buried her head in the sand, and kept herself occupied. Ludwika felt unprepared for what was about to come and hoped against better judgement that nothing would happen at all.

Manfred didn't come alone. He had brought a young civilian woman with him who took Michal's place in the translation when they settled for their talk about the future on the bench behind the barn. This suited Ludwika much better. Michal always made her so self-conscious and awkward. But it had become almost unnecessary to have someone interpret anyway. She understood most of what Manfred said and she knew and said the right words, only her pronunciation often let her down.

"I must leave Poland in due course," Manfred said, very formally. "My mission here is almost complete and I am being promoted. I have a new assignment that will take me to a different part of the Reich. I cannot bear to leave you behind," he said and looked at her with sad eyes. "Would you do me the honour and come with me?" he asked.

"Where to?" she asked. She thought he had a nerve to tell her to follow him blindly without even telling her the destination and in what capacity? As his mistress? His wife? A maid?

"That is not certain, yet," he said. "I will go ahead and you would be collected to join me when I am established in my new location."

"And what would be my status?" she asked him.

He smiled bashfully.

"I would like to take you as my wife," he said but without looking at her and before she could reply he continued: "That will demand a lot of formalities, though, and the prospects of getting permission for this from my superiors and the administration are uncertain. It isn't hopeless, though. I may have found German blood in your ancestry, in which case full naturalisation to become a German citizen should be possible. In that case, I would be free to ask for your hand in marriage."

Ludwika was overwhelmed with conflicting emotions. Who would have thought that his interest in her should be so genuine and deep? Yet, the obstacle to an official union between them sounded frightening. The force of German law, even for a loyal soldier like Manfred, was disheartening. She shouldn't have been surprised about that. Of course, the racial segregation laws would affect both of them. She had deluded herself thinking that his protection in the village shielded her from everything.

"All is not lost," he said when he saw her long face. "Due to your cooperative nature and pro-German attitude, I was able to secure an official permit to employ you as my housekeeper when I take up my new position. Until the issue of your racial heritage and naturalisation is cleared you will be required to continue to wear the mandatory 'P' on your clothing. I will not force you. Should you accept these conditions then I can start the proceedings."

It was a lot to take in.

"What about Irena?" she asked.

"I'm afraid it wouldn't be practical to bring her along with you," he said, sounding very formal. "You wouldn't have the time for such a responsibility."

Ludwika's head sank.

"You will be doing her a favour," Manfred explained. "In Germany, Irena would not be seeing much of you. It will fall on your family here to take care of her from now on. It's for the best, particularly if we can't prove the German blood in your ancestry. We know nothing of her father, so I understand. She is better off here. Your entire family will be more secure once you are working directly for the German Army."

The way he put it there was really no decision to be made and yet it was the toughest one of all. It broke Ludwika's heart to think that she would not be taking her daughter with her. Given the circumstances it was, however, what any sensible woman and mother would have to do. It was the best for everyone. She consoled herself that the girl was young and would have Stasia and her grandmother to take good care of her. She would soon be back, wouldn't she? Ludwika realised that despite her hurt and sadness, she was lucky to have been offered such a chance to help her family. She would be doing the right thing. Knowing that would help her aching heart to get over the pain.

"Yes," she said timidly and took his hand. This time it was his turn to be coy and look nervously at the interpreter for disapproval. There was no reason for this as the woman smiled benevolently at the couple and quietly walked off to give the lovers a minute to themselves.

"Ilse is a kind woman," he said, nodding his head towards the direction she had gone.

He leaned in and kissed Ludwika, very passionately this time. After a few minutes he stopped and got up and, with a meaningful look in the direction of the translator, he added: "I have duty to attend to. You will hear from me soon. Be prepared to be collected at any time. I may not be able to warn you before things are going to happen. I also may be forced to go on ahead without saying goodbye to you first. Always be prepared!"

He embraced her quickly, smiling like a young boy on his birthday. "I'm so happy!"

He turned and hurried towards the translator. Ludwika stayed on the bench a little longer, taking in the big decision she had just made, and worrying how to break the news to her family, particularly Irena. She heard his car disappear before she had even left her seat.

Ludwika's days in Poland were numbered. The gravity of her decision began to sink in. She looked at the farm and the fields that had been her home all of her life. She knew next to nothing about the world beyond the nearest towns. Her father had taken her to Krakow once and to Lodz. She'd seen the mountains in the south of the country but nowhere else. Leaving here was not a choice she would have made if she could have avoided it. She was happy here but she had to go. If not, her whole family would be in peril. She wondered what her father would say to his daughter marrying a German, an enemy. Franiciszek Gierz was always so balanced and thoughtful, a gentle father and a far-sighted man. He had taught her the importance of doing the right thing. It was his wisdom that had made Ludwika the grounded woman and the protective mother that she was. Instead of scolding his daughter for falling pregnant out of wedlock, he had been practical and had instructed the entire family to keep totally quiet to all accusations, provocations and name calling. He led by example and Ludwika knew that were it not for him, Irena might have a different life. Because of him she was not the 'bastard child' but a valued little girl in the Gierz family and in the neighbourhood.

Surely he would approve of Ludwika's choice to go with the German. Her father probably would have liked Manfred if only he didn't wear a Nazi uniform. Her father would be able to see the human behind the clothes, see the logic in Ludwika's decision and be as happy as she was that the help and the opportunity came from a man whom she actually might grow to like.

Ludwika dreaded telling the others, though. She went to the stalls instead and tended to the animals. They couldn't judge her and they always were so happy to see her. She sat down in the corner of the shed and began to sing the song about the goose, the fox and the hunter. That song had been her favourite, too, when she was a child.

After Irena had gone to bed, Ludwika gathered all the adults in the kitchen to tell them about her situation.

"Do you know what you are doing?" Stasia asked, concerned. "You'll always be a collaborator. I don't think when this is over you can ever come back here. You know, when our people return. They'll know what you've done and how and why we were spared. This situation is only a temporary one; we will be liberated one day. Don't sell out yet!"

Ludwika sat silent and listened. It wasn't as if that thought hadn't occurred to her.

"Does it look to you as if this occupation is 'a temporary one'?" Michal stopped Stasia in a mocking tone. "Poland has been conquered and divided plenty of times over the centuries but this is very different. Two sworn enemies made a deal: the Communists and the Nazis. Nobody is going to come to our rescue this time. It's been half a year and nothing has happened. Instead, they take our children and keep us as slaves. Don't listen to her, Ludwika. Go and save yourself. You know it will benefit us here on the farm, too. You're doing the right thing for all involved. And if things really should one day go back to 'normal', you'll still be better off in Germany – I tell you that."

"She can never come back, though," Stasia said. "People don't forgive a traitor. She'll never be able to see Irena or us for that matter. If the family gets reunited, she won't be part of it."

"It's a risk I'd take if I were her," Michal said. "Untersturmführer Tischler is a powerful man if he can protect us. He's young and he's not one of the foot soldiers. I've heard that Himmler personally reviews all candidates to that rank; high flyers who are groomed for even better positions. Whatever happens, he has a promising career ahead of him, and as his wife or protégé, Ludwika has got it made. And don't forget the benefit for us here. With the protection of that German we can even think about starting up a resistance group."

"What do you say, mother?" Stasia asked.

"I think that Michal is right," Agnieska said from her praying corner. She had been kneeling in front of the Mother Mary statue with a rosary in her hands for a while. "The situation in Poland is at least going to last a long time."

"Didn't father always say it's best to hold out?" Stasia said.

"I wish your father was here to tell us what to do," Agnieska agreed. "You're right, he was always one to think furthest into the future. That was easier before the Germans came. The way they are being now, with their ideology and ruthlessness. . . Old rules don't apply here and we're all left to guess what is best and what will happen."

"In all of Polish history the country survived," Stasia insisted. "Ludwika, you should hold out. Manfred doesn't seem the vengeful type. If you turn him down he's not going to be spiteful."

"History is a funny thing," Agnieska said. "You see: I thought I had seen it all. Twenty years ago Germany and Russia fought on our land. We never expected the rain of shells, the level of destruction and how they scorched the earth behind them every time they retreated. Now that they have agreed to simply go halves, what prospects have we got? Predicting the future is a futile business. There is a good chance that there will never be a country called Poland again, at least not the way we know it. If Poland re-emerges from the ashes, it might be a tiny little region around Warsaw. Our home might become part of the Reich forever."

"Still," Stasia almost shouted. "It's too soon to know for sure. It's like we're giving up now."

"It's Ludwika's decision," Agnieska said. "I'm sure she knows what she's doing. I'm starting to agree with her. With all that we know about Manfred and the politics, this is a good bet. He seems a nice enough man, at least to us."

"I've noticed one thing," Piotr said. "Manfred said he worked to set up the German occupation here. If he is going to work somewhere else, maybe the Germans have their sight on somewhere else? His new job, could that be a different country to invade?"

"That's a good point," Michal said. "I was thinking the same. It's been half a year and nobody has come after Hitler. He might feel it's safe to take some more."

"And if he does, maybe that will push his luck too far and get his enemies to unite and attack him," Stasia said. "You see, there is hope that this nightmare can come to an end. Don't go Ludwika! Don't sell yourself."

"Think of Irena," Stasia said with a crack in her voice. "She loves you so much. She needs you."

Ludwika swallowed.

"Irena is almost all I can think about in this," she answered. "Irena is young and impressionable and will get over our separation very soon. Children are quick to adapt and she has you and mother to take care of her. Maybe one day she can come and join me and Manfred in Germany."

"How can you make such a heartless decision?" Stasia asked and looked away.

"It's not heartless. It's the only decision I have left," Ludwika said. "Every other decision I could make bears more risks and dangers. A lot of things can happen that will prove this to be wrong. I don't want the Germans to take Irena to complete strangers and I don't want a German family to take away our farm. If the Germans leave and I am branded a traitor then Irena will still be here with you and the farm will still be ours. That would be a prize worth going for. Now let's not talk about this anymore. This is hard enough for me as it is."

A heavy silence fell over the room; everyone was thinking about what had been said. Despite the difference of opinions a sense of acceptance was beginning to settle. Stasia, with a tear in her eyes, got up and hugged her sister from behind. Ludwika briefly touched her sister's hand and stroked it without looking up from the table.

"I think I can do with Slivovitz," Michal said.

Agnieska brought the bottle to the table.

"Me, too," she said. "Me, too."

The days that followed were tense and full of anticipation. Ludwika had decided not to tell Irena of the changes ahead. There was no way of knowing how long it would be before Manfred would collect her and she didn't want her daughter to be worried ahead of time. It would be bad enough when it happened. . . the faster, the less painful it would be. She tried to see every day as a gift and spent as much time with Irena as possible. When she saw how fond Irena was of Michal, how she marvelled at his talent to pull faces, how he and Piotr both had become such great father figures, Ludwika would feel more and more assured that things would turn out fine.

The longer the wait was, the more Ludwika was at ease with her destiny. To keep her mind positive she tried to imagine where Manfred would be taking her? If the postcard from Bavaria was anything to go by she might be seeing wonderful places. Those mountains had to be as high as the Tatra Mountains in southern Poland.

She didn't have to wonder long where Manfred would take her. On a Tuesday, soon after his visit the radio announced the surrender of the Danish nation to the Germans after an invasion that had only taken hours rather than days. This had to be where Manfred was heading, and where he would take her. She wouldn't be seeing any mountains there. Ludwika marvelled at the speed with which the Germans had swallowed up another nation. It didn't look as if anyone was able to withstand them. Seeing where armed resistance had left Poland, she wondered if it, too should have surrendered like Denmark did to cut its losses. Would the world wake up now or continue its sleep and let Hitler have his ways in Europe?

The atmosphere in the village was depressing. The gloating German settlers went about their business as if the world truly belonged to them already. Even Magdalena Weber, one of the friendly settlers, who always emphasised that she had not known that her new farm had been forcefully taken from Poles and how sorry she was about it, even she seemed secretly pleased about this new German victory.

"Why wouldn't she?" Agnieska said in her defence when Stasia commented about Frau Weber. "She hasn't seen how it happened. All she did was take up an opportunity given to her."

"Now that she knows at what price her good fortune came…" Stasia started, but Agnieska stopped her.

"If Frau Weber and her family went back to Germany someone else would come and take the farm. Whether it's her or not makes no difference to us or the people the Germans took the farm from. Same with us, if we refused our privileges," she added. "You said so yourself."

Stasia fell silent.

Chapter 4

The next day at noon a car came to collect Ludwika. The driver was a young German soldier who was very complimentary about her language skills and who expressed his delight that she had her suitcase packed already. After all, they had a train to catch in Breslau. He handed her travel documents and a train ticket to Hamburg and smiled at her with big blue eyes. He couldn't have been older than nineteen and he looked the part of Hitler's tall, blond and athletic ideal man.

"It will be a long and arduous journey," he warned her. "It will be best if you bring refreshments."

He was as friendly and polite as Manfred, which reassured Ludwika that not all Germans were as nasty as the soldiers and some of the settlers. Agnieska rushed into the kitchen to prepare snacks while the driver waited for Ludwika to say her goodbyes. She cringed at that prospect. Michal and Piotr were out in the fields and Stasia was in the cow shed with Irena.

"I don't think I can," she said to her mother when she came back with the snacks. "Tell her that I'm on a long holiday. Tell her I love her and I will see her as soon as I can."

"No, you need to speak to her," Agnieska insisted. She was welling up. "Irena will never believe me that you went on a holiday without saying goodbye to her. She needs to hear it from you."

"I can't," Ludwika said fighting the tears. She managed to pull herself together quickly and said. "I promised myself I will never cry in front of that child. She mustn't see me like this and worry about me. Let her think I'm heartless and that I have selfishly gone on a jolly. It will help her transfer her affection to Stasia and you."

Ludwika took her suitcase and went to the door. She turned around briefly to wave at her mother. "Thank you," she said, instead of a goodbye. She could not make her mouth form those words. Saying them out loud would force them both to think about the magnitude of this moment. She quietly went to the car and waited for the driver to start the engine.

She looked ahead of her without turning back to the farm once. She didn't look right or left. Instead, she hummed the song about the goose, the fox and the hunter, to calm her nerves.

"Worrying has never done anyone any good," her father used to say. "When something awful happens you have to deal with it. Do your best and hope it is enough."

She remembered those words now and she thanked him mentally for preparing her so well for life and its many challenges.

"You mustn't cry over spilled milk," he had also said. To live that motto was much harder today. Not crying about leaving her daughter behind and the rest of her family was very difficult, however good her reasons for it were and as she sat in the car she tormented herself, wondering if she really had done the right thing by Irena. Who was to say what was best for her child, the damage was always going to be the same: an abandoned girl without any parents.

"My name is Aki," the driver said and stretched out his hand while driving. "It's short for Joachim."

Grateful, she shook his hand and listened as carefully as she could to his descriptions of the architecture in Hamburg: the impressive palatial buildings, the many bridges and canals, the Alster Lake, which wasn't really a lake but a river, and the friendly nature of its people.

Ludwika nodded and hoped she would remember his descriptions of Altona Station in Hamburg and the way to the address she had to find once she arrived. He had been very good to her. She wondered if he was treating all Poles with the same courtesy and kindness or only because she was of interest to Manfred. What would the people in Hamburg be like?

Thanks to Aki, the journey to Breslau went by quickly. His chatter didn't leave her much time to worry about the path ahead of her. Or about what Ludwika was leaving behind.

Breslau showed the volatile nature of politics: it had once been Polish, now it was almost completely German. It gave her hope that she had made the right choice; even if it did mean going against her own country.

Ludwika had never travelled far from her village and was in awe when the driver took her past the town hall: it was like a castle to her, only more elegant, and reminded her very much of a postcard she had once seen of Prague. The large market square with the cobblestones and the elegant street lamps, the trams and those tall, spruce merchant buildings – it was all very impressive and helped distract Ludwika from the deep well of sadness in the pit of her stomach

"I thought you might like to see the town," Aki said and smiled at her as she managed to snap a little out of her misery and became somewhat more animated. "The architecture here is similar to that of Hamburg," he explained. "Breslau was once part of the Hanseatic Trade League, the same as Hamburg."

She felt empty, but let him carry on, nodding numbly to his words.

"I'm glad you were so well prepared and had your suitcase ready to leave. Now we have some time before the train must depart. I can show you the rest of the city," Aki said and drove towards the University, the river and along a beautiful park. When he dropped her off at the train station she was still sad and scared, but also excited. Maybe there was hope.

Her ticket was second class, but she didn't dare sit in those compartments with the fine people. Her clothes were scruffy in comparison. Even though it came from Lodz, the train was a German express which connected Berlin with Bucharest. Many people had fallen asleep due to the long journey. She didn't want to wake anyone and make a spectacle of herself, so she stood in the corner behind the mail carriage until the ticket inspector bullied her into her allocated seat.

"You're in the way," he said and shooed her along until she was at the right spot. She sat down by the door of a six-seater compartment, next to a large man with terrible breath. Cowered in the corner for the next four hours, Ludwika saw nothing of the landscape outside. It was getting dark now anyway and the rhythmic movement of the train made her drowsy and nod off. She was grateful for being right by the door as she could lean against the partition and away from the man without seeming to be bothered or offended by his spilling over onto her seat. Occasionally people got up to use the rest room and some kicked her shin or fell over her legs. She always apologised as if it were her fault. There were not many stops though and she was surprised when they arrived in Dresden just after midnight, much sooner than she would have thought.

In Dresden a group of soldiers took up a few compartments in the same carriage as her. Seeing the men in uniform did not remind her of her Manfred – she could call him that now, couldn't she? It reminded her of the men who had driven through her village and ensured 'law and order'. The men here were, however, remarkably well behaved – so unlike the Polish soldiers she had once encountered in the streets of Lodz. Everything went quiet soon after the train had left the station. It was a huge relief. The big man next to her seemed a blessing in disguise, too. Behind him, she felt relatively safe and hidden away from the world.

The train rolled into Berlin-Anhalt in the early morning hours, with the city still asleep. Her connection to Hamburg was leaving from the Central Station. Manfred had drawn a map, showing her how to get from one station to the next. It was simple, given the short distance, the few turns and the width of the streets. She walked past the Potsdamer Platz, which was bustling with traffic. She never had seen so many buses. There were impressive buildings everywhere she looked, such magnitude – it was intimidating. There were recruitment posters on the walls and other adverts, all looking glossy and shiny. People were so well dressed, men in uniforms or suits, women in fine modern clothes; even the newspaper boys seemed smart – or was she just imagining that? The trees lining the big avenues gave the city an air of luxury and as she walked past a huge beautiful park towards the Brandenburg Gate Ludwika felt small and unimportant, scared and out of place, yet, also in awe. The Reichstag building and what it represented instilled more fear in her and she walked steadily on until she finally arrived at the Berlin Hauptbahnhof. Everything was so tidy and well looked after, she noticed. How could a country so close to hers be so different? And busy…

People bumped and ran into her and nobody apologised. Some swore at each other and one even pushed her aside. She found a quiet corner by the lavatories and stood there until her train was ready for boarding. An entire section of it was filled with soldiers, more lively than the last lot and up for mischief, it seemed. Again, Ludwika felt fear flood her body, and she clutched her suitcase as if it were her father's protective hand.

She didn't have a seat reserved for this part of her journey and had to find one, hoping it would be away from the soldiers, the noise and any hostile people. She was lucky to find a compartment with a kind-looking woman who had four children with her. Being in a party of five in a six-seat compartment meant nobody else would be joining them. That was a huge relief. Having children around always eased her tension. The mother seemed hardly older than Ludwika, yet she had three boys and one girl who had all passed the toddler stage.

"You're just what I needed," the woman said with a huge sigh of relief. "Martin needs the toilet and I was wondering how I should manage the other three when I get to take him."

"I'd be happy to watch them," Ludwika said smiling. The mother halted when she heard the accent and then looked long at the 'P' that was stitched to her arm.

"I can't do it yet," she said, speaking slowly to make sure the foreigner understood. "We're still in the station," she said. "You mustn't use the lavatories when the train is stationary – did you know that?"

Ludwika couldn't make out if this was meant to be rude or helpful. The woman seemed of rather dark complexion for a German herself. She was very pretty. No wonder she was blessed with this many children at such a young age. She was probably one of the first to have found a husband, one of the first ones off the shelf.

"Thank you," Ludwika replied. "Very good to know."

The company of children reminded her painfully of Irena and to distract herself she started to sing to them, a nursery rhyme about little Hans – the only one she knew in German. The little girl joined in and so did one of the boys. Ludwika had been so used to having plenty of children around her; she could imagine that Irena was standing behind her, with a bunch of other village rascals. The mother still looked suspicious at Ludwika but as soon as the train had started she ran towards the toilet with Martin, the oldest of her boys. He had soiled himself by now, unable to wait and she had to clean him up and put some fresh clothes on. Ludwika smiled at the obedience to rules the young mother had demonstrated by not going to the bathroom, even though it was a child emergency. It occurred to her that from now on she would probably have to conform to the same bureaucracy and strictness.

By the time mother and son returned Ludwika had already made good friends with the remaining three, who were busy teaching her more German nursery rhymes. Martin, the young boy in new clothes, also joined in. The woman watched in awe as her children were completely taken in by Ludwika, almost oblivious to their mother. Once the inspector had seen and validated all of their tickets, the German woman took out a book and read. Ludwika froze when she saw that it was a book written by Adolf Hitler himself.

She heard her father's encouragement in her head to keep going and not to worry about anything before there was a need for it. It was true, the woman would mean her no harm, not while Ludwika was taking care of the children.

After the singing had stopped the children told her about their grandparents' big villa by the Alster in Hamburg and how they looked forward to eating ice cream at its shore. The mother had obviously decided to leave her to it and only occasionally spared a glance around the compartment, the rest of the time her head was turned towards the window and deep into her book. Undeterred, Ludwika was grateful for the children's company and the happiness it brought her. The oldest boy, he looked about six, asked her to read them a story from their book and she happily obliged. It would be good practice for her. She found it very difficult, however, and the children didn't seem to understand her renditions of a German folk tale.

The mother put her book down now and took the seat beside Ludwika.

"Don't give up so easily," she said. Ludwika couldn't make out if the woman was scolding her or meant to encourage her. The tone was harsh but the face seemed benign.

Ludwika started a different fairy tale, and every time she mispronounced a word the woman would step in and correct her with surprising patience, while one by one the children fell asleep in their seats.

"You're not bad at all for a foreigner," the woman whispered. "Your German will get better over time. Don't lose heart and keep going, then it will become easier and soon take care of itself."

She looked her up and down.

"Where are you from, Ludwika?"

"Poland," she replied, a little nervous.

"I know that, but which city?" the mother asked.

"Near Breslau," Ludwika decided on.

"Are you Jewish?"

Ludwika jerked and shook her head vehemently.

"No," she said quickly.

"Then I've got to thank you," the mother replied, relieved. "My name is Irmingard. Irmingard Danner. You saved my life by giving me those two precious hours to read." She looked towards the door and then she added in a low voice, so that nobody could hear: "My husband Erich has been hassling me to read that Hitler book for weeks now. My father-in-law works for the publishers and is a big shot in the party, too. He's bound to ask me questions about it. I can't make myself read the damn thing. Don't you, too, find politics is so boring? As hard as I try, after ten minutes I can't remember what I've read earlier. Today was the first time I could concentrate and I will be able to say at least a few intelligent things about it and make my husband proud."

"You're welcome," Ludwika said. She was feeling a lot better.

"You have a great way with children," Irmingard observed. "Are you trained as a nanny or something? I wish I had someone like you around every day. We have a governess, but she is awful with the children. I'm so disappointed with her – and she came with the highest recommendations from our friends, one wouldn't believe it. I know the children are young and impressionable and need discipline to function but they are scared stiff of her and don't seem to behave any better once she's gone. Martin always interrupts me when I read a story to them. Not once did he do that with you, and do you want to know why? Because he doesn't want to upset you. He cares for you and respects you, more than with his own mother – or the strict Fräulein No Smile. That's what they call their governess."

"Thank you," Ludwika said humbly. "I'm not trained to look after children professionally. I usually work on a farm."

"I would hire you tomorrow," Irmingard said. "You wouldn't consider it?"

Ludwika didn't know how much of her relationship with Manfred she was allowed to reveal to a stranger. This woman seemed nice, but at the end of the day she was German and had connections to the Nazis. Who could say if she wouldn't interfere to get her way, and then what would become of Ludwika's family?

"I am to become a maid in a German household," she said, fearing that even that might have been too much. Could she track Ludwika down from this statement?

"What a shame," Irmingard said and laughed. "Of course, the good ones area always taken already."

She got out a pen and paper and wrote down an address, and a telephone number.

"This is where I and the children will be staying for the next three weeks," she explained. "Should you find yourself free at any time and would like to earn a little extra, get in touch."

Ludwika took the piece of paper and put it safely away in her suitcase.

"Thank you," she said. "Very kind of you."

"It's such a shame those racial laws are in place now," Irmingard said in a low voice again. "I mean, I don't understand about politics and I am sure there are good reasons for them to be made. But for people like you, it really doesn't make sense to me."

She shook her head at the ways of the world, then grabbed hold of her book and started to read again.

Ludwika stared out of the window. She could see little of interest, mostly green grass or fields of heather. Her thoughts frequently returned to Przedborów and Irena, but she wouldn't allow herself to become sentimental. That would be of no use for anyone. Irena had enough people around her and she was safe. That was all that mattered, it was more than many could say of their daughter. Instead, Ludwika tried to think ahead and began to wonder what this Hamburg might look like. It was hard to imagine a city built around a lake, with the Elbe and its harbour in the city as well as the canals and probably millions of people. If it was anything like Breslau then it had to be beautiful.

She wondered if Manfred would be waiting or if he was working in Denmark or Norway and would make her wait for him in a lonely flat. The world was scary one minute and then exciting and full of possibilities the very next. She had to concentrate on the good parts to keep going, she reminded herself time and time again. If Manfred wasn't there, maybe she could go and visit those children after all. Of course, maybe Manfred wasn't in another country at all and was doing a different administrative job in Hamburg. She would prefer that. The thought of him leaving her alone in a strange city was not very comforting, nor was the idea of him being there, either. Although he had been kind and lenient towards her, he might change. Ludwika scolded herself: she had to stop these thoughts and go back to thinking about the wonders of Hamburg. That would be much healthier and useful, but it was hard to keep the gloom from her mind. She tried desperately to visualise the place. If these children liked the city, then it couldn't be all bad, she told herself. The driver, Aki, had been besotted with the place, too. She settled into a comfortable state of fragile but contained optimism and slowly fell asleep.

"You've got to wake up," Irmingard said, shaking Ludwika. "We're almost in Hamburg. I didn't know where you had to get off. I thought you said you were going to Altona but my brain, I keep forgetting things. I was no longer sure."

"Yes," Ludwika said, coming to her senses. "Altona."

"Thank God," Irmingard said. "The next stop is the Central Station. We have to get out here. It was nice to meet you. Remember to give me a call if you are free. Even an afternoon would do wonders and give me the chance to have my hair cut without having to worry that the children are being chained to their chairs and locked away." She laughed. "Best of luck in this wonderful city. You will love it."

She turned to get her children to walk towards the exit. They didn't want to go.

"See what I mean?" Irmingard said and pointed at them. All four were looking at Ludwika with disappointed faces.

"I'm afraid Ludwika has further to go. She needs to stay on the train until she gets to Altona," Irmingard explained. "Hopefully, she will come and visit you while she's here."

The children cheered up and voiced their approval.

"Off you go now," Irmingard said.

"Thank you," Ludwika said and waved briefly at the children. Then she sank back down and didn't look that way until the train had moved out of the station and the carriages had filled with new passengers.

When she got her suitcase from underneath the seat she found that Irmingard must have dropped her book and left it on the train. Ludwika picked it up and had a look at it. She took it and put it in her suitcase. She might as well use it for reading practise. She opened it where the bookmark stuck out. It wasn't a bookmark as it turned out. Irmingard had left a note for her and a few Reichsmark.

Thank you for being so kind to my children. Now that I have 'lost' my book on the train, you have an excuse to come and visit us. My father-in-law will love you if you come carrying that book and you will be welcomed with open arms.

Fond regards

Irmingard Danner.

The train inspector announced that they would shortly be arriving in Hamburg Altona, the final stop on this journey. Everyone gathered their belongings to get ready to disembark.

Ludwika put the book and the note away and instead took out Manfred's hand-drawn map to help her find the way to her new residence. He had neat hand writing, she noticed. When the train stopped she stepped onto yet another clean station platform and braced herself for what was going to happen next. Her German adventure was about to begin and she hoped that it would be as good as it promised to be. All Ludwika could do was embrace the situation, ignore the ambiguity and dangers and hope for the best.

Chapter 5

Manfred's map of Altona was not as useful as the one he had made for her transfer in Berlin. The roads around the station were narrower, forked more often and many of the turns were not at right angles. Ludwika became confused and kept getting lost. The first few times she simply retraced her steps and found the right turn on the second attempt. Then she needed help. She approached a mother with two children who came her way. Ludwika felt safe whenever a child was around. The woman, however, stared with open disgust at the 'P' on Ludwika's coat and rushed past, dragging her children as if to protect them from an infectious disease.

Ludwika tried to find the way on her own again, staring at the map, helpless and increasingly worried that she might never find it. What would happen to her if she couldn't re-unite with Manfred? She had almost no money and as she was wearing the nasty 'P' mark hostels might even refuse her business.

At last an old man stopped and took the map out of her hands. "You're almost there," he said laughing. "You confused Klopstockstrasse with Klopstockplatz. 'St' means street, 'pl' means platz. You were so close, you silly girl. Just turn back and you are on the Elbchaussee. I guess another two blocks and you're there."

"Danke," Ludwika said and she wanted to hug her saviour. She wouldn't have known what to do without him. She had lost all of her confidence to approach people after the way the woman earlier had treated her.

"Anytime," the man said with a wink and moved on.

Elbchaussee was beautiful. The houses were magnificent: villas or apartment buildings many storeys tall and all built in the wonderful architectural style that she had seen in Breslau and Dresden: white large bricks, some painted in other, bright colours, the windows were huge, often arched and everything looked so opulent. Trees lined both sides of the road and there was a park, too. This was a fine place. She wondered how she would fit in.

Manfred lived in one of the apartment buildings. Some of the flats had small balconies and the walls were so white, it had to have been painted recently. She had to push a large, heavy wooden door open to get to the staircase and then go up a flight of stairs before she found the door with 'the name Tischler' next to it. The tall ceilings made her feel small. She knocked at first, reluctant to use the doorbell.

It wasn't Manfred who opened the door but a woman in her forties. She looked unhealthily skinny and exhausted, her dark hair untidy and her bony face dirty. She waved Ludwika in and led her across a small corridor into a modern kitchen.

"Where is Manfred?" Ludwika asked confused.

"Untersturmführer Tischler is not here," the woman said. "I'm Eva, his housekeeper."

"I don't understand," Ludwika said. "I thought I would be doing that."

"You will," Eva said. "I'm here to show you the ropes so when he comes home next week or the week after, you will know everything you need to know."

"Thank you," Ludwika said, relieved to have company and a helping hand, at least for now.

Without further introductions, Eva explained to Ludwika how to use the cooker and then showed her round the flat, which was larger than Ludwika had thought. The living room was huge but felt somewhat overcrowded with furniture: bookshelves, armchairs, a leather sofa and a writing desk. The dining room next to it had a large central table that left little space for anything else. The size of the rooms and the height of the ceiling impressed her. The flat had its own bathroom and toilet and one large bedroom.

Was she meant to share that with Manfred? She knew that part was coming but relations between Poles and Germans were expressly forbidden. Until she was naturalised there was no way that Manfred would break those rules, not with his position and career to lose. There had to be somewhere else for her to sleep.

As if she could read Ludwika's mind, Eva raised her eyebrows suggestively and walked back to the kitchen. Ludwika followed, hoping for an explanation.

Eva took scissors and began to cut the 'P' off Ludwika's clothes.

"No, you mustn't do that," Ludwika protested. "I'll be arrested."

Eva shook her head and smiled.

"Don't worry," she said. "Herr Tischler said to do this. Your status is in dispute and until it is decided you don't need the 'P'. You can carry a letter from the authorities that states so." She stopped and looked directly into Ludwika's eyes. "Always have that letter with you in case you are questioned."

Ludwika looked at her with suspicion. She found it hard to believe that the 'P' could go and began to wonder if the housekeeper was trustworthy. Could Eva have been Manfred's love interest before and was trying to harm her rival? Unlikely. Manfred would neither have gone with a woman who looked so Jewish nor would he let her teach the new woman in his life. This didn't make sense and it frightened her. Why wasn't he here to tell her everything in person? Ludwika didn't like this one bit.

Eva seemed to understand what was going through Ludwika's mind and produced the letter from a kitchen drawer. It was written in a very official tone with words she didn't understand, though. It was possible that Eva was speaking the truth, but it was difficult to be sure. Eva was about to throw the 'P' out.

"I'll hold on to that," Ludwika said and kept it.

"As you please," Eva said, taken aback. She got up and put on a coat.

"We haven't got much time."

Ludwika searched the room and saw a clock in the corner on one of the kitchen units. It was four in the afternoon already.

"There's a curfew for Jews," Eva explained. "I have a long way ahead of me and I often need to walk all of it. An inspector can force you off the tram because you're Jewish if he feels like it and then you'll have to walk. Nothing you can do about it. Nobody's going to stand up for us. The Grindelviertel, where I live, is five kilometres from here."

If Eva wasn't staying here but in a Jewish Quarter, where would Ludwika stay?

"I'm going to show you the shops on the way to the tram," Eva said. "Take your suitcase with you. I'll walk you to your hostel."

She locked the door to the flat and handed Ludwika the key. "Be here no later than eight in the morning."

They walked along the beautiful Elbchaussee. Ludwika felt exposed without her 'P', as much as she had felt exposed when she had worn it. Fortunately, Eva walked confidently and with big strides, as if she had nothing to fear. There were a few small shops within walking distance. The market and the more specialised stores were all located around the train station.

The hostel was a cheap-looking, run-down building, lying hidden off one of the big roads. The receptionist checked Ludwika's papers. She was a large woman, maybe 50 with a grey headscarf and a hostile look.

"Where is your 'P'?" she asked abruptly. Ludwika showed her the letter.

"I see," the woman said suggestively. "Sign here," she said, pointing at a guest book.

Ludwika had to share one washroom and two toilets with the rest of the all-female inhabitants. The dorms slept up to eight women – all of whom looked foreign and spoke different languages. Ludwika kept to herself for now and observed quietly. When she opened her suitcase Hitler's book was visible and was noticed. There was some whispering. Nobody spoke to her after that.

Exhausted from all the travel and emotionally drained, she fell asleep, despite some heavy snoring, giggling and whispering that endured all through the night. Used to farm life she woke at five the next morning. She washed and left the hostel at six, taking her luggage with her. . . just in case. She didn't think it would be there on her return. Ludwika made it to Manfred's flat in less than twenty minutes, deposited her belongings and then went out to buy some food. Delicious smells wafted from the bakeries and she had to try some of the pastries on offer. The saleswoman smiled broadly at Ludwika's excited face and recommended a bun with a cinnamon filling. "We make the best Franzbrötchen in town," she claimed and handed it over proudly.

Ludwika was starving and yes, this tasted delicious. How different life was without the 'P', even when she spoke with an accent.

Back at the flat she waited for Eva. She was about to start cleaning on her own to pass the time when she realised how tidy everything already was. It seemed pointless wasting her energy. Eva had emphasised how specific Manfred was in his wishes and Ludwika feared she would only do it wrong. She took out the Hitler book to see if she could understand any of it. There were too many words that made no sense to her. She needed her dictionary. She looked up a few of the strange words but soon got bored doing this. Ludwika didn't care for Hitler's childhood and his family. She flipped through the pages to look for something that might grab her fancy. The first chapter that seemed of interest was "Race and People". She didn't get far into it before she had to close the book and put it away; this was worse than she had expected. What had happened to Poland and its people had been planned and published all along? How far would the Germans go to implement it all? Ludwika was afraid to even think about it.

She couldn't wait for Eva to come now and show her the ropes. She had to do something to occupy her perturbed mind and so she got the broom out and began to sweep the kitchen floor. When Eva came in soon after, the Jewish woman laughed at Ludwika's feeble attempt and took hold of the broom.

"You mustn't direct it that way," she said and demonstrated the movement in the air. "And there is a tiny gap between the cooker and the unit next to it. No crumbs must ever get between them. It's impossible to move the unit and the gap is so narrow that you can't get in there either. Always start by the cooker and push the dust away from it, understand?"

Ludwika nodded.

Eva went on to explain a lot more specifics and made Ludwika write them down.

"When I'm gone you will have to do it exactly the way he likes."

Ludwika didn't think her Manfred would be so strict. He had always been so gentle. She dutifully made notes, as requested.

"Before Untersturmführer Tischler moved in there was a Herr Manhart living here. He was secretary to a party official and I thought that he was very pernickety but in comparison to Herr Tischler, he was easy going. You'll see."

There were specific instructions for almost every piece of furniture and all parts of the flat. Ludwika found it amusing. It didn't matter to her one bit. If Manfred wanted her to be so exact in keeping everything tidy, it was no problem for her. She would go mad on her own anyway and needed things to occupy her. She couldn't afford to hang around and let her mind wander. Keeping busy was the best one could do.

In the afternoon Eva took her leave.

"I'll come by again tomorrow and on Monday. After that you're on your own. Herr Tischler will send you a telegram when he gets back. There is money in the kitchen drawer. You need to write down every pfennig you spend in the booklet next to it: what you bought and exactly where."

Again, Ludwika was amused. Manfred wouldn't be so tight with her – she was sure of it; not after the way he had showered her with privileges. She had no intention to take advantage of his generosity anyway and had nothing to hide and nothing to spend the money on. Everything she needed was within these walls – except her family and Manfred, of course.

When Eva had gone, Ludwika felt restless. To keep the worry over Irena at bay she went through the flat, looking for anything to distract her. She had a good snoop around. In the living room Manfred had stored a lot of books. Mostly dry reference books and political titles. The bottom shelf, however, was very interesting: it had plenty of children's and song books. He must have kept them from when he was a child – which, admittedly, wasn't that long ago. She smiled. Manfred was probably still a little boy inside. She loved the thought of that.

She began to sing the songs from the book, which got her in a better mood. She left Hitler's book on Manfred's desk and put the song book in her suitcase instead. It was time to go back to the hostel.

The walk along the beautiful Elbchaussee was uplifting, too. It was a huge road but much calmer than the streets of Berlin had been. The trees and the green patches were soothing. Eva had mentioned that it was not far to the river from here and Ludwika made a mental note to explore the area some more soon and maybe sit down by the water one day. The temperatures were milder for the season than in Przedborów.

At the hostel nobody spoke to her, as before, and so she spent the evening trying to learn the lyrics to some of the songs. If she were ever to visit Irmingard Danner and her children, that would come in handy. Ludwika planned to visit them. She longed for children. . . for Irena. Already the big city felt lonely and she began to miss her family and daughter more than was good for her. She mustn't allow herself to get sentimental and look back. Ever.

After a long sleepless night during which her mind drifted back to Poland, despite her best efforts, Ludwika looked forward to the crunchy sweetness of her Franzbrötchen in the morning and to keeping busy cleaning the flat. It didn't matter that it was still perfectly spotless. She had to do something.

Eva watched as Ludwika worked her way through the rooms.

"You catch on fast," Eva said. "Herr Tischler will be pleased."

Ludwika wanted to know what Eva would be doing from now on but didn't dare ask. A hard-working and competent woman like Eva should be able to find work easily. On the other hand Ludwika knew that Jews were made to clean the streets and do all the really dirty work. At least that was what they were forced to do in Poland or the areas that once had been Poland.

"I wish you luck," Eva said. "I don't think I'll be coming Monday now after all. You don't need any more reminders. You have your notes. It will save me the long journey."

She put on her coat and went to the door.

"One last piece of advice: keep to yourself in the house. Herr Frei next door is very ill and stays in the apartment all the time now; his daughter comes once a day to look after him, usually in the afternoon; her husband was arrested for being a communist, so better avoid her. Frau Ziegler downstairs is a widow; her husband died in Poland, so stay clear of her, too. That won't be difficult; she works nights at the hospital. Herr Stahmann is at the front, so his apartment is empty right now. I found the best way to keep them happy is to clean the staircase even when it isn't your turn. Do it after Frau Ziegler has gone to bed and before Herr Frei's daughter comes in the afternoon. In fact, all errands are best done in the mornings.

Ludwika nodded. "Thank you," she said.

Eva turned and opened the door to leave.

"Maybe we can meet up some time?" Ludwika asked, sad to see yet another familiar face go.

Eva gave a wan smile. "If you want to come to the Grindelviertel, please call in." She wrote down her address. "It's not going to do you any good to be socialising with the likes of me. If you're lucky and get your naturalisation then you'd be stupid to risk your reputation by associating with Jews. Herr Tischler will make that clear to you. It's one thing to have a Jewish servant, but to be friends with me can only bring trouble."

Ludwika sat down, deflated and worried. She longed for Manfred to return so he could do exactly that: explain everything to her. The world was so difficult to figure out. He should never have left her here to her own devices like this.

Conscious of her duties, Ludwika continued to clean and tidy, buy groceries, in case Manfred should return unexpectedly, cooked and tidied after herself. She had never been alone for such a long time, it scared her.

The evenings in the hostel continued to be awkward. She had tried to strike up conversations with the other girls, but none of them was willing to become friendly with her. They would speak if spoken to, answer with short replies about where they came from and what they did for a living and then leave at the earliest opportunity. Ludwika remembered what her mother Agnieska had told her a long time ago: once you have a certain reputation, it is impossible to get rid of it. She also remembered her father, who had told her not to worry too much about what other people thought of her.

"They think what they want anyway," he had said. "It is foolish to hope that you can change their mind with words. Maybe with deeds you can and even that is overly optimistic. Always do the best you can."

It was easily said. She was in one of the largest cities in the Reich and had never been so lonely. It began to matter to her what those girls thought. They were foreigners, too: some Italian, some French and one girl from Slovakia. They seemed to be treated with a fair amount of respect. To an untrained eye the Italian women in the hostel could look Jewish. Everyone dark skinned was regarded with suspicion, that much was obvious when you observed people's reactions on the street. Even Irmingard, from the train, probably was sometimes questioned about her racial heritage. There had been a hint of Slavic in her features. Maybe that was why she'd been reading the Hitler book – to convince others of her loyalty to the regime.

Chapter 6

According to the newspaper boys the German invasion of Norway had gone smoothly for the Reich. For Ludwika, that meant that Manfred would be travelling on from Denmark to help with the establishment of the occupying administration in some of the conquered territories there. He sent her a short telegram to that effect, with no date for his expected return, no information about money and no news about her prospects of becoming a German or getting married. She would be a stranger in a foreign place even longer, in a state of limbo. When Manfred had kissed her and declared his feelings for her she had begun to warm to him. He had been kind and he was a strikingly handsome man but it was impossible to forget what the Germans had done to their neighbours: he was one of them.

By late April Ludwika had been alone in town for several weeks. She thought of the May celebrations at home that had always given her and Irena so much pleasure. On the first day of May, girls would carry pine or evergreen branches decorated with ornaments and ribbons to symbolically announce the arrival of spring. Who could say if it would be celebrated this year?

Ludwika had started several letters to her family but never sent one of them. She had heard in the youth hostel that the German mail was being censored and she didn't know if what Manfred had done for her was strictly legal. After reading the Hitler book she was deeply concerned. Manfred had never told her exactly what his job was and she began to wonder if he really was as mighty and powerful as Michal had suggested. He was far too young for that in her opinion. If her letter fell into the wrong hands and exposed Manfred's preferential treatment of her family it could affect all of them badly.

Besides, every time she had started another letter she had to stop herself anyway. Unless she was married or had something definite to report, she might only upset her ever-worrying mother with news about her isolated and uncertain life. What could she tell them? What had the Gierz women told Irena about Ludwika's disappearance? She was dying to know. Yet, giving them her address here in Hamburg could also lead to trouble. A letter from Polish farmers might draw also unwanted attention. She settled for a picture postcard of Hamburg's harbour, which she sent home. She didn't sign it and wrote just a few lines about the beautiful city, her good health and her love for the local baked goods.

Disheartened by Manfred's telegram, Ludwika used the last of her pocket money to seek out Irmingard Danner. Instead of going to Manfred's flat one Sunday morning she took the Straßenbahn across town to the Alster. She couldn't believe how huge and long the lake was, and as people had said: right in the centre of the city, surrounded by houses, hotels and merchant buildings.

She arrived at the west side of the lake, which was also where the Danner residence turned out to be. The houses on this side were huge mansions and villas. Some buildings were clearly embassies or of administrative nature with flags hanging outside, others seemed private, yet were equally grand. It was a long way up the shore to the address. The road was not directly situated by the lake as she had expected but set slightly back from it. The Danner mansion had a massive front garden and was three storeys tall. . . similar in style to Manfred's apartment building but detached and with the feel of a villa or a manor house. All this space for one family? Ludwika wanted to turn on her heels and go back home. She couldn't speak to people who lived in such a noble house as this, or could she?

She rested on a bench by the lake to consider her options. After a lot of soul searching and battling with her loneliness, she at last found the courage to ring the doorbell. She had come all this way, it seemed silly to go home without trying. Ludwika had given up making friends with the people in the hostel; she had to take this chance. If things with the Danner family should become awkward, she had her letter from Manfred as security and she could make her excuses as soon as she had returned the book to its rightful owner. Standing in front of this intimidating mansion brought back the dreadful words from the chapter about races and the German feeling of superiority. It was scary. The man who owned this house had published the book, or at least helped. The gravity of the situation hit her, but it was too late to change her mind: a liveried manservant opened the door and asked her what her business was. When she told him he smiled, took the book from her and let her stand outside.

Ludwika heard loud noises and screaming from inside the house and within moments Irmingard and all of her four children came rushing to the door to greet her.

"Oh, how I hoped you would come," Irmingard said and just about stopped herself from hugging Ludwika. "You kept us waiting," she added, pretending to be hurt.

"Goose, fox and hunter," Martin called out. "Goose, fox and hunter."

"Quiet, young man," Ludwika said with a smile. "You mustn't make a spectacle of yourself."

"Goose, fox and hunter," Martin kept chanting loudly and his siblings joined in.

Ludwika looked helpless at Irmingard, who seemed equally powerless to stop them.

"I don't really know how to behave in such a fine house," Ludwika said. "Won't we upset someone with our singing? Aren't there people working, making money or writing speeches?"

"You're funny," Irmingard said. "Today is a Sunday and nobody is 'writing speeches', but you're probably right. This is not the greatest place for a reunion. Let's take a stroll by the lake, and I can show you an area where children can play. There is also a pier where we could hire rowing boats and enjoy ourselves. I couldn't row by myself but if it's the two of us, we should have a jolly good time."

Ludwika nodded, still nervous and intimidated by the power that the house and such wealth represented.

"Wait here," Irmingard said and went inside, taking the children with her. A few minutes later they all came out, dressed with light coats and shoes, appropriate for the mild winds that were blowing today.

The children took Ludwika by their hands and led her impatiently towards the water. They knew the way and began to sing the song about Little Hans. Irmingard followed them, a few steps behind.

The footpath by the water was full of people out for a Sunday stroll. The children soon joined others and threw pebbles into the lake and watched the sailing boats in the distance.

"What kept you so long?" Irmingard asked when they had a moment to themselves. "The children were asking after you almost every day."

"I'm sorry," Ludwika said. "My new position has kept me very busy. It's a long way from Altona to here."

"Well, I'm very glad you came," Irmingard said and looked around her to see if anyone could hear her. When she was satisfied that nobody was listening, she added: "It's been so boring for me here, I can't tell you: the children feel the same. They mustn't run in the house and must watch out for the flowers in the garden. They are meant to study every day – at their age!"

Ludwika didn't dare comment. As much as she agreed, she couldn't say anything disrespectful about Irmingard's family. Irmingard looked expectantly at her friend, then she suddenly froze.

"Where is your 'P'?" she asked in a concerned whisper. "Are you mad taking that off?"

"I have a paper that grants me special exemption," Ludwika whispered back and handed Irmingard the document. "Please have a look. I have the 'P' in my pocket in case I'm required to sow it back on. I even brought the sewing kit."

Irmingard had a quick look and handed the certificate back.

"That's good news," she said, still keeping a low voice. "They might make an exception for you and declare you German. That would be marvellous. That will make it so much easier for you to see the children, too."

"Have you read the chapter about races in that book you left on the train?" Ludwika asked, trying to find out where her friend stood on the matter.

"I told you I don't hold much for politics. Whatever I've read on the train, it's long forgotten," she said. "My father-in-law was pleased that I knew some trivia about Hitler's family and could name a few chapters in the book but since then nobody has questioned me. Why do you ask?"

"If your father-in-law published this book he won't want me speaking to your children. My race is inferior to him. The Nazis have terrible plans for Eastern Europe," Ludwika said.

"Now you're making me depressed again," Irmingard scolded her. "Don't you start talking about politics. Look, not everything in that book needs to be taken seriously. You're already exempt from whatever plans there might be, so stop worrying about it. Anyone who takes that noisy bunch of rascals out of his house will have the blessing of my father-in-law. He might even help you with your application. You better make his acquaintance soon because we are only here for a few more weeks."

"Why, where are you going?" Ludwika asked.

"Back to Berlin of course," Irmingard said, rolling her eyes theatrically.

"I thought you didn't like it here?" Ludwika commented.

"I don't, but in Berlin I don't like it much more. There I have to go to party meetings with my husband and I never get a minute to myself. But enough of our doom and gloom," she suddenly stopped herself. "Let's go and find the ice cream vendor. You'll see how mad the children go for it."

On the way further up the shore Ludwika was reflecting on what she'd been told. It seemed a risk to take for a Polish woman to meet with a party big wig. If he was one of those who hated the Poles, too, all of her hopes could come to a quick end. Who was to say that Irmingard could predict his response to Ludwika? On the other hand the man might be able to end her worries in one swift movement. If only she had seen Irmingard's father-in-law and had a better idea of what he was like, and if she knew more about Manfred and the actual power he had.

"Do you get on with your in-laws?" she asked Irmingard, testing the waters.

"Yes, they are lovely people," Irmingard said. "They never had a daughter and treat me as if I was one of their own. They are extremely formal, though, and stiff. If you were German you'd know about the different mentalities in Hamburg and Berlin."

"What does your husband do?" Ludwika asked.

"He's a member of the Reichstag," Irmingard said. "One of the youngest ever. They say he is a high flyer. Unfortunately, it means we had to give up our residence in Hamburg and go to Berlin where we don't know anyone outside the party circles. Politics is all I hear about, day in and day out."

Her rant was interrupted by the children spotting the ice cream vendor and breaking into a run with loud screams and shouting. They laid siege to a man with a bicycle that had a small swan shape attached to its steering wheel. Inside the swan were two tubs of ice cream. There were already plenty of people queuing. Irmingard got her purse out when she caught up with her children and bought them all a scoop of lemon ice cream, including Ludwika, who never had one before in her life. It tasted delicious.

"We were lucky to have caught him," Irmingard explained. "It's early in the season for ice cream." She sighed. "Isn't life wonderful some days?"

Ludwika nodded with a broad smile and a twinkle in her eyes while enjoying her ice cream. If only she had Irena with her, this would be bearable indeed: the thought of her daughter stung badly.

When they had finished, they walked up the lake a little further and found the pier that hired out rowing and pedal boats. They spent an hour on the lake with the four children, the two women rowing cumbersomely before returning to the shore.

"It's late," Ludwika said. She was exhausted. "I must make my way back to Altona. Thank you so much for the ice cream and the boat trip."

"You did most of the rowing," Irmingard said, "I should thank you."

She shook Ludwika's hand. "Please come back to visit soon. Next time we can go the other way to the Jungfernstieg and enjoy all the amusements. They have ice cream there, too."

The children joined their mother, making urgent requests to see Ludwika soon.

"I will try," she promised and walked towards the Straßenbahn.

Irmingard came after her.

"I almost forgot," she said and handed Ludwika a few banknotes. "I wanted to give you this in case you are short of money."

Ludwika had no choice but to accept. Her money was about to run out and Manfred had not told her how he planned to stock up her funds. She looked uncomfortable though and her "Thank you" almost got stuck in her throat.

"It's the least I can do," Irmingard said. "The hours you babysat for me on the train, now you came all the way here to return the book. Think of it as an investment. I need to make sure you have the funds to visit us again."

Ludwika reluctantly put the money away.

"Thank you," she repeated, this time in a clearer voice.

"You seem a wonderful person," Irmingard said. "If all your people were like you, then maybe we wouldn't have the problems we have. I'll have a word on your behalf with my father-in-law. What else are his political connections good for, if not granting me a favour for once? After all the tedious hours I've spent at party meetings, I certainly deserve it."

Ludwika felt the fear when she heard Irmingard's intentions. She wanted to ask her to let things lie, but couldn't get those words out either.

"Stop worrying," her father reassured her in her mind, and so she did. She nodded her gratitude and then walked away.

The children fell into a rendition of the song about Little Hans making his fortune in the big wide world. She turned around and waved at them, then began her walk back to Altona.

The route took her through the Grindelviertel – the Jewish Quarter – and past Eva's street. Ludwika only realised where she was when she saw hateful writings on the walls, broken windows and some damaged buildings. The quarter scared her; there was hardly anyone on the streets and those who were seemed fearful and hurried on their way, not looking up and keeping close to the walls. Without realising it she copied their behaviour and walked in the same awkward manner, without stopping to visit Eva as she had intended. She wasn't sure that it was safe to be here, or whether her visit would be welcome. The Jewish woman had been so difficult to figure out.

Ludwika wondered if things would get easier for her if she were to be naturalised. Since she had removed the 'P' nobody had treated her particularly nicely. She had to ask people for the way a few times and they had been helpful, despite her accent but not enthusiastically so either.

Everyone still seemed rather reserved and distant, not the way she knew it from the village back home.

Ludwika tried to clear her mind and just observe the beautiful buildings and the people around, something which was easier to do once she'd left the Grindelviertel behind. There was something about the better parts of the city that did agree with her, despite her fears. The reserve in people gave her the impression that they were more civilised than other Germans. Maybe she was fooling herself with such thoughts, but it gave her some comfort.

By the time Ludwika had reached the hostel it was late and her feet were aching. Tomorrow she would remain in Manfred's flat cleaning, she promised herself. All outdoor errands could wait for a few days she reckoned. Besides, he was miles away in Norway and would never know. The other hostel residents were ignoring her, as usual, and Ludwika settled on her bed and soon fell into a welcome asleep.

The next morning she went past the bakery for a Franzbrötchen and then continued straight to Manfred's flat. When she opened the door she found a thick envelope on the floor. It was stuffed with money and a short note from a friend of his named Dieter who had come to deliver it.

She would not have to worry about her finances anymore. It was a huge relief. Reassured that she was taken care of, she set about her cleaning with full enthusiasm.

Chapter 7

Days went by without her seeing anyone apart from the sales people in the shops. No letter or word from Manfred. The daily routine gave her comfort and, thanks to the specific instructions she was never short of tasks. Carpets needed to be carried down and dusted weekly, bed linen changed and washed so it would be fresh every week. . . Manfred wouldn't come back to stale-smelling sheets. Every day she had food prepared in case he would come home unexpectedly. Then she ate it herself the very next day and began the same process all over. She longed to hear Irena's voice singing, to see the fields around her farm, exchange jokes with Stasia and hear her mother's endless prayers. The loneliness gnawed at her and made her desperate for human contact. The Danner girl began to remind her of Irena, even though they didn't look that much alike. When the weekend came Ludwika couldn't bear it any longer and decided to visit Irmingard and the children again. The German woman was odd but probably the closest she had to a friend right now and Ludwika missed having children around her. This time she took the Straßenbahn from Altona to Klosterstern, which was very near to the Danner residence. She arrived at the villa soon after lunch time. She was devastated when she was told by the housekeeper that the family had taken a trip to the sea and would not be back for several days. Ludwika thanked the woman and then went for a stroll along the lake.

Deflated from not being able to see the children her mind filled with darkness. What was the point of this life in Hamburg and the 'golden cage' Manfred had put her in? The isolation and the separation from her family were too painful. Why had he brought her here if he wasn't even going to be around? Didn't he know what he was doing to her? Didn't he love her at all? If he did, why had he forced her away from her family if he wasn't going to be with her either? Every day she was alone she suffered. The gentleness that she had seen in him gave way to a vision of this man who was nothing more than a bureaucrat, making irrational demands and blindly executing orders of his cold-hearted superiors. Was her being here really protecting her family?

It took much will power but eventually Ludwika managed to put these gloomy thoughts aside. The sun was shining and there were even more people out than the previous Sunday. Children screaming and playing, sailing boats out in the distance, lovers rowing together and groups of youths playing ball by the grassy shore: The happy atmosphere was infectious and who was to say that Irena wasn't enjoying a sunny day at home with some of her friends?

Instead of walking home via the Grindelviertel, Ludwika decided to take the route through the quiet city centre towards the harbour area. There were few people on the road today and she stopped to admire the town hall and the tall and magnificent buildings around it with their small towers, the large windows and their exquisite classic designs. Once again she was surprised how safe the people seemed to feel. There had been next to no air raids in Germany and compared to her life in Poland this didn't feel like war at all.

She bought an ice cream and walked slowly towards the harbour. A group of Hitler Youth walked on the opposite site of one of the many canals between the lake and the river Elbe. They seemed cheerful and full of beans.

The distance to the harbour turned out to be further than she expected and Ludwika was exhausted once she got there. On the other side of the water ships were loaded. She watched as smoke billowed from an iron works and sparks flew high into the air as welders set to work but those impressive views were spoilt for her by the grim presence of German destroyers further along in the harbour. They were a reminder of the deadly force of the Reich. With Denmark and Norway conquered, the battleships must have returned to secure the homeland. As if that were necessary. The power of Germany and its military might was disheartening. Even if she were to join the nation by marrying Manfred, it was unsettling to see the weapons of the Fatherland so close. . . machines that could crush resistance so effortlessly.

She didn't stay long, despite her exhaustion, and followed the road that ran parallel to the river back home to her hostel in Altona.

Two weeks went by during which Ludwika had not gone to see Irmingard again. After long deliberation she had convinced herself that it was a lucky sign that the Danners had been by the sea that Sunday. The risks of an association with them outweighed any possible benefits. Manfred was her best bet here in Germany and she decided that she would rely solely on him. Better the devil you know than the devil you don't. Manfred had seen to her safety in Poland. Now, she was safe and cared for, even if it was lonesome. Irmingard might mean well but who knew what the rest of the Danners were capable of?

While awaiting Manfred's return, Ludwika had become somewhat careless in the cleaning of the flat. It was a thankless, repetitive task that seemed to have no purpose at all until he came back, and week after week there was no sign of that happening anytime soon. Instead, she read most of his children's books and spent days sitting by the river. When Manfred at last announced his return with a telegram, she had to hurry herself to bring the flat up to scratch. The dishes had piled up and there were crumbs in the gap between the cooker and the kitchen unit that she could not get out. Would he spot them? Despite her concerns, she was looking forward to have some company at last.

She stood by the window waiting nervously for him, looking down on the road. When he emerged from the army car that dropped him off he immediately looked up and spotted her. He waved and walked hurriedly to the entrance. She could hear his fast steps climbing the stairs. Ludwika opened the door. He nodded formally, then walked past her into the kitchen. All the while he beamed silently, smiling at her with complete joy and happiness.

Ludwika was lost for words and smiled back, shy and curious as to what news he would bring and how the next phase of her life would play out.

He looked at the food she had prepared, which was still standing in pots on the stove, and he nodded his approval. He took the lids off and sniffed each pot.

"Smells delicious," he said. "Bravo."

"Sit down," she invited him and began busying herself at the cooker. "You must be hungry. It will be ready to serve in a few minutes."

Instead of sitting he looked around the room, swiped the surfaces with his hands to look for dust, checked the gap between the oven and the kitchen unit and then walked around the other rooms. She was shocked at this inspection and his blatant display of control. Disappointed and concerned, she left him to it and concentrated on the food. If he was that pernickety she better not mess the food up, too.

Manfred returned to the kitchen and sat down. His plate was already on the table.

"Not bad," he said. "A few minor corrections aside, you did a good job."

He dug into his food and chewed, demonstratively assessing and deliberating its quality without in the least looking worried that it would offend her.

"I can taste the Slavic influence," he said. "The stew suffers from the overuse of the spices."

"I'm sorry," she said.

"Don't worry," he said and smiled. "Next time make sure you bake a cake and make some of your famous snacks. What about the gingerbread and poppy-seed loaf? I was hoping you'd have your specialities ready for me."

She listened and nodded with a sunken head. This was not the welcome she'd hoped for. Where was the charming and caring man she'd met in Poland? There, he had made her feel like a princess. Here, he was a pedantic teacher who looked down on her.

"I will make them tomorrow," she promised, squaring her shoulders. After all, she had to be grateful for everything he did. She had to swallow her pride and recognise that he was still benign in his intentions and an ally she must keep.

"That's more like it," he said and smiled at her. She looked down, staring at his black uniform with the lightning bolt SS on his collar. She marvelled at all the stripes, armbands and decorations. She had no idea what they meant. There were so many already, more than the last time she had seen him. How was that possible? The uniform made him look dashing and intimidating at the same time. He rose and stood in front of her, only now taking his cap off. He raised her chin until their eyes met. Very slowly he leant into her and gently kissed her.

"I've been waiting for this a long time," he said in between kisses. "Every day I was dreaming of kissing you."

She tensed up. This was where she would find out what type of relationship she would have with him. She was at his mercy: in his flat, in his employ and in his country. He didn't have to marry her, he didn't have to ask her, he could just do as he pleased. She knew it and there was nothing she could do. As if he could read her mind, he withdrew.

"Don't be scared," he said. "I'm a gentleman."

Manfred opened a bottle of wine and poured them both a glass.

"Time to celebrate my return," he said. "Prost! To the future!"

She toasted him and drank. The wine tasted very sweet.

"I'm afraid I have to report a minor setback in our venture to have you naturalised," he said. "There were some complications. My request has been denied at this instance and you will be required from now on to continue wearing the 'P' on your clothes."

She nodded. She had half expected this to happen at some stage anyway. Part of her was almost relieved – the part that felt loyalty and allegiance to her people in Poland and the part that didn't want to dream big dreams. She remembered how people treated her differently with the 'P' sewn to her clothes. Life would be more awkward now.

"I have some good news as well," he said and stood up. "Let me get out of this uniform first and unpack."

He kissed her on the forehead and went to the bedroom. She sat on tenterhooks while he was taking his time getting changed.

When Manfred returned he was wearing a fresh uniform and handed her a big sack of clothes.

"They'll need washing," he said before attaching the swastika armband and the other decorations. Then he refilled his glass.

She hadn't drunk more than a sip of hers but now took a big gulp. She looked at him expectantly and nervous.

"Ach, yes," he said and toasted her. "The good news."

He took another sip of his wine. "Have some more, too," he encouraged her. She was getting scared.

"You don't have to worry your pretty head," he said. "The reason our request was denied is that there was a different enquiry about you. Erich Danner, a Hamburg representative in the German Reichstag has requested all of your files for inspection. I spoke to him briefly this morning on the telephone and he has told me that you have become friendly with his wife and children. He and his father are looking into your case now. This means a short delay to the process for now and better prospects for a positive outcome overall.

The Danners have a different kind of influence that is more advantageous for your case," he added cryptically.

She doubted that and cursed herself for being so naïve and ever making contact with Irmingard. So the politician's wife was going to fight Manfred over who would get Ludwika as their pet? Did he know that Irmingard wanted Ludwika as her nanny? Manfred needed her to be German to make her his wife. To be looking after the Danner children Ludwika could remain Polish, could she not?

When she told him about her fears and worries about Irmingard's motives he laughed.

"I don't think the Danner family will want to have a Polish employee," he said. "They would prefer you to be German for that, too. You never know where the racial laws are going these days. A committee is currently working on a unification of all the regional and local laws, so that we have one rule for all. When I worked in the Sudetenland we had the idea of making all Jews wear a Judenstern. Why not introduce that everywhere else? There are going to be many changes."

"Would you want me to work for the Danner family?" she asked. "They live in Berlin."

"It is a definite possibility," Manfred said. "Until I know about your racial status we cannot get married. You could divide your time between Hamburg and Berlin."

She looked surprised at him.

"It looks as if I'm going to be working abroad a lot," he said. "I'm only going to be here for a few days before I have to leave again."

"Back to Norway?" she asked.

"Maybe," he said, winking at her. "Maybe somewhere new? I don't know, only that the Reich needs me. I'd feel safer if you were with people who can take care of you while I'm gone. Eva can always clean the flat here while you're in Berlin. My assignment in Denmark and Norway was a relatively short one. My next one could take longer."

She sat there in silence.

"Don't worry your pretty head," he said. "It will all turn out just fine for us. Trust me."

He kissed her on the lips and held her in his arms. Although she could not make out whether she could trust him entirely or not,

Ludwika felt safe and protected in his arms and held on to him tightly. There was nothing else to do. In a hostile country, he was her only hope.

An hour later, after she had done the dishes and tidied up, he sent her home to the hostel so he could get back to his work. He had told her nothing about his time in Denmark and Norway. What he had said about implementing racial laws across the Reich and his commitment left no doubt about how dangerous he was. Would she be safer with the Danner family, she wondered? The decision about her fate was not in her hands – or was there something she could do? Should she sit back and hope or try to find out more from the Danners about their plans for her and maybe bring forth a specific outcome?

Without realising it, Ludwika began to hum nursery rhymes until the bewildered looks of passers-by dragged her back to reality.

She pulled herself together and walked with a steady pace towards the hostel, reminding herself of the futility of worry. It would all work out, she told herself. It simply had to. For Irena's sake.

The few days she had with Manfred went by quickly. He spent a lot of his time at home writing reports and paid little attention to her, other than suggesting what dishes she should cook and checking up on her house work. He also went out, not telling her where he was going or when he would be back. He came home late each evening and sent her home after she had tidied the kitchen. His mind was pre-occupied and the advances she had feared would come never materialised. When she emptied the wastepaper basket she found a page he had written about the problem of the gypsies and other undesirables in the Reich. Although he had only written a paragraph on the sheet, it filled her with dreadful ideas about the nature of his work. That weekend Germany began its invasion of Holland, Belgium and France. The papers were full of praise for the formidable army and its rapid, successful campaigns Manfred left soon after the beginning of the military operation without the opportunity to say goodbye to her. She arrived at his flat in the morning to find a short note on the kitchen table, together with some money.

Dear L,

I shall miss you dearly. Take good care of the apartment until I come back and, of course, take good care of yourself.

Yours, M.

She was relieved to learn that he still seemed besotted with her. His tone, somewhat abrupt, remained romantic.

At least she had a lot to do to keep busy after he'd lived in the flat for a few days; she had bed linen to change, clothes to wash and to give everything a good tidy. He had bought her two cookbooks which she read thoroughly and began practicing from. She was reading all recipes in it to find out what spices and dishes Manfred might be used to. It gave her an idea how she could adapt her own dishes into more palatable and acceptable versions for him. She could take her time with all this; she knew it would be weeks before he would return.

The rapid invasion of France scared her, though. She only heard the newspaper boys shout out the headlines, without ever buying a paper or getting to know more than the hearsay in the hostel. Who had ever heard of one country invading this many others in such a short period of time? What was happening to the world and why was nobody actually doing anything about it beyond empty declarations?

Chapter 8

As Ludwika had come to expect, she didn't hear from Manfred for a very long time. She had tried to ask him about her family but he had cut her short whenever she broached the subject. He was always tired or not in the mood for heavy conversations and kept her busy with the housekeeping. Now she had no idea whether she was allowed to contact her family. Time with him had run out so abruptly without her finding answers to any of the subjects that mattered to her. The checks on her racial background were still ongoing and with the uncertainty over it she didn't have the confidence to keep asking. She didn't want to rock the boat by pestering him and now he was gone and it was too late.

The solitude soon turned into the biggest challenge for her, though. No singing and radio broadcasts could save her from the dark cloud that the loneliness brought with it. In the hostel, Ludwika still kept to herself. Many women had come and gone since that time she had been seen with the Hitler book. That incident was long in the past now and yet, it worried her too much to try and break the ice. She feared those confident and loud women who seemed to understand this world so much better and who seemed superior and able to harm her. How could she trust any of them? In her eagerness not to show weakness, Ludwika probably appeared disinterested and unapproachable to them, which was why they never made an effort with her, either. There was fraternisation going on between the boarders, it just didn't include her.

Ludwika would need more entertainment if she was going to spend such long stretches of time by herself. She overheard two women in the hostel talking about a sailing regatta on the Alster the coming Sunday and decided to go along. The days were getting hotter and the lake had a soothing effect on Ludwika every time she saw it. As it was in essence a river its slow but constant flow reminded her of the phrase 'water under the bridge'. It meant that everything would come to pass eventually, even her present sadness.

On the day, the Alster was surrounded by masses of people. In her naivety she had gone to the Jungfernstieg, the southern shore, thinking it would be the best location to watch the regatta. It was, but consequently it was impossible to get anywhere near the front of the quay to see the race. It was hopelessly overcrowded. Ludwika had to walk a long way up by the west side of the lake to find a spot that allowed a good view that hadn't already been taken. She was wearing the 'P' again since Manfred had told her to do so and today she felt the difference it could make. Back in Altona, the shop assistants and people who knew her seemed to turn a blind eye to it and didn't treat her all that differently. Occasionally, there was the odd stare on the street but the stigma was altogether bearable. At least it showed them that she wasn't Jewish. Here at the Alster people noticed the 'P' much more and they seemed to mind. She could hear people whispering, pointing fingers or hissing swear words under their breath. She kept her head low and focused on the sailing boats. She could bear it while the race was on, she told herself; she wouldn't be staying for long.

The boats were magnificent to watch and many of the men sailing them were handsome athletes. There were so many boats on the water, it was an amazing spectacle.

A mild breeze kept the temperatures soothingly warm. It had been worth coming out here, despite the simmering antagonism. The sound of children playing and singing made her feel better.

The race leaders were approaching her corner of the lake now to navigate a buoy close to the shore. People were moving in on her to see better and there was some pushing and shoving. Ludwika withstood it at first but started to feel that some of it was deliberately aimed at her. She wasn't tall enough to see much with such a big crowd around her anyway and so she backed off and walked further up the shore. A group of Hitler Youth walked towards her. She stepped on the grass to let them pass, her heart beating faster.

"Get lost," one of them hissed as they moved by, and he shoved her half-heartedly with one arm. Ludwika was paralysed by fear, trying to catch her breath. Fortunately, the group continued to the shore to watch the race. As soon as they were out of sight she started walking away from the lake as fast as she could.

Ludwika didn't know the area that well, but she needed to feel safe, to find somewhere to re-capture her spirits. She ran for several blocks. The lake was behind her, which meant that she was walking westbound. At some point she would have to turn south to get to Altona, but there still was time. After a few more blocks she started to feel calmer. The elegant apartment buildings and the broad, tree-lined streets made her feel safe, She stood still for a moment to let all the tension and fear fall off her shoulders. Nothing really had happened, she told herself. It was a small incident that didn't matter.

Ludwika continued on her way. If she kept heading south she should come to the harbour, she figured. The route took her through the Grindelviertel. She had not realised where she was until she recognised the swastikas and abuse scrawled on walls and doors. The roads here were completely deserted and she had a feeling that something terrible had happened only recently. She could sense the tension in the air and wondered if those Hitler Youth might have had something to do with it. Ludwika turned a corner onto the street where Eva lived. Anti-Jewish slogans had been daubed on the walls and pool of blood lay at the entrance to a building. Suddenly she heard loud voices and a commotion on the other side of the road. Two men came charging out of a building and crouched down by a tree. She looked closer and realised that there was someone lying on the ground. Now she could spot droplets of blood trailing from where she stood across the street to where the men picked up a body and dragged it into the house, the door quickly shut behind them.

Ludwika heard a window open and a woman shouting at her: "Run away, quick!"

The tone in the voice was shrill and alarming. Ludwika looked around to see where the threat might come from but couldn't see anything suspicious. Her heart raced, she was confused and it took time for her to spring into action and run.

"The other way!" the helpful voice from a window above directed her. Ludwika ran as instructed, despite not knowing why or what from. She heard the sound of engines, fast and urgent, nearby. She stopped to discern where the noise was coming from, as her heart thumped in her chest. Just then, a large door opened in front of her and a woman stuck her head out and waved to come in. Ludwika ran towards the door, which was the entrance to a yard and a secondary building. Her saviour closed and locked the door, then signed her to be quiet. Through a peephole in the door the woman watched what was happening outside. Ludwika's heart was racing. She heard the cars driving past the building and the engine noise slowly disappearing. After a few minutes, the woman turned to Ludwika.

"They're gone. Must be someone else's turn today. You better wait before going out there again," she said.

"Thank you," Ludwika said. In the darkness of the yard it was hard to make out the features of her saviour.

"I mean it," the woman said. "You're a fool to walk around here on your own."

Ludwika nodded. The push she had got from the Hitler Youth seemed harmless in comparison to what was going on here. Eva had warned her; the last time Ludwika had come through this area should have been enough to alert her to the dangers.

"You can come with me if you want," the woman said. "It's my brother's birthday and we're having a little get-together. One more person won't make a difference." She stretched out her hand. "I'm Anna."

Ludwika shook the hand.

"I'd be grateful, thank you. I'm Ludwika."

"Where are you from?" Anna asked as she led the way up the flight of stairs.

"Poland," Ludwika said. "Now I live in Altona."

The light from the windows in the staircase gave her a better view of Anna, a forty year-old slim woman, her face aged by fear and poverty.

"What are you doing here in the Grindelviertel, then?" Anna asked, surprised.

Ludwika didn't want to admit that it was an accident for fear the woman might throw her back out onto the street.

"I've been looking for my friend Eva. She used to work in Altona with me. I wanted to pay her a visit."

"If I were you I wouldn't come here again," Anna said brusquely. "The Gestapo come regularly to beat up people or to take them away. You never know who it's going to be next. The best thing is to keep your head down and hope for the best. You could easily be mistaken for a Jew, so unless that's what you are, you should thank your lucky stars and stay in Altona, where it's safer."

Ludwika nodded, waiting for Anna to tell her to go. Fortunately, that didn't happen. Instead, she opened a door and invited her into a large apartment full of people. Someone was playing the piano, a handful of people danced in the middle of the room, near the wall stood a table with cake and there was more food in the kitchen. Ludwika guessed about 40 people had squeezed inside. None of them was wearing the black Jewish clothes she had expected to see. Some of the tunes sounded familiar. She tried to engage with some children but they were busy in a world of their own, chasing each other and being terrible rascals.

Ludwika sat on a chair in the living room, near the piano, trying to understand the lyrics. They sounded German at times but had to be Yiddish: those languages did sound alike. A group of old women sat on the sofa, clapping along to the music. Anna had disappeared into the kitchen and never came back. The mood was lively, undimmed by the brutal events that had taken place on the street outside. Ludwika admired the unbroken spirit of those present. If she lived in the Grindelviertel she wasn't sure she would cope so well. Despite the festive atmosphere, she felt unsafe and after half an hour Ludwika silently left the party. She wanted to go home, away from the people who had kindly helped her but weren't really interested in her beyond that.

Back on the street she contemplated going to Eva's home to say hello, but she dismissed the idea, remembering how odd Eva had been to Ludwika. She didn't belong here, she didn't understand the mentality of these people who had angered the Germans and were subject to so much hate; it was best not to get involved with them. Eva and Anna had said so themselves. Although her parents had never said a bad word about the Jewish people, many others had, and Ludwika wondered if there could be truth to it. She didn't want to think badly of anyone. She just didn't know what to believe any more.

She walked as fast as she could, eager to leave the Grindelviertel behind, hoping that out of sight could become an out of mind. She swore to herself that she would never put herself in harm's way so carelessly. She would never come there again.

How foolish she had been not to value her safety. Even without the naturalisation, working for such well-connected people as Manfred would provide its own protection. She couldn't wait to return to his flat and do the chores the best she could.

Chapter 9

A few more weeks passed without word from Manfred. The newspapers were still full of praise for the German Army and its continued successes in France. She understood this meant he would be a long time from coming home. He seemed to spend a few weeks in each new occupied territory and then move on. She wondered how that could be of use. Why not keep him in one place when he had found his bearings?

At last in July the papers announced that the French had capitulated and that the war between the two nations had ceased; it could not be long before Manfred came home now.

Two days later, Ludwika arrived at the flat to find two soldiers waiting for her outside the building.

"Untersturmführer Tischler was killed in a traffic accident in Lyon," they informed her. "We are here to collect his work documents so the family can come and take care of his other belongings. Please go ahead and open the door."

Ludwika did as she was asked, her trembling fingers struggling to work the key in the lock. Poor Manfred. Not just sadness hit her, but fear too, of the uncertainty this would bring to her life and that of her family in Poland. She stayed in the kitchen, shocked, grieving and worried all at the same time while the men searched the flat thoroughly, opening every drawer and looking in every corner and nook. She would have a lot of tidying to do when they were gone. She wondered who she would be working for once the Army had assigned the flat to someone new.

When the men were finished they took the keys from her and asked her to leave. Ludwika did as she was told, scared of what would become of her now. She didn't have enough money to return to Poland by train. She didn't even have enough to continue to pay for the hostel. She realised that she would have to find work elsewhere but she didn't have an official work permit and had no idea what was expected of her now.

"Who will be living here next and when will they come?" she asked the soldiers.

"We don't know," they said, disinterested.

"Without a key I can't clean the flat when the new tenants come," she pointed out. "What am I supposed to do?"

"That's no concern of us," one of the men replied. He looked through his papers as if he was searching for orders or instructions with references to her. He shook his head and said: "You can go home now."

She did as she was told and returned to the hostel. Ludwika lay down on her bed and cried. Only now did it dawn on her that she knew nothing about what had happened to Manfred. Had he died instantly or had he suffered? She felt sorry for him, regardless of her ambiguous feelings. The incident in the Grindelviertel had brought everything into perspective for her and she would have liked to have seen him and shown her gratitude for protecting her from the hostile world around her. She thought of the devoted look on his handsome face and of his tender kisses and felt sad that such a young man had come to such an untimely end. Ludwika remembered her drowned brother. That had been such a waste of a life, too, and so many more lives were being wasted now.

The cold hand of fear gripped her heart as she wondered what would become of her family in Poland now, without Manfred's protection? Agnieska, Stasia and Irena? So many questions with so few answers. . . the two soldiers had told her nothing. And she still didn't know what had happened to her father.

She lay down and sobbed into the bedspread, her tears dampening the sheets. Once the initial turmoil had eased, Ludwika calmed herself and assessed her situation. She couldn't afford to dwell on misery. Until she had the funds to return to Poland and could ascertain that it was safe for her to do so she was stuck here. She needed to find out whether her family was still in Przedborów and if she was branded a collaborator now before considering such a step. Ludwika put on her better dress, took the Straßenbahn and went to the Danner residence in the hope that their offer of employment was still good. It was her only option now.

Herr Erich Danner Senior was happy to receive her. It was Ludwika's first time to be allowed inside the villa. A housekeeper led her through an enormous reception hall into a smaller room with a desk, behind which ran a large book case that covered two walls entirely. Herr Danner was seated at the desk and politely stood to shake her hand; that was a far more respectful gesture than Ludwika had anticipated. He indicated two visitor's chairs on the opposite side of his desk.

"Please, Fräulein Gierz, sit down."

She did as she was asked and waited for him to continue.

"What can I do for you today, or rather, what can you do for us?" he asked her and smiled. He was tall, grey-haired with broad shoulders, athletic looking for a man well over fifty but his formal attire and behaviour were that of a scientist or a politician. He wore a wing collar shirt beneath a dark, tailored, three-piece suit with a gold watch chain looping from his pocket. He was intimidating and welcoming all at the same time. He looked at her expectantly and when she was too shy to answer he laughed, his bright eyes twinkling beneath bushy grey eyebrows.

"Has the cat got your tongue?" he asked. She tensed up even more.

"Fräulein Gierz," he said. "You seem in distress. "Why don't you tell me what weighs so heavy on your heart?"

She tried, but instead of words tears flooded from her. His brow creased with concern.

"Fräulein Gierz, you need to help me out here. You don't have to fear anything from me. My daughter-in-law holds you in high esteem and has requested that I help you in any way that I can. Unless you have committed a crime you can tell me anything."

So she told him about Manfred's death and the difficult situation she now found herself in because of it.

"Now don't you worry, as it so happens my family has kept an eye on you all along," he said. "Unfortunately, we cannot prove that you have German blood, but I can certainly make sure that you get a work permit. Thank God you aren't Jewish. I had my concerns and checked."

Ludwika felt a huge sense of relief and dried her tears.

"Wouldn't it be possible for me to go home to Poland altogether?" she asked. "I miss my family so much."

His brows creased again, this time however he looked angry.

"I'll get you on the next train to Berlin where you can start working immediately, helping out Irmingard with the care of my grandchildren," he said. "Your family has coped without you, they will have to continue to do without you but my Irmingard has been a mess of late. Don't you be ungrateful to the hand that feeds you and pays for your train ticket to Berlin."

She nodded obediently glad that he hadn't withdrawn his offer altogether.

"I assume you have no further business to attend to and need nothing more than to collect your belongings from your current residence?" he asked.

"Yes," Ludwika squeezed out the words. Though he was being kind, Herr Danner had a confident and powerful presence that convinced her that being on the wrong side of him could have fatal consequences. In short, he frightened her.

"I hope this will take care of your immediate needs," he said, handing her a few small banknotes. "Come back tomorrow afternoon. I will have made all necessary arrangements by then."

She got up and curtsied.

"I'm very sorry for your loss," he said. "By the sounds of him, Untersturmführer Tischler was a great young man and an asset to the Reich."

She nodded humbly and avoided eye contact.

"Try to be strong," he said, "Your tears won't bring Manfred back."

"Thank you," Ludwika said.

Once she was outside the building the magnitude of the conversation began to sink in: Danner had rescued her. What an odd sensation to grieve for one man and be saved by another, hours later. It was too much to take in. Life on her own without Manfred would have been impossible. God only knew what the German authorities would have done to her. Ludwika was so relieved and happy that she managed to push aside the upset of the past few hours. She had to look forward. If Herr Danner had been truthful and his daughter-in-law Irmingard really did have such a hold over him, then maybe he would extend a protective hand over the Gierz family in Poland, too. If so, then her life in Germany still had a higher purpose. Maybe she would even be allowed contact with her family, or to visit them or return to them once she had earned enough money?

Lost in these daydreams, Ludwika had started walking towards Altona again. She stopped when she realised that she was getting close to the Grindelviertel and turned on her heels. She took the Straßenbahn instead, where a woman told her off for singing. Ludwika hadn't even noticed how she had started humming tunes again. The momentary joy was too big and the rude comment couldn't dampen her mood.

She treated herself to one last Franzbrötchen and walked to the harbour to watch the boats. She'd be back here many times with Irmingard. This was safe, it was not a goodbye.

Herr Danner Senior was not there when she arrived with her suitcase the next day. The housekeeper, however, had specific instructions for her.

Ludwika was given a ticket to Berlin and a piece of paper with the address of the family residence and instructions on how to get there.

Her train did not leaving until the following morning, so Ludwika had to go back to the hostel for one last night.

The train journey the next day was pleasant. She was booked on an express train and sat in a compartment with people too preoccupied with reading to bother with talk, which suited her fine. Ludwika even had a window seat, so she could admire the lush landscape outside that swept past as the train carried her towards Berlin. She thought of Irena and then of the four Danner children Ludwika would have as company. It wasn't the same as having Irena, but, under the circumstances, she couldn't ask for much more.

Chapter 10

When Ludwika arrived in Berlin, Irmingard was waiting for her, at the end of the platform with the children, who sang her the song of the goose, the fox and the hunter. Ludwika had to fight back tears of joy at the sight of them all.

"Thank you," she said to the children. "You did that very well. You all have the potential to become famous singers. Maybe you should start a Danner choir?"

Irmingard was the first to break ranks and hugged Ludwika, her body stiff as if this was awkward for her. Ludwika was grateful for it all the same.

"Thank you so much for coming," Irmingard said. "I'm so sorry to hear what happened to your Manfred. We'll take care of you now. You're one of us," she said. "Isn't she, children?"

The children agreed loudly and made a big fuss over Ludwika.

"We'll have to walk," Irmingard said. "We're too many for a taxi. It's not far, though."

Berlin was much livelier than Hamburg. The calm reserve of Hamburg people that had often confused Ludwika was replaced here with an exciting and dynamic atmosphere. It was intimidating, but she found it refreshing at the same time.

"You're going to stay with us," Erna, the youngest, said.

"Am I?" Ludwika asked, exaggerating her surprise for comic effect. It felt so good to care for a little girl. It helped with her pain over the separation from Irena that would not go away.

Erna laughed. "Yes, you are. When father and mother go out in the evenings you are going to look after us and can read us stories and bring us to bed."

"Aren't I lucky?" Ludwika said.

"Our governess Fräulein Stirner always made me go to bed at six but I am older now and I hope you won't be as strict as she was," Erna said.

"We'll see about that," Irmingard interrupted. "Frau Stirner only did as I told her. I'm going to tell Ludwika to do exactly the same."

She winked at Ludwika to show she didn't mean it.

"Ludwika will know these things anyway because it is scientifically proven that children need a certain amount at sleep and at your age a child needs to go to bed at six. There are rules and best practices for everything. Aren't there, Ludwika?"

"Yes, of course," Ludwika quickly agreed, but she winked at Erna.

The walk to the new residence led them through the centre of Berlin. She recognised the Reichstag and the Brandenburger Tor: she adored those wide tree-lined avenues and the magnificent classical and palatial buildings on either side.

"Not far now," Irmingard said. "We live near water here, too. Right by the Museum Island. It will come in handy for you on days when it rains. You just need to cross the bridge and take the children to one of the many museums, rather than having to stay indoors all day. Erich was very lucky to have found this apartment for us. We have an entire floor to ourselves. It's not as grand as the house of my in-laws, I must warn you. Erich Senior bought the flat and the furniture for us but Erich's wages from the Reichstag don't allow for quite the same level of comfort. We have a housekeeper who also does some of the cooking but you and I will have to share the rest of the chores."

Ludwika thought of Manfred and his pernickety ways. The man had kept one woman busy full time only for his demands. She wondered how the Danners would run their household.

"For the next two years the children can share their bedroom," Irmingard continued, "then you may have to share with Erna so we can make it a boys-only room."

Ludwika liked what she heard. However much work there would be for her, she would never be as lonely here as she had been in Hamburg.

"You will like it with us," Irmingard said. "The timing is so perfect. Our housekeeper has been ill all week and I could only do the chores when Herr Gabler was here. I've been begging Erich Junior to ask his father for more funds so we can hire more help, but to no avail."

Ludwika looked questioningly at her employer.

"Who is Herr Gabler?" she asked.

"Ah, Herr Gabler is our home teacher," Irmingard explained. "He prepares the boys for school. Martin will start this September; the twins Max and Fritz will go next year. Then it will be Erna's turn. So you have your work cut out for the next two years at least. I'm still trying to persuade Erich to have Herr Gabler continue teaching the boys. Public schools can be so hit and miss. Many of the good teachers are at the front and I don't want my children to have a second-rate education. Erich says that if Martin doesn't do well we will take him out of school, but I say: Why wait until the damage is done? Especially, when we have such a talented teacher on our hands already?"

"Do you like Herr Gabler?" Ludwika asked the children.

They fell very quiet.

"Herr Gabler is wonderful," Irmingard answered for her children, her face slightly blushed. "He is very strict. He is retired and is doing this as a favour to Erich Senior. Erich Junior thinks that Herr Gabler is too good to be teaching only a few pre-school children and instead should be instructing entire class rooms. Erich thinks, as a member of the Reichstag, he should not be keeping someone to himself that could benefit many others. Fortunately, when we came to live here after the elections in '38, I made my Erich promise that our children would get the best possible education and this is what Herr Gabler is; even if he can be very demanding."

She had directed her last sentence at the children who suddenly seemed very sheepish.

"He always hits us with a stick," one of the twins said. Ludwika could not tell them apart, yet. "I'm sure you deserve it," Irmingard replied. "When I went to school we were always hit with a stick if we didn't behave. Herr Gabler is very old fashioned and I appreciate that. If you don't want to get hit, all you need to do is to behave. It's not that difficult."

The children fell silent again.

Ludwika looked at them and noticed Erna's face betraying some discomfort.

"Do you need to go?" she asked. Irmingard looked surprised and said: "Nonsense, she's been before we left. She can't possibly need to go again. We're home soon anyway."

"I better take her into that coffee house and take her to the toilet," Ludwika said.

"She needs to learn how to pace herself," Irmingard insisted. "When I was her age I was going like clockwork."

Ludwika took Erna by the hand and pulled her into the building to the toilet. Irmingard looked angry when Ludwika and Erna came back out.

"If you are going to spoil the children then you have to bear the consequences," she told her. "I'm washing my hands of it."

"Erna is not the first child of that age that I know," Ludwika replied. "I agree that children need discipline but when it comes on its own it is the best kind. She will learn how to pace herself much better in a year or two. She is just a little too young for it yet. That's what I believe, but of course you are her mother and know best."

Irmingard pondered on that and instead of replying, said: "Let's keep going. We're only a few blocks away from home."

Their home was on a busy crossroads by a bridge onto the Museum Island. It was a large stone building with a classical design, large arched windows and a huge entrance door. The apartment was on the third floor with views in several directions. The kitchen was large enough to fit a dining table even though there was a separate dining room. The living room was twice the size of the dining room. Then there was Herr Danner's office, as well as a library, three bedrooms and a bathroom. All of these were big rooms with high ceilings, filled with elegant ornaments and furniture that sat on expensive carpets. Ludwika was in awe and intimidated at the same time. Her bedroom was the smallest, but big by her standards.

Erich Danner had the same striking features as his father - the big nose and well-defined cheekbones. His chin was dimpled and his brow furrowed between bushy eyebrows. He was athletic and tall, with the same blue eyes as his three boys.

"Nice to meet you," he said, shaking hands. He appeared preoccupied and looked pleadingly at Irmingard. "I must apologise but I'm in the middle of a big project and must return to my office. My wife will make all the necessary arrangements with you. I look forward to seeing you at dinner."

With that he withdrew.

Irmingard sighed. "Typical Erich: always so busy and wrapped up in his politics."

She leaned towards Ludwika and whispered: "It is a shame, because all he ever does in the Reichstag is vote 'yes' for what the Government proposes. It's all a big boys' club and I don't think any of his efforts are really going to impress or even interest anyone.

What he does is nothing but a hobby, when he could be enjoying himself and taking advantage of all that Berlin has to offer. He loves the museums and art, but now that so many of the artists have turned out to be Jewish or degenerate, he hasn't been once to an exhibition."

She shook her head. "What a crazy world we live in these days."

Ludwika nodded as if in agreement. "You look tired. Would you like me to cook dinner?" she asked, wanting to change the topic.

"No," Irmingard said. "I need you to take care of the children."

Ludwika laughed. "I think I can do those two things at the same time. Your kitchen is big enough."

Irmingard looked astonished. "Are you sure? I can't even do one of them right," she said and giggled. "That would be marvellous. I would so like to take a bath and relax. We have to go to yet another party meeting tonight. I had such a busy day and my feet are killing me. If I'm not careful I'll fall asleep during those speeches, and Erich will be cross."

"Go ahead," Ludwika said. "I'll help you with the bath, too, if you need it."

"Thank you," Irmingard said. "You're worth your weight in gold."

Ludwika asked the children to find their favourite books and stories and then sit in the kitchen, waiting for her. Irmingard seemed surprised when the four children did as they were told by their new nanny.

Ludwika promised to read each of the stories if there was enough time.

"That would be more likely if some of you could help with the cooking. There's no need for you to do anything. You can just sit and watch me and we sing. If you are big enough to use a knife and cut some of the vegetables or find me ingredients from the larder, we might get enough time for an additional story. What do you say?"

Martin volunteered to cut the vegetables. He was quick to catch on and figured out how to do his tasks with little guidance needed. The twins went into the larder and looked for whatever Ludwika was asking for. Erna took the ingredients they had found and handed them proudly to Ludwika. By the time that Irmingard came out of the bathroom the kitchen smelled of chicken stew.

"What is that in the oven?" Irmingard asked.

"I am baking an apple strudel as well," she said. "A house should always have a cake or some pastries in case you get visitors or feel faint during the day."

"You are amazing," Irmingard said. "Please never leave us."

Erich Danner joined his family in the dining room.

"It smells delicious," he said when Ludwika served him his meal. "Maybe you can give my wife some lessons when the children are with Herr Gabler."

Irmingard shot him an angry look. "There is no need to be so mean," she said. "If Ludwika can look after the children and cook at the same time, I don't have to. I am pulling more than my weight with all the political rallies that we go to. Your father has been so kind and generous to us but you refuse to ask him to hire a cook for us."

Erich looked angry.

"Father bought us this apartment and the furniture," he said. "And he pays for Herr Gabler, who doesn't come cheap. That is more than enough. We live quite comfortably, especially now that we have such a competent new governess."

He ate his entire meal without saying another word.

Irmingard sulked, too, and only the children and Ludwika chatted happily away as if there was no tension at all.

"I'm very impressed," Irmingard said to Ludwika when the family had finished eating. "I was worried you would make everything too spicy or creamy. I was only in Poland once and the cuisine was not becoming. Your cooking is almost German. Well done!"

Ludwika silently thanked Manfred and his cookbooks. She still had them in her suitcase and would be able to make good use of them.

When she went to bed that night, after Erich and Irmingard had returned from their evening out, Ludwika felt content and safe for the first time in a long while. She just hoped that her family in Poland was, too.

Chapter 11

The summer passed quickly. The Danners allowed Ludwika to write to her sister Stasia to tell her all the news, but she never received a reply. She was very concerned about this and every day when the postman came she looked expectantly through the letters.

"There could be many reasons for this," Irmingard said when Ludwika mentioned her worries. "No news is always good news."

Ludwika shook her head.

"What if they've been deported? Manfred said he would make sure that wouldn't happen, but now that he's dead, maybe they lost the farm and have been forced to move?"

"I'm sure that if they were treated well all that time before, they will continue to receive those privileges. There is no need for the authorities to waste time and change anything that was working. And if they had moved, then the letter could have come back to you with 'unknown address' written on it," Irmingard pointed out. "I'm sure they heard your news but aren't able to write back. You really amaze me with your worrying over nothing."

"You're right," Ludwika said at last and wiped her tears away. "There is no point in worrying."

"That's better," Irmingard said. "Now that we cleared this up, I will leave you to your own devices. I have an appointment to have my hair done."

Life with the Danners was easy for Ludwika. The housekeeper came early mornings to make breakfast and left in the afternoon, usually around the time that Herr Gabler arrived. Ludwika prepared the other meals and when the children were being taught in the afternoons, she ran the odd errand and helped with the cleaning. As friendly as her employer was, Irmingard tended to complicate things and tried to point out errors wherever she could, whether they were true or not. The fact was the Danner household ran much smoother when she wasn't around to interfere. Even Herr Danner occasionally sneaked out of his office when Irmingard was gone and played the piano.

"Don't tell my wife," he'd say. "She'd be furious that I can take time out of my day to spend on my hobbies. If she knew I can make a little time for myself each day she would surely tell me how I ought to spend it and I would never get to play the piano."

Ludwika would smile knowingly and take the children to the playground, so there would be no witnesses to his time out of the office.

Herr Gabler, the tutor, was a tyrant of a man. Arrogance personified, he demanded complete submission from everyone, including the Danners. He had a walking stick which he used to discipline the children. Gabler would pace the room, his large paunch straining against his waistcoat as he played with his monocle. He would throw fiery looks at anyone who asked him anything. Even the most innocuous of questions could make people feel uncomfortable for asking them. At the same time he was never short of stingy remarks and insults, calling the children to reason and moderation.

"I'm hungry," he once said to Ludwika after one of his lessons. "Go and find me something, but not some of your Polish snacks; I want something tasty and proper."

She curtsied without giving him a reply, turned around and came back with a piece of apple strudel that she had cooked from a recipe in Manfred's cookbook. He devoured it in a manner that did not befit his alleged high social standing.

"Did you make this?" he asked.

"Yes."

"Is there more?" He sounded like a small child himself as his eyes shone with pleasure.

Again, she walked away without replying and came back with another big slice and put it on his desk.

"So much about the moderation you teach," she said drily and left. He blushed and then dug into the strudel as if nothing had been said.

From then on he treated her with a sudden and unexpected courtesy, as if her defiant remark had impressed rather than insulted him.

Ludwika could see why the children hated him, though. He ruled them by fear and they were always very timid when he was expected, which was about three times a week. They had no defence against his scolding. Ludwika liked to listen in on the lectures and often hid behind the door when it was ajar. Her maths and reading skills were poor and she could learn a lot from his teachings. She wondered if he knew about this and had spotted her through the small gap in the door: if so it probably flattered him.

When he gave difficult lessons he would send Erna out to stay with Ludwika. At other times he would give the older ones a task to do and have a one-on-one with the little girl. Ludwika was impressed by how much reading and counting the young children were capable of, long before their formal school education was to begin. She had to hand it to Herr Gabler: his methods worked.

When all three children were in the living room for their lessons, Herr Danner would often come out and keep Ludwika company in the kitchen. He would ask her questions about Poland and her family.

"I need to know these things," he said. "We're making racial laws and I haven't even been to Poland. My wife has been there once and she didn't like it much. I am to discuss the Führer's ideas and how to implement them, so it would be a huge help for me to see how different you Slavic people really are."

She told him as much as she knew, always tempted to beg him to find out about her family but was too scared to overstep the mark and lose his goodwill.

"Would you say that the Polish person is hard-working and goal-orientated or is he more under-achieving and lazy?"

"Hard-working, of course," Ludwika said quickly.

"Looking at you that seems certainly true," he said. "I hear that Untersturmführer Tischler thought you were of Germanic blood anyway: a shame he could never prove it. It would make everything so much easier," he said. "Imagine if a ban on foreigners were imposed to use the trams and trains? How would you be able to take the children to the Zoo? We need to do something about that before the laws close in on us."

Ludwika felt a surge of hope when he spoke like this, but then nothing ever came of his promises. The same initial enthusiasm ended without results when she finally dared to ask if he could find out more about her family and their situation.

"Naturally," he said. "I'd be happy to."

Weeks went by and he never mentioned the subject once. She doubted he even remembered. Clearly he was occupied with other issues. He seemed naïve and sweet at times and in such a threatening world, his gentleness was hugely appealing. Irmingard was a poor match for him, and he tended to blossom into a warm and chatty man whenever his wife was out of the house. If she was present, he resorted to being quiet and blunt. Irmingard's many rules and her constant nagging only succeeded in driving him away from her. If Ludwika and she were real friends, she would tell Irmingard to ease off before she damaged her marriage. As things stood, Irmingard seemed to struggle too much with her own life to take notice of other people, including her husband.

Ludwika sometimes wondered if Erich liked her. His behaviour certainly indicated an interest but it could well be only scientific. When he once caught her listening in on a lesson by Herr Gabler he smiled instead of being cross with her for not doing her chores. Manfred had been stricter with her than this, maybe because of his military background.

Christmas and New Year celebrations in the house went well. For the Danner family it meant everything was taken care of by Ludwika, and for her it meant she was distracted enough not to fall into the dark hole of sentiment. The tree, the carols, and the midnight Mass – all was reminiscent of home. Memories of Irena opening presents, of her brother Franz when he was still alive, her mother singing carol after carol. . . it was a difficult time and were it not for the smile on Erna's face, Ludwika would not have been able to bear it. A new year was about to begin, too. What would 1941 bring for her and the world?

One day in early January, Irmingard came back from the hairdresser with her hair dyed blonde.

"I'm fed up being looked at with suspicion," she said. "I can prove my Arian lineage with documents going back several centuries but that doesn't stop people from staring. Now at least they will leave me alone."

Ludwika understood. She felt those suspicious stares, too, when she was out and about.

"You are exaggerating," Erich said.

"I am not," his wife insisted. "Don't you like it?"

He hesitated before saying: "I do like it but it will look as if we have something to hide."

"I don't care," Irmingard said, angry.

Ludwika consoled her. "I understand how tormented you must feel," she said. "I often wish I was blonde."

"How about we treat you to the same extravagance for your birthday next week?" Irmingard asked.

Ludwika was delighted by the offer and by the fact that her employer had remembered the date. This would alleviate some of the looks on the street and it would be a luxury she thought she'd never enjoy. What a fantastic gift.

"I wish you wouldn't dye your hair," Erich said to her one afternoon as they sat together in the drawing room. He'd taken the opportunity for some surreptitious piano playing while Irmingard was out shopping and Herr Gabler was teaching the children.

"I understand," she replied. "It is too expensive, I guess, and the salon will refuse to treat a Polish woman."

"No, it's not that," he said and shifted uncomfortably on his seat.

"Why not then?" she asked, perplexed.

"I think you are prettier the way you are now," he said. "Irmingard looks dreadful with the yellow paint. Everyone can see it's fake. That's not the woman I married. She doesn't get bothered on the street, as she claims. She is vain and is just using this as an excuse to try something new. Please don't make the same mistake and destroy your beauty."

"There is no use in me being beautiful," she replied. "Nobody benefits from it. The dye may help me look after your children more easily when I'm in public. I don't think they need to witness any more of the harassment I get, not if that could be avoided."

"Stay beautiful for me," he said, moving from the armchair in which he was sitting to join her on the chaise longue. "I have a friend who will take up your case to become germanised. You can't help the odd look or two on the street, but without the 'P' you will be living a different life than you are now. It will be worth it."

She was lost for words at this forward complement. What was she to think of that?

"Thank you," she said. The hope of becoming a German citizen was too much to allow herself to dream about. What would it mean for Irena and the rest of her family – would they be made safer as a result? Would they become Germans, too? If it didn't come true again she couldn't bear the disappointment.

"It's wrong to assume that the Nordic race consists only of blond people," Erich said. "The Führer himself has dark hair and a toned complexion. I don't see the ugly Slavic features in your face at all, which makes me convinced you are from better stock."

As he spoke, his fingers caressed her cheekbone. Ludwika was scared. She had read the racial laws when they were laid out after the invasion of Poland. Relations with a German were punishable by death. She had no way of refusing him, but she didn't want this. It was dangerous. If anyone saw them she could be killed. He, too, would lose everything he had worked for - his career and his family. She drew away, timid and frightened.

"Come here," he said, pulling her into his office and closed the door.

"Don't," she said. "Think of Irmingard and the children. We're breaking the law," she said, hoping to make him see sense.

"Don't worry," he said. "I don't work for the Reichstag for nothing."

"Your wife...," she said, "...if she finds out."

"She won't," he promised. "She's too self-absorbed to even think it."

He leaned in and kissed here, which sent pulses of unexpected pleasure coursing through her body. It was wrong but it felt good to have another human touch her, want her and caress her. Ludwika realised she was helpless; resisting would only make matters worse. She relented reluctantly, frightened of being caught.

As if he could read her mind he said: "The children's lessons will go on for a while and Irmingard won't be back for hours. She's clothes shopping: this is safe."

He locked the door to his office and began to quickly undress her. To her surprise, he was a skilled, passionate and considerate lover. It was somewhat spoilt for her by fear and guilt but it hadn't felt like a violation. He held her close for long after they had finished. She felt strangely protected and ashamed for it. Irmingard had been her saviour and here Ludwika was, sleeping with her employer's husband.

"You're not the first," Erich said, as if he could read her mind. "My marriage has been a sham for a long time now. Don't think you've ruined it. If anything, you are able to prolong it by taking care of the children. If it were not for you, Irmingard and I would be arguing all the time. You've brought harmony to a place that was a battlefield. Don't feel bad about what happened between us. It is a wonderful thing."

What could she say to that?

"Thank you." It was her reply to almost everything these days. Ludwika got up and dressed. Erich hid the used condom in a box in his desk and put his clothes back on, too.

There was a knock at the door. She ducked and hid behind the desk while Erich arranged his clothes and then opened the door, calmly and as naturally as if he had nothing to hide. It was Erna, who'd been dismissed from class and couldn't find Ludwika.

"She probably went out for some groceries or for a breath of fresh air," Erich said. "Go back to class and wait for her there," he suggested.

When Erna had gone back to the living room, Ludwika quickly sneaked out and disappeared down the staircase. She waited for a few minutes before she came back up and entered the flat as if she really had been on a walk. Her face was flushed and she thought that everyone could tell her shame.

She busied herself in the kitchen, making another cake. Erna never reappeared and neither did Erich. When Herr Gabler was finished with his lesson the children never asked where she had been and Ludwika was left to try and behave as if this was just another day; however, a lot had changed.

Chapter 12

Erich never missed an opportunity to make love to her in his office, even though those occasions were very rare. The Danner residence had many visitors and he was a cautious man. When they finally were alone together he was always affectionate and it seemed he wanted to be close to her, too. It didn't feel like he was using her, it felt as if he was in love. Yet, despite the unexpected intimacy between them he avoided her questions about her family or of securing a German passport for her. She never dared to push him on the issues. She had seen that nagging like Irmingard's only made him stubborn. She could only pray that he would make good his promise. She felt she had good reasons to be optimistic.

Irmingard was pre-occupied of late and seemed to have forgotten all about having Ludwika's hair dyed. Ludwika's birthday went by without a celebration or even a mention of it from her employers. A few weeks after the day, in February, Irmingard announced that she was pregnant again and made a huge fuss about it, demanding special food for her ever-changing appetites, more time for rest and she refused to go to any more political rallies and evening outings. Erich was delighted about the new arrival to their family at first and gave in to all of her demands, but her moodiness soon poisoned the atmosphere between them.

"I know the Führer wants children but I asked Erich to be careful," she complained to Ludwika one afternoon. "Four is more than enough, especially since he still refuses to hire more help."

Ludwika knew how careful Erich could be, so she knew he had to have done it on purpose. Poor Irmingard seemed tired and exhausted from this pregnancy, not at all as happy and radiant as Ludwika had felt when she was expecting Irena. "I'll help," she offered. "You don't have to worry about a thing."

Irmingard smiled weakly, but her eyes were sad.

She seemed to resent her husband and as soon as he was out of the door in the evenings, she would put on her coat and sneak out to the cinema, demanding that Ludwika wouldn't tell him about her nightly escapades.

"I need to get out of this trap," she said and disappeared into the night.

To complicate things further, Herr Gabler would continually invite Ludwika to sit in on his lessons.

"I've spotted you so many times hiding behind that gap in the door," he said. "Not so much lately but still often enough to assume your mind is thirsty for knowledge, a sign that you need stimulus. If Herr Danner doesn't object, it could be very beneficial."

"Oh I don't know," she said evasively. "I wouldn't find the time."

"You seem to find the time to go for a stroll and fresh air increasingly more often when I'm in the house," he said suggestively. "You can't possibly be that busy if you have time for that."

She froze. He couldn't possibly know, could he?

"I fear that my presence during your lessons would have an adverse effect on the children's discipline," she answered. "I always make them laugh and you are ever so serious."

"Let that be my concern. Ask Herr Danner," Herr Gabler said. "Let's hear what he has to say on the matter."

Ludwika mentioned it to Erich the next time they were alone. He would hear none of it.

"There is no way I would let you spend time with Gabler when you could be with me. Don't you understand how much I need you? I never get to touch my wife these days, especially not since she is pregnant. Without our meetings my life is nothing but coldness and hard work. Politics is a demanding business with tough decisions to be made every day. We need to put our hearts second and our rational mind first. Don't think that I'm enjoying the harsh rule we must implement. Even when I spend time with the children, Irmingard has asked me to be strict and set boundaries. I'm never allowed to be soft and gentle. You are the only person who knows the real me, the only one who understands."

Ludwika doubted that she knew him at all. Right now she was as puzzled and surprised as she could be. She thought he loved his work for the Reichstag and that he was behind all their decisions. Now he voiced regrets. What else was he unhappy about? He seemed to run deeper than she had thought. She swore to herself to be very careful with him from now on. Her life in Berlin was too good to lose. She could only hope that Erich wouldn't snap and make a rash and stupid mistake. She mustn't anger or provoke him and for that reason she had to decline Herr Gabler.

"With Frau Danner being pregnant, I think it would be unwise to commit to regular lessons," she said to Herr Gabler. "I'm so grateful for your kind offer but there won't be many walks in the future," she assured him.

From that point on, when she and Erich were intimate during Herr Gabler's lessons, she took groceries from the apartment with her in a basket and pretended that she had bought them on the market fresh while the lessons were in progress.

Herr Gabler threw her suspicious looks all the same. Ludwika couldn't imagine how, but she knew that the tutor was on to her and Erich. She continued to behave as if nothing were the matter but her abrupt manners with Gabler probably confirmed his suspicions that she had something to hide.

Ludwika became uncomfortable in his presence.

"When the twins go to school in September, Gabler will be a thing of the past," Erich said. "I'll 'volunteer' him for the public schools. It's time he shared his talent with a wider audience. He has a lot more potential; maybe if he is being kept occupied that will stop him from snooping around my business."

"Aren't you scared he might expose us?" Ludwika asked. "He seems to know something."

"If he knew and wanted to do something about it, he would have done so already," Erich replied. "He's just trying to get back at you for standing up to him. Men like him come across as being strong and patronising but when it comes to taking on a member of the Reichstag he will have his tail between his legs and behave. Don't you worry about it."

The cat and mouse game in the Danner household continued for several months. Irmingard grew large but never let that stop her going out. Ludwika wondered if she, too, had a lover. Maybe both of them were cheating, not just Erich. She hoped that was the case. She also hoped that Erich hadn't forgotten about her papers. He was always angry about his wife and so she never dared ask him about her problems. It tormented her not to know anything about her family and Irena and be in limbo about her future.

German and Italian military might swept through the Balkans and Greece, with nothing in sight to stop them, attitudes in the Reich were hardening towards foreigners. Twice she had been refused custom in a coffee house and a restaurant when she took the children out for walks or excursions. The stigma of the 'P' sewn on her clothes was becoming a greater burden every day. She became painfully aware of her position as a privileged slave whose cares and worries were totally secondary to the Danners. Her best option was to lay low and not provoke their anger by repetitive demands or questions. She was lucky to be in the position she was, and that type of pestering behaviour might make matters worse.

"It's not safe for you to make all these 'extra shopping' trips anymore," Herr Gabler said to her one summer day after he had finished his lessons. Ludwika had been with Erich and she was still flushed, unable to cool down sufficiently in the boiling June heat.

She froze, wondering what he meant.

"I'm sorry to be so blunt," he said, playing with his monocle, "but your people are being dragged from the streets and their homes and forced to work for the big factories over here. You must have heard about this, even if you have been spared witnessing it yourself. There is so much hard labour to be done in Germany and all of our strong young men are fighting somewhere for our future. I worry about you, Ludwika. Please be careful on the streets and everywhere else. Your good fortune hangs on a very thin thread, don't be mistaken by any reassurances you are getting."

She nodded, too shell-shocked to even come out with a "Thank you."

When the Germans attacked Russia in late June and more men left their families for the front, women were encouraged to support the war effort. Posters everywhere in the city invited them to share the burden.

"They have a nerve," Irmingard said when the two women walked past one such advertisement. "I'm carrying enough of a burden as it is." She pointed at her huge belly. "I think it's twins again, or the baby is a monster. Either way," she said to Ludwika, "you will have to stay with us much longer than we had thought."

That at least was music to Ludwika's ears. Her position was safe.

Herr Gabler on the other hand continued to warm Ludwika whenever he got a chance to speak to her alone.

"I know from a reliable source that the number of imported workers from the East is rising dramatically," he said. "It's no longer just the big factories who order them. In some places the workers are locked away in camps, but not everywhere. The more of you are visible on the streets, then the more aware the population will become and the stricter the implementation of all the rules about interaction between Polish people and Germans. You have to be very careful. You don't want to end up in one of these camps and be working day and night in a factory, do you? There is one such camp here in Berlin, not far from here in Oranienburg, right next to the Heinkel factory. I have it on good authority. Please, be careful."

She thanked him and tried to shrug it off, but she was getting infected by his doom and gloom.

"I don't know what you have been promised and whether Herr Danner has enough influence but, if I were you, I would try to be outside as little as possible."

She nodded thankfully. If only it was up to her, she thought. Ludwika would stop seeing Erich and going out on the streets at the drop of a hat. Sadly, all of this was out of her hands.

The next time she saw Erich, she urged him to speed things up for her German passport and work permit, telling him about what she had learned.

"You are so sweet," he said, kissing her forehead. "You have nothing to worry about. Those camps are for criminals and for Roma and prisoners of war. Gabler and his scaremongering mustn't upset you. He is an old fool who probably has a crush on you. That's all."

However, Ludwika could not help feeling that the teacher was right and probably her only true friend left. Erich seemed too naïve to see the danger and he made nothing but empty promises. She had to do something herself.

With the little funds she had saved, mostly from Manfred's housekeeping money and Herr Danner senior's generous cash injection, Ludwika went to a hairdresser to have her hair dyed. Unfortunately, the salons around the city centre refused her service. One was kind enough to direct her to a barber who might be persuaded to 'perform the procedure'. She walked up north, following the directions she had been given, only to find herself in the Scheunenviertel, a Jewish quarter. The familiar hateful graffiti on walls and the odd atmosphere on the road reminded her of the drama in the Grindelviertel in Hamburg and her resolve began to crumble. Ludwika's instinct was to turn around and run away, but she pulled herself together. She knew she had to go through with it. Irmingard insisted that she had a much easier life since her hair had been dyed. That couldn't have been made up just for effect, as Erich seemed to think. Ludwika believed her and so she braced herself and continued walking until she found the man in question, sitting in one of the salon chairs, reading a paper.

"I can't help you," the barber said abruptly after she had explained what she wanted, and he turned back to his reading.

"Please," she begged.

He put the paper away and glared at her.

"Do you know how many people in Berlin and in this quarter currently want their hair dyed blonde? There's too many of you and too little dye to go around in these parts. Look at my empty business – does it seem to you I have dye to spare? Even if I had some left, I couldn't give it to you, a stranger who isn't even one of us."

He directed that last part at her 'P'.

She looked at him as if this wasn't real. He couldn't refuse her as well. He had to know what she was going through. They were both victims of the same tyrants, were they not? She didn't move.

"Don't you have ears?" he shouted. "Get out."

His aggressive tone startled her and she turned and left, upset by his unkindness and now completely unsure what to do next. One thing she did know, though, was that she had to get out of the Scheunenviertel. She walked steadily back south when an army truck passed her, causing her heart to pound. This was too similar to the Grindelviertel in Hamburg. Ludwika managed to keep walking, but her knees were jittery. With every step, she felt as if her legs would give in and she might fall to the pavement. When she heard that the truck had stopped not far behind her she doubled her steps, desperate to get away. The next street corner was not far ahead. It would be her opportunity to get off this dangerous road; she would be safe. Yet, she couldn't help wondering what the soldiers wanted here. She couldn't resist turning back to find out. Maybe it was all harmless or maybe it was time to run. She had to know.

Ludwika saw the soldiers surrounding a building while a small group of them went through its front door. Although nobody paid her any attention, at the sight of their rifles, she panicked and began to run, heading for the safety of the road on her left.

"Halt!" One of the soldiers screamed behind her. She was too far away from the building they had encircled, this couldn't be meant for her, she told herself and kept running. Just as she was about to turn the corner, she heard the command "Feuer" behind her and then a salvo of shots, followed by a sharp sting somewhere above her knee. Ludwika's leg gave way and she fell to the ground, head first, cutting her face in the process. Before she had a moment to recover some of the soldiers gathered around her.

"Don't move," one said, aiming his rifle at her. The other searched her and found Manfred's letter.

"Polish," he said to his comrade. "Stupid cow for running away."

She was about to say something but the sight of the rifle silenced her.

"Do you want to call a doctor?" one asked the other.

"Are you having a laugh?" came the reply. "For her? No, she'll be fine on the truck. Better find out whether she is who she says she is. What's she doing around here unless she's Jewish, too? Better have that checked out."

They dragged her roughly over the pavement and lifted her onto the truck. Ludwika was in agony but that didn't seem to bother the brutes handling her. The throbbing pain around her knee felt like hammers hitting her repeatedly with every beat of her pulse. She tried to touch the wound but she was unable to as the soldiers hauled her towards the truck. It was excruciating. She vaguely noticed that something was wrong in her mouth; her upper lip was swollen and her cheek, which had scratched along the cobbles, was bleeding. Her leg was wet, so she guessed the wound down there was bleeding, too, but not a lot.

The strangest thing was that none of that mattered. Her pain was the least of her worries. She was in much graver danger now that she was in the hands of such merciless killers. She should have listened to Herr Gabler; how stupid of her to come here of all places, she scolded herself. Would Erich's influence be enough to get her out of this? She had her doubts.

Ludwika sat alone on the truck, waiting while the soldiers stormed the building. At least she could put pressure on her wound and stop the bleeding. Oh, it was sore. Outside she heard loud commands and shouted warnings from the soldiers; shots rang out, followed by screams and crying. Ludwika cowered in the corner of the truck, terrified.

There were a few more shots, then the truck was filled with a group of Jewish men and women, only some of them in traditional attire. Some men had their curls and beards cut off, their faces bleeding from the rough and humiliating treatment. Soldiers joined them and then the truck started its journey to a police station. She saw the Jews being loaded onto a bigger truck while two men compared lists and crossed off names. She was the only one left, still cowering in the corner.

"Get up," ordered a soldier. He waved impatiently at her from the outside.

She tried to move forwards but could only slide sideways and drag the wounded leg behind.

"Oh for crying out loud," the man said and boarded the truck. He pulled her roughly along the bench and then held her armpits as he slid her down onto the tarmac.

"Damn it," he said when she fell to the ground, unable to support her body weight. The fall hurt but it was nothing in comparison to the pain she was already feeling. The soldier carried her inside the police station where he put her into a holding cell and locked the door before she got a chance to speak to someone. Ludwika knocked on the door but the only response she got was a cold "Shut up."

She felt too weak to pursue this further. Left alone, she sank on the bed. She studied the wound, it was not as large as she had expected given the pain she was feeling. It looked like a bullet had grazed her leg At least the bleeding wasn't too bad. She doubted she would die from blood loss but she felt dizzy all the same. She ripped part of her jacket off and pressed it firmly onto the wound to stop the bleeding.

Her face hurt and felt strange. There was grit in her mouth - or was it something else? She felt with her tongue and found a gap. A tooth must have shattered when she had fallen to the ground. The others didn't feel right either. Some might have been chipped; how badly she couldn't be sure. She wondered if Erich could help her now.

Chapter 13

Nobody came for what seemed ages. Were it not for the pain, Ludwika would have preferred it that way. She remembered Herr Gabler's warnings about the camps and factory work and feared for the worst. Eventually, a doctor was brought in to examine her knee. She tried to tell him and the soldiers that accompanied him about her position with Erich but they shushed her.

"That's not too bad. . . just a good graze," the doctor said to the soldiers as if she weren't even there. He opened his bag and got a bottle of disinfectant out, a needle and bandages. "You'll need to hold her down while I stitch her up," he said and dabbed alcohol on the wound.

The pain was excruciating. Ludwika managed to hold still, realising that resistance was only going to prolong the process, but she screamed in pain until the soldiers pushed a cloth in her mouth to stop her. It was over quickly, though. The doctor remarked how lucky she was that the bones and the patella had not been hit and splintered. He was very rough when making the stitches. Then he bandaged the knee and left without bothering to examine her face.

Ludwika was on her own again and was kept in her cell without food or any further attention. At least she was able to stretch out. She could have felt safer if she had company, though. A part of her was assuming the worst, while another was sure that Erich would eventually come after her and sort out the mess she was in, once she had the opportunity to mention his name. Had they not seen the letter from Manfred? Although it was out of date, it showed that she was regarded as an asset to the Reich by an Untersturmführer; she was not an enemy and not a Jew. And she was working for a member of the Reichstag. Her captors had to be made aware of it. If only someone would speak to her she could clear things up. This had to be a big misunderstanding. Whoever they had been searching for in that house in the Scheunenviertel, it wasn't her and that had to be known by now.

She couldn't make sense of the world any more. Having lived near the German border all of her life, she had known many nice and peaceful Germans. What had befallen the nation?

How she cursed that stupid idea of having her hair dyed, and how she hated that Jew who had tossed her out of his shop. It was his fault that she had been out on the street in the first place. She was beginning to wonder whether maybe the Jews were really to blame for the mess in Europe. Could an evil so big have suddenly appeared without any reason? She didn't know what to think any more. As the hours progressed and she wasn't released, Ludwika's heart sank. Of course, Erich wouldn't be able to save her. Herr Gabler had been right. Why would a man of such great promise and social standing risk being associated with a Polish woman who had been arrested in the Scheunenviertel? The scandal would be too great; he would have to distance himself from her. This meant also that she would probably be sent to a camp and never be able to see Irena or the Danner children again, never get to return to Poland or to that comfortable house in Berlin. Her life was over.

Then her hopes rose again. Erich was a member of the German parliament. He had to have powerful friends and influence. He had assured her so many times that he would protect her and that it would be possible for him to do so. Maybe this would be easy for him to sort out, if only she could alert him to her situation.

The night dragged on, not helped by the pain and the constant back and forth of her worry. None of her father's wisdom could stop that now. She was in the hands of the authorities and her case was weak.

The next morning, at last a policeman came in to her cell and wrote down all of her details: name, place of birth, Nationality and home address. When Ludwika tried to explain that she was working for a member of the Reichstag he looked at her suspiciously and noted it down without asking her any further questions before making his exit.

She waited, still in agony and without food, for several hours. Then the man came back.

"We spoke to the family in question. Herr Danner has confirmed that you were working as his governess," he said. "I don't know how you bewitched the man but he was willing to go to considerable length to have you released."

Her heart beat faster with excitement. Erich had kept his word.

"I don't know why you're smiling," the man replied. "Once I told Frau Danner that you've been fraternising with the Jews, resisting arrest and were shot fleeing from the authorities, she reined her husband in. She said that with an injury you were no longer of any use to the household. She is heavily pregnant, she said, and needs someone who can look after her children, not one who gallivants through the Jewish quarter."

"What about Herr Danner, what did he say?" Ludwika asked, holding on to the name as her last straw of hope.

"He said that he believed you of good character and of German ancestry. Therefore, you should be considered as suitable for Germanisation. Untersturmführer Tischler had confirmed this before his death in France but sadly the relevant documents were lost."

She was touched at Erich's efforts but she could tell by the look of the man before her that it had not been enough to save her.

"The trouble is, you need a working permit," the man said, bluntly. "If we issue you with a permit it will be made out to you as a Polish National and that brings you under the jurisdiction of a different department. We will have to send you to one of the detention camps for Eastern Workers. Only yesterday, a whole bunch of you were sent from here to a camp in Oldenburg, together with the Russian prisoners."

Tears poured down her face. This could not be happening.

"If we forget about that, you still have charges against you for fraternising with Jews and resisting the authorities. Unless you can prove your German ancestry quickly you will be sentenced as a Polish woman and the outcome then is also your deportation to a detention or work camp."

She looked at the man with astonishment. He had delivered her verdict with the utmost neutrality as if he didn't care one way or another, as long as the law was kept and regulations adhered to. He didn't seem to think this was cruel or heartless. He seemed devoid of human feeling.

She wondered how long they would allow her to recuperate before moving her. It was mildly reassuring to know that Erich had cared and was trying to help. In effect, however, it amounted to nothing. Who would have thought that Irmingard would drop her like a hot potato?

It was also the first time Ludwika had heard that there had been actual proof of her German ancestry. Manfred had confirmed it, the policeman had clearly said that. If the documents had been lost, maybe they could be found or new documents could be produced. If

Erich knew about this then he had to be close to finding the document or proof or whatever it was they needed. She seemed so close to reaching her goal: a German passport meant not only her own survival, it would also protect her family and the farm, the main reason she had come here. If only she didn't run out of time before the bureaucratic trap fell shut on her.

The waiting and isolation were torture. Every time someone came near her door Ludwika jumped up, only to crouch down in disappointment again when they walked on. She still was in great pain. Her knee was weak and movement of her leg was very painful.

After the soldiers had gone she was finally fed: a small piece of chicken, ham and bread. Then she was left alone again, forced to wait and hope that all would turn out fine.

On the third day in her confinement she had a visitor: to her surprise it wasn't a member of the Danner family but Herr Gabler. She hurt herself trying to get up when he walked into the cell.

"Stay down," he said. "There's no need for formalities any longer. Not in here, you silly woman."

She looked at him searchingly, trying to figure out what he had come for. Was he gloating?

"My dear Fräulein Gierz, I can only imagine how difficult your situation here must be: the not-knowing, the wondering and worrying. As I've grown older I've become a very impatient man and cannot bear suspense at any cost. I've come here today to put you out of your misery."

She looked even more puzzled. What on earth was he on about?

"I have learned much more about your current state than even the police know at this moment."

He walked back and forth in the cell and looked at her with pity.

"Frau Danner is aware of your liaison with her husband," he said. "She once came back unexpectedly from an errand and heard you two love birds through the office door. She is probably pleased about it since she has begun an affair with someone else herself and it is likely that said man, a soldier on the Russian front, is the father of her unborn child. I understand he was on leave around the right time for that."

"How is that going to affect me?" Ludwika asked, worried and confused at the same time. She realised this had to be bad news in any case, but she had no idea what it would mean in detail.

"In light of her own indiscretion Frau Danner needed to secure her marriage and has approached me to testify against you should it ever come to divorce proceedings. She hoped that my promise to do so would act as a guarantee for any rash decision on behalf of Herr Danner, should he discover her affair."

"I'm still not following you," Ludwika said.

"I covered for you, of course," Herr Gabler said. "I did not want to get involved in a domestic argument and did not want to hurt you. I can't see how she would leave her husband or vice versa. She is so used to the luxury and he can't risk a scandal. So I denied all knowledge of your affair."

He stopped and looked at her angrily.

"I warned you repeatedly to stop this foolishness before it got out of hand. If only you had listened. Without my cooperation Frau Danner needed a different proof so she positioned herself outside the house with a private detective. The two of them entered the flat after a considerable wait and then quietly searched it, all rooms bar the office. They then waited outside until the lessons were almost over. Frau Danner returned to the flat and found you back in the kitchen, claiming you had gone shopping when she could confirm that you had not left the house all afternoon."

"What is she going to do?"

"She is going to do nothing," Herr Gabler said. "I told you, she needs her bargaining chip should things go wrong for her. She told me triumphantly and scolded me for not being a better spy. Herr Danner, however, might well do something. Unfortunately, Frau Danner can be a bit careless when it comes to covering her tracks. Herr Danner found out about the private detective his wife had hired and asked me if I had been approached by said gentleman. I hadn't, but Frau Danner had mentioned the name of the detective, so I knew that Herr Danner was on to her."

Ludwika still looked stunned. Where was this leading?

"Herr Danner told me and the police yesterday that he would seek to get an exemption for your case that would allow you to work for his family. Given what I know about the mutual spying and given what he stands to lose I wondered how genuine his statement was.

His wife knows about your liaison and has a detective to back up her story: this didn't make sense. So I conducted a little investigation myself. With the excuse of looking for reference books in the office I have searched his desk and found a letter he had composed to the police, recommending that you were actually not to be exempt but to be sent back to Poland instead. His family no longer required your services. I guess he meant well, hoping you would be reunited with your family, as you so dearly want. As soon as he sends the letter you are on the next train out. Only it won't be to Poland as he naively assumes. It will be to a work camp, as I've told you repeatedly."

Ludwika shook her head.

"That can't be," she said. "It can't."

"I'm afraid it can," Herr Gabler said. "For what it's worth, I shall be very sad seeing you leave. I would have been happy to help you if I could. I wish you luck. At least now you know where you stand and don't have to harbour false hopes or worry for nothing. You're no stranger to hard work, so I'm sure your life in the camp will be more bearable than it is for others. People will like you, wherever you go. Chin up and don't ever give up. A strong woman like you has everything at her disposal to survive. Don't cry over that spineless wastrel."

"I won't," Ludwika said, bravely. "I'm crying over my daughter and my family."

"You have to let go of that, my dear Ludwika," he said, clicking his heels like a soldier. "They are out of your reach and will have their own resources to work with. Your worry is only costing you strength. You need to solve your own problems and fight to survive. I'm sure they do the same wherever they are now. Pull yourself together. You are better than Frau Danner, who whines day in and day out. Do your family proud by being resilient. I know you have it in you."

She nodded. He was right: it was all she could do. His tone was harsh but she felt his care for her and it gave her new strength.

"I'm worried about the Danner children," she said. "What did their parents tell them about me?"

Herr Gabler's face twitched uncomfortably.

"They told them that you had gone back to Poland because of a family matter."

Ludwika nodded in acceptance.

"Good," she said. "Promise me to support this story at any cost. Don't tell them I was shot or what is happening to me. I don't want the little ones to find out and be sad. Let me have that little comfort that they are spared the awful truth."

"Of course," he said. "I never planned to tell them anything. I'm there for their mathematics and their reading skills, and nothing else."

"Herr Gabler," she said, looking at him with pleading eyes. "You are a good teacher. Please don't be so hard on them all of the time. Try to make them feel like they are worth something, too. As a teacher you can do that. The Danners spend next to no time with them; it's as if the children aren't worth their bother. You do, so please show them that you are enjoying their company. It will mean a lot. They need to learn but they also need a childhood and happy times. There is so much tragedy and pain in the world."

In response, Herr Gabler noisily sucked up air into his nostrils.

"Thanks for your honesty," she said.

"You're most welcome."

He took her hand and kissed it.

"In that same spirit: remember, you are strong and a formidable person. Best of luck to you."

He clicked his heels again and then left.

Ludwika understood her situation at last. Misled by false hopes and promises she had allowed herself to become weak and deluded. Now that she faced a tougher future she was ready to meet the challenges full on.

Part 2

Chapter 14

The next morning an official told Ludwika what she already knew: there was no need or place for her in Berlin, so she would be joining an initiative to balance the workforce within the Reich and be transferred further west where manpower was needed. She would continue her recovery there until she was able to make her contribution to the Reich.

She listened to the man without much emotion. She felt numb, but resolved to face whatever was coming her way. The constant worry about losing her privileges and safety and about the fate of her family had caused her a pain of its own. In a perverted way this felt better as she was no longer running away or chasing false hopes. It was as her father had said: all the worry had not protected her. In her case, her worry had caused her to do a stupid thing and go to the Scheunenviertel where she was shot and arrested.

Herr Gabler had been a godsend with his honesty and encouragement. If he believed that she would manage in this work camp then maybe there was a chance that she would. It was lucky that Ludwika had sent that letter to Stasia when her life was at its best. If her family was still on their farm they would not have to worry about Ludwika, they would never know of her current misfortune and neither would the Danner children. All of them could continue with their innocent belief that Ludwika was taken good care of and that maybe one day she would return.

She took comfort in the fact that the people who cared for her were spared the awful truth.

An hour after the official had left, Ludwika was escorted to an army truck full of prisoners. They made room for her on the bench after she had been lifted on. Nobody spoke until the truck reached a goods depot where the prisoners were loaded onto freight trains and locked in. The people were kind enough to let her sit in a corner with her leg outstretched. There were no seats, no windows and next to no light. After an initially subdued and quiet atmosphere in their wagon, once the train was well on its way, people began to slowly talk to each other. She could hear Russian and Polish being spoken in the distance, and German men nearer by, all speculating about what was to come.

She tried to blank everything out but it was impossible. She was tired and her body felt hot and feverish. She nodded off and slept for most of the journey, which had a lot of stops. She had terrible nightmares that the other passengers shunned her for coming to Hamburg with Manfred; they spat at her and treated her like a collaborator and traitor. When she woke up she saw thought she could hear someone say that they were in Hamburg but maybe she was only imagining that, too. She couldn't see the outside from where she was sitting and she was too frightened to speak to anyone, worrying that her dreadful dreams might come true if she let on anything about her past.

Late afternoon, the train came to another stop in Oldenburg, a town in the Northwest of Germany and further away from Poland than she had ever been. The goods wagon was opened and their group was loaded onto a convoy of trucks that drove them to various camps. A few Russians were unloaded at a primary school building that had been converted. Ludwika and a group of Polish and Eastern Europeans were taken to the Lindenhof, a restaurant in the centre of town with guest rooms and a dance hall. The new arrivals were led into a large dining room within the restaurant where a committee of soldiers and civilians were inspecting their papers and assigning them jobs.

When it was Ludwika's turn, an abrupt woman demanded to see her wound. Ludwika uncovered it for her.

"Bending down might be a problem," the woman said without any real emotion. "I'll get a nurse to have a look at you later. Maybe we can make a splint or something for you. You'll work in the canteen until you can bend and bear weight."

She made a few notes, then she said: "Your bed is in the woman's section in the dance hall."

She wrote something on a small form, stamped it, handed it to Ludwika and nodded towards the exit behind her.

"Next!" she shouted, already looking for the next worker.

Ludwika limped slowly through the door in question, down a long corridor until she saw a door that said 'Dance Hall'. The room was huge and filled with makeshift beds and mattresses. A small part of it had been divided off for women. Ludwika made it to one of the beds and lay down. Although there were only the new arrivals in the hall, most of the bunks seemed to be taken already, indicating that more people would be arriving later, probably after their shifts had finished. So far, everything seemed humane and not too bad. Before she had time to give her situation much more thought the promised nurse arrived and fixed her leg with a splint made from two old planks. It was makeshift but it did the job. Ludwika was surprised and pleased.

"I damaged my teeth," Ludwika said to the nurse, who was about to leave.

"Let me have a look," the woman said and examined the mouth with her fingers.

"I'm surprised you're not in more pain," she said. "You've broken large chunks off. They'll have to come out or the exposed nerves are going to kill you."

"Thank you," Ludwika said and sank back on her bed. At least there was some medical care for them and food. She had feared worse from what she had heard about the German and Russian prisoner of war camps in the Great War. This didn't feel like a prison. People were free to walk around. The slip of paper she had been given said 'work permit'. She thought of Herr Gabler and smiled. She would do as he had asked her and be brave and strong.

When the other women came back from their work Ludwika was shooed off her bed and she had to take one of the less comfortable mattresses by the drapes that divided the hall. There was a draft, which was probably why it had been left vacant.

"How long have you been here?" Ludwika asked the woman who looked the least unfriendly, in German and then in Polish.

The woman was in her twenties, like Ludwika, small, bony with dark curly hair. She looked tired and sad but less aggressive than the women who earlier had told Ludwika to get off their beds.

"Two months," she answered in Polish. "I was working in a hotel in Hamburg before then. They took me a few weeks after the invasion."

"How is it here?" Ludwika asked. "I've noticed there are few guards. Aren't the Germans scared we'll run off?"

"Run off?" the woman said and laughed. "Where would we be running to? What would you be living off? Unless you know someone who can take you in and hide, the police will have found you before you got to the edge of town."

"Then it's not too bad in here?" Ludwika said, her hope rising.

"It depends on how you view things," came the reply, "and what they're making you do. I'm working in a hotel here. The people are not very nice but I get food on the table and I even get to keep a little money. Others have to dig out soil to help build a road through the city. They work hard every day. I wouldn't want to swap with them."

"Thank you," she said. When the woman didn't say any more, she added: "My name is Ludwika."

"I'm Halina," the woman replied. "The rules for us Poles and for the camp in general are hung up on a pin board in the hallway. Read them yourself, I'm too tired to explain everything to you today. I've got to lie down now."

"Thank you," Ludwika said and got up and limped towards the pin board. The strict and threatening tone of the rules didn't surprise her, few of them were new to her anyway: no fraternisation with Germans, sexual relations with Germans bore the death penalty, there was a curfew in place and plenty of rules about the general housekeeping and the hygiene in the camp.

Ludwika returned to her bed and quietly observed who was friendly with whom and how the women in this section went about their business. She followed them to the dining hall where their evening meal was served: an indefinable stew with bread. The new arrivals were taken to the restaurant kitchen where they had to do the dishes, even Ludwika with her limp. By the time the entire camp had been fed and the kitchen work was done it was dark outside and Ludwika fell exhausted onto her bed. Her leg was sore.

She was awoken early to start her morning shift in the kitchen. The camp inmates were served a small portion of porridge each before being sent on their way just after sunrise. Ludwika found that standing up for a long time was difficult and that carrying the dirty dishes to the sink was also challenging. She was careful not to break anything and not to be seen as disobedient. After the team had finished tidying up the kitchen she was given a huge pile of potatoes to peel, sitting on a chair next to a serving trolley for the peeled potatoes and a bucket for the skin. In the middle of the room a group of Polish women sat on a table, doing the same. They were chatting and laughing, while she was all alone. They didn't seem to care. An hour into the repetitive and boring task, the nurse interrupted her and asked her to come along.

Ludwika was led into a small room with an examination table, a sink and a desk. Without an introduction, a man in a white coat opened her mouth and examined her teeth.

"Lie down on that table," he ordered. Ludwika did as he said. She knew what was about to come. This was no dentist and there was not going to be gas or pain relief.

The nurse took a leather belt and strapped Ludwika to the table before holding her mouth open while the doctor fitted a metal mouth guard. Ludwika's shoulders were pressed down. She caught a glimpse of the pincers before she felt the pulling and wiggling on her teeth. The firm grip made the already mashed and fragile tooth fracture some more and she screamed as pain shot from her nerve.

"Quiet," the doctor ordered and wiggled some more. The pain was unbelievable. The constant pressure on her nerve almost made Ludwika faint. When the tooth finally came out, luckily in one piece, the pulsating ache in her jaw began to subside. Without pausing the doctor then extracted the second tooth, this one was harder to move and required more wiggling. Ludwika felt as if her jaw was breaking, but it was the tooth which broke off.

"Three molars missing," the doctor said as he removed the mouth guard and the belt. "From now on you're better off only opening your mouth a little when you speak or laugh."

She wondered whether he was serious or mocking her.

"Bite on that cloth to stop the bleeding," he instructed her and gave her a small wrap of tissue.

The nurse helped her up and led her back to the kitchen to finish peeling the potatoes. The other women looked at her with a mixture of sympathy and amusement as she walked past their table. Ludwika ached all over. She had the urge to hold her cheek but needed both hands for the potato peeling. She couldn't risk failing her mission and being branded a lazy, unproductive worker. She had to make herself indispensable here, so she would be spared the hard labour of road construction.

Ludwika was good at cooking and she had to make sure that this was noticed and acknowledged. She felt better having this plan; it made it easier to ignore the whispers between her colleagues. The dull pain in her jaw decreased throughout the afternoon. Her cheek was swollen though and she couldn't easily speak. When it came to dinner time she couldn't chew or swallow, and gave her food to Halina, who greedily dug into the extra portion.

A few days went by, during which Ludwika made no new special friends. The kitchen staff spoke little with each other and if they did, the German woman who had processed her on her arrival would come in and reprimand them. There weren't many laughs to be had. The shift pattern allowed them an hour during the afternoon to sit outside in the sun. The workforce would split into groups of smokers or established friends. As the new girl, Ludwika didn't find an ally easily and, suspicious of everyone, she kept to herself. Sadly, she was working in the kitchen whenever the other camp inmates returned from their respective jobs, which made socialising with any of them harder.

There had been some flirtatious looks from men but since relations between inmates were also forbidden she was not inclined to respond to any of them.

Her best friend of sorts became the German overseer, Marie Schiessler. The two of them were the odd ones out. Seeing Ludwika's dedication and obvious talent in the cooking department, Marie made unprecedented complimentary remarks and involved her in the forward planning of menus.

"I'm so fed up with the lazy and work-shy people in here," Marie complained often. "The second you don't breathe down their neck they sit in the corner giggling like schoolgirls. They don't seem to realise how important our work is. We need to build those roads. If only more people worked like you then I wouldn't have to waste my time and could do something more constructive myself."

Ludwika didn't agree but kept her opinions to herself. Marie interpreted the silence as humbleness and assumed they were thinking along the same lines.

"The Free State of Oldenburg has a proud history of supporting the National Socialists," Marie bragged. "It was the first place in the Reich to have had a NSDAP government. In 1932, even before Hitler became our Chancellor. I wish this dedication would rub off on everyone here. It really should."

When she had finished with her rant she showed Ludwika the picture of her husband, Hermann, who was stationed in France.

"Isn't he a handsome man?"

Ludwika nodded. He wasn't all bad, although it wasn't clear how recent the picture was. He looked a lot younger then Marie looked now.

"Have you got anyone at home?" Marie asked her.

"No," she replied. "It's just me."

She didn't want to share her story and bring up old memories. It was better neither to think about the past, nor about what was happening in Poland. The less facts that she had, the less she would worry. It had not done her any service in Berlin. This was her life now. The sooner she began to accept it and get on with it, the better it would be. The new focus on the present helped her to feel better about what she could not change. There was no way she would find out about her family from here. She tried to see the tough overseer Marie as another human being, a woman in love and not just a mean dictator.

"There must have been someone," Marie insisted. "A pretty girl like you must have had her chances. What about that fellow that wrote that letter for you?"

"What letter?" Ludwika asked, confused.

"You gave me a letter from a German Untersturmführer who wrote about your ancestry," Marie said. "I can't remember now, it was probably a lot of rubbish but it showed that he was keen."

Ludwika shook her head.

"He said that he wanted to marry me," she said. She was about to talk about his accident in France when she realised that Marie's husband was stationed there and she didn't want to worry her. "He died," she simply said.

"There you are," Marie said. "We all have our bundle to carry. Whatever came of your German heritage? Do you really have German ancestors?"

"Yes, about three generations back or so," Ludwika said. "Manfred dug that up, but my employers in Berlin lost the documents that proved it."

"What a shame," Marie said. "Well, I always had my suspicions about you. You're so hard working, I'm sure that is your German blood."

Ludwika struggled to let the implied insult to her fellow Poles go. Even if she had a German passport she would always feel Polish and be proud of her nation. Marie might be a hard worker but she didn't do anything physical herself. With all the hard labour the Polish men were forced to endure every day to build a road, you could hardly call them lazy.

"Sometimes I think yours is the best way to be during a war," Marie would say. "Being separated from the ones you love is the worst. If you have nobody to lose, then you're less vulnerable. I hope it won't be long now before the war is over."

"Me, too."

The other inmates noticed the friendship between Ludwika and Marie and kept their distance. Sometimes they'd call her names for sucking up to the Germans but they were too scared of the consequences with Marie to go overboard with it.

Gradually, Ludwika was removed from the hard legwork and began overseeing the kitchen work, freeing Marie to do other duties. Once she established that she had free rein in the kitchen, Ludwika started talking to each one of them individually to learn more about them. . . their likes and dislikes in the kitchen. One girl said she hated doing the dishes because of the way it made her hands all wrinkly and look old. Another one had sore knees when scrubbing the floor and would rather do the dishes. With all this information she sat everyone down one evening and announced changes that accommodated most of these wishes. When Marie was out on errands, Ludwika also allowed her staff to chat. Within a few weeks the atmosphere had changed completely. Although they still distrusted Ludwika as a person of authority and kept their distance from her, the kitchen staff got on with each other much better and things got done much faster.

"I don't know how you do it," Marie said. "I'm glad to see discipline and efficiency in the kitchen at last."

Chapter 15

Christmas 1941 was business as usual. The inmates had to work all day and there were no celebrations or exchanges of gifts. Only a few of them sang Christmas carols on Christmas Eve and prayed. The money that everyone officially earned was heavily taxed and deductions were made for food and accommodation. There was next to nothing left. Few shops on the outside would serve inmates and what was available to buy was of low quality. Many hoped that the ban to send money home to loved ones would be lifted and, for a time, they saved everything they could.

It was known that in a different camp, which housed French, Belgian and Dutch people, celebrations did take place. Through the occasional contact with them at the road construction site, it had also transpired a long time ago that those inmates received better food and higher wages. Everyone seemed happier when the festive season was over: Ludwika certainly was. This Christmas had been the worst in her life.

"In my family we didn't give each other presents either this year," Marie told her after the event. "We've donated to help the soldiers at the Russian front," she said proudly. "The poor men are stuck outside of Moscow and have to fight in the freezing winter. Everyone is sending clothes and socks to keep them warm. One of my neighbours even gave up her mink coat."

"That's very generous," Ludwika said, who was increasingly skilled at making diplomatic statements. The situation in Russia gave many prisoners new hopes that perhaps the tide of the war was turning. Like everyone else in the camp, Ludwika hoped that Germany would be forced to its knees by its enemies soon and Poland liberated. The madness in Europe had gone on for too long. Thoughts of freedom seemed far-fetched, though, given the continuous successes of the German Army. The sudden halt of progress outside Moscow seemed a singular event rather than the foreboding of a change of fortune.

"The good thing is that we are getting more workers sent from Russia and the East," Marie said. "I've got to find someone from this camp whom I can trust to look after my father," she said. "Have you any suggestions as to who would be suitable?"

"I don't trust many people in here," Ludwika said. "What's wrong with your father?"

Marie swallowed, finding it difficult to speak.

"He isn't very well. He was a hard-working carpenter all of his life but soon after my mother died he started to become ill and had a brain tumour removed. That was four years ago and he's a little slow since then. I used to send a worker from the Drielake School Camp to help him in the house so I would only have to look in on him once or twice a week. The Drielake Camp was full of French prisoners and is just a few roads from where he lives. Now they've moved those inmates and replaced them with the Russians, all of who are working on the road. I've got to find a spare set of hands from here, I guess."

"I would do it," Ludwika offered, "if you can spare me in the kitchen; or maybe Halina, the Polish woman who works in the hotel?"

"The hotel won't give her up easily and I would hate to lose you in here."

Marie hesitated.

"Unless you only go every other day and I get someone else to go in between," she said. "Yes, you could still keep the kitchen under your control and you would notice if the other girl didn't care well for my father. That's an excellent idea. I'll take you to him during our break and show you what needs to be done."

Fritz Kröplin, Marie's father, lived a two-kilometre walk from the camp. The flat was above his old workshop, which was now used as a storage space by a furniture shop nearby. He suffered from bad headaches and often spent entire days without food or drink in the darkened living room. He was only in his fifties but bore the signs of a much older man. Ludwika noticed that the kitchen and the floors were clean but the living room was untidy with plenty of newspapers and books around, empty glasses and even some dinner plates. She immediately started to pick things up and carry them over to the kitchen.

"Thank you," Marie said and sat down with her father.

"How are you feeling today?" she asked him.

"Much better," he said. "The headaches have gone but I still feel a bit dizzy when I get up, so I stay down as much as I can. I've been thinking of getting a pot so I don't have to walk to the toilet so often."

"I'll get you one," Marie promised.

Ludwika started to tidy the papers and books into piles and wiped the dust from the table and the desk.

"She's very industrious," he said. "Where did you find her? I like her."

Marie smiled lovingly at him.

"For you, I will have only the best," she said.

The man seemed a gentle soul, grateful for everything anyone did for him.

Ludwika couldn't help wondering how Marie could have ended up so harsh and judgemental. However nice she was to her father and Ludwika, she was heartless towards all the other inmates.

"She has a great smile," Herr Kröplin said, studying Ludwika. "That will bring a little sunshine into this dark flat."

"Would you like me to open the curtains?" Ludwika offered, walking towards them.

"No, no," Marie said. "He needs it dark. The sun hurts his eyes."

"I see," Ludwika said and instead of opening them, she checked that they were shut as best they could.

The year of 1942 brought a big improvement of her lot. Ludwika enjoyed the next few months that gave her regular breaks from the camp and got her outside, walking. She was often stopped by patrols and was scared every time, despite having the right papers to prove that she was allowed on the streets. It was a fact of life around the camp, but one which Ludwika never got used to.

Spring was on its way and it got warmer, leaves began to bud on trees and she couldn't help feeling happy over these little things. Not that Oldenburg was a friendly place for foreigners. The population kept a close and suspicious eye on its guest workers; most of whom stayed in groups on their way to the construction site and to their camps. It seemed that the justice department was only looking for an excuse to prove the undeserving nature of its helpers and clamped down on them with draconian punishments. A Frenchman who had an affair with a German woman was hanged; the woman was sentenced to prison after having her hair cut off publicly and her name published in the local newspaper. Another man had been hanged for stealing, even though he was known in his camp as being honest. Ludwika knew that her chances of survival hung by a thin thread.

Working for Fritz Kröplin, however, was very easy and enjoyable. Away from the claustrophobic camp and the inmate politics, this was her little refuge. Uncomplicated and grateful, he let her get on with things and made no demands. Unless she offered to do something for him he would never ask for it. He was usually too ill to speak much to her and so just lay there. Occasionally, he would ask her to sit down, take a break and tell him stories about the outside world and her life.

"I'm not a good storyteller," she said.

"I'll be the judge of that," he said. "All I need is a little distraction. You don't have to come up with a punch line. Anything is better than staring at the ceiling, hoping the pain is going to stop."

So she told him about the ice cream vendor in Hamburg with the swan on his bicycle, about the sailing race on the Alster and about the day she got shot and arrested in Hamburg. He was a good listener.

"Thank you," he said. "Those are some adventures. What is life like for you now?" he asked.

"I must be grateful," she said quickly.

"You don't have to be so diplomatic with me," he said. "I'm not one of them."

She knew that but she was not willing to take a risk by stepping out of line. Maybe he wasn't a Nazi, but his daughter was.

"I'm lucky," she said, and to some degree she felt it.

One day he asked her to switch on the radio.

"You must be feeling better if you can stand the sound," she said,

Together they listened to a news broadcast about the latest military successes of the German and Japanese armies.

"Now turn the dial slowly to the left," he said.

She did as he asked but she didn't understand why.

"Go back all the way to the right now," he asked her.

The dial reached the previous position where the news continued.

"Keep going," he said, "keep going."

She turned the dial further until she noticed another radio station. The voice was distant and faint and didn't make sense to her at first: a well-spoken male voice spoke of the heavy losses that the German Army had suffered and how the Reich was already on its knees. She couldn't imagine how someone could get away with this. She looked questioningly at him.

"It's the British Radio," he explained. "It's illegal to listen to it, so don't mention it to Marie. It's useful to hear what the enemy is saying. It is all lies of course. Both stations are big mouths who say what they want us to believe, but I guess between the two I can figure out what is really going on in the world."

She switched the radio off.

"If it's illegal I won't have anything to do with it," she said.

"Then at least you need to switch it on and turn the dial back to the official German station," he said. "Marie mustn't see the dial anywhere else. Nobody can hear us on the outside. We only need to make sure Marie doesn't find out. Apart from that, we're safe."

To Ludwika it all seemed too familiar: taking risks, stepping out of line and dealing with secrets. She was not being foolish again; she had sworn that to herself. She made a point of leaving the room whenever Herr Kröplin asked her to switch the foreign broadcast on.

Marie was delighted at how well her father and Ludwika got on and praised her frequently for her commitment and sincerity.

"I've made a formal request on your behalf," she said. "I want this issue settled once and for all."

Ludwika looked confused.

"What do you mean?"

"Your ancestry of course," she said. "If we can get you to join the Reich as a citizen, we must. People like you don't grow on trees. Father won't live forever and I cannot send you back to the camp. My Hermann has some friends in the right places, maybe we can find that document that they lost in Berlin and make you an honest German woman. You deserve it. Father has never been happier."

Ludwika hated the rollercoaster of emotions that followed. Her hopes for complete security and stability were raised again but it also brought with it the fear that they would be smashed. In the past, the moments when she dared to dream of a better life for her and her family at home had always been followed by disappointment and disillusionment. She didn't want that to happen once again. She said her humble "Thank you," but tried hard not to let herself get carried away by high hopes.

As had happened in the past, nothing came of the enquiry. An entire long summer went by with Ludwika on tenterhooks. Every day she arrived at Herr Kröplin's apartment she looked for a note from Marie. Every time she saw her overseer she waited for an announcement of good news. Every evening she sank on her mattress, tired and disillusioned. All Marie's promise had done was to stir up emotions that she would have rather left alone.

Herr Kröplin could be invisible when he was poorly and not speak to her for days. The summer heat especially caused him great distress. When he was better, he was a great comfort, by being so kind and caring.

Marie was increasingly busy as new prisoner and forced labour camps were established in Oldenburg for which her advice and expertise were needed. A constant stream of Russian prisoners of war, convicts and more exiled Eastern Europeans forced to work in Germany arrived week after week and with it came a surge in suspicion and hostility from the locals. Executions of thieves and alleged criminals increased dramatically and the authorities began to fence camps with barbed that had yet to be secured. All inmates were required to have a permit if they were outside the boundaries for some time, but now failure to have such a permit often resulted in people being shot on sight. Halina had witnessed one such event and she was a changed woman since. . . much more timid and compliant.

Ludwika was painfully aware of the danger of walking through the increasingly hostile town every other day. She had seen a German girl, not older than ten years old, being brutally beaten by a soldier for throwing food over the fence for the Russian prisoners. She feared that her own luck could be turning again and was frightened. When she told Marie about her feelings and asked to be excused from her work for Herr Kröplin to be spared the walk through town the German woman got very angry.

"You can't abandon my father now that he got used to you. I've given you these privileges because I thought you appreciated them. Don't disappoint me now. A few stares on the street won't harm you."

It was not how Ludwika saw the situation but she obediently continued with her work. Marie clearly was not to be moved on the matter. The summer turned to autumn and with the colder temperatures and less sunshine, her soul felt bleaker, too.

Another Christmas, 1942, and New Year came and went. It was surprising how fast it had approached. When Ludwika was a child, the days leading up to Christmas had been so slow and heavy with anticipation but this year she had hardly spared a thought for it and she was unprepared for the turmoil that hit her when it came round.

Again, no celebrations were allowed. Ludwika lay on her mattress alone, imagining her family celebrating without her, Irena treating Stasia as her mother now and Michal as her father figure. She thought of the children in Berlin, who would be singing Christmas carols, now with a baby by their side. She hoped her voluntary travels to Germany had secured her family's position, despite Manfred's death. It was the hope that sustained her - that and the consolation that she had done everything to her best ability and with the best of intentions.

The New Year in the camp started badly. Deliveries fell way short of the expected amounts to feed the inmates. Food ran out long before the next supplies were expected and all the kitchen staff could do was to reduce portions, add water to the soup and serve mouldy bread. The inmates shot hateful looks at her and the women who served the meals, as if it was their fault. People bickered over portion sizes, and greedy bullies and thieves stole from other people's plates. Heating in the camp had also been reduced. Cold and hungry inmates soon let their frustrations spill over into aggression. When Ludwika raised the issue with Marie, the German woman only shrugged.

"There are so many more of you," she said. "How do you expect us to feed everyone? It will have to do."

The Western prisoners, who were in separate camps and were treated preferentially, had less restricted access to the outside. However, even they seemed to be feeling the effects of this increased austerity, too. There were more alleged thefts and execution announcements amongst their number.

Fritz Kröplin covered his face with his hands when he heard the official news broadcast about the German surrender at Stalingrad in February 1943. It was the first time such a defeat had been acknowledged publicly by the German station itself.

"It was bound to happen," he said. "Hitler took it too far, too quickly. God help us if we get back what he gave out."

Ludwika silently agreed.

The foreign radio station always presented a much bleaker picture of the war than the German broadcasts. It gave Ludwika a surge of hope, despite her resolve not to get carried away by optimism. So far, the war had lasted three years and little had stopped the Germans. Was this situation in Russia really only a minor setback, as the Germans said, or were the British broadcasts true and this could be the end to all the madness? If so, what would happen to her beloved Poland? Would it be liberated or swallowed by the Russians whole?

Chapter 16

It was on that very day, whilst making her way home to the camp, Ludwika saw the man for the first time. She would never forget it; he was the most handsome man she had ever seen. As she stood outside Herr Kröplin's house, he walked by on the road, pulling an empty handcart. He moved forcefully, with long strides, whistling as if the cold did not affect him and if this wasn't really hard work at all. She knew there was something special about him before she even saw his face closer up. When she did, it almost made her forget the freezing cold winds.

He had black hair and a dark complexion, with the exotic looks of those foreigners she had seen on her trips to Lodz and Krakow. He had to be Italian or Greek. Ludwika's heart beat faster and she felt embarrassed, worrying that he had noticed her staring. Despite the temperatures, she felt a surge of warmth beneath her winter coat. She had stopped walking and stood transfixed. She realised before managing to make a fool of herself and started walking home, in the same direction as he had gone. He stopped just ahead of her, busy steering the cart so it would fit through the narrow passage between two houses.

Ludwika loved the way he moved, so confident and effortless, and he was a very good whistler, too. He noticed her catching up with him and stopped so she could walk past. He was wearing a cap, which he lifted it in a gesture of respect. Ludwika got a glimpse at his eyes: they were a mesmerizing hazel colour.

"Nice to meet you," he said in an accented German. She couldn't figure out where he came from and what that would say about his status within Oldenburg. His voice was deep and soothing, as if she had known it all of her life. Ludwika nodded shyly and continued walking, probably a little too hastily. She had to, though. Men had only disappointed her. Besides, liaisons with almost every type of man were forbidden in the Reich for her and she could lose too many privileges to risk it. She couldn't speak to him. It was too dangerous in too many ways and she had to forget about him as soon as she could.

She was surprised when she arrived back at the camp so quickly. Ludwika had walked almost without paying attention to her surroundings, so deep in thought was she about the man. She couldn't sleep either that night, constantly tossing and turning. She knew she was in trouble.

The thought of the man was difficult to shake off over the next few days. His dreamy eyes haunted her and she couldn't stop wondering who he was and what his story was likely to be. She had been so electrified by her infatuation that she had not dared look at him closely enough to identify insignia or marks on his clothing. Was he Jewish? She was no specialist on racial features, but he reminded her a little of a Jew she'd seen in Berlin and the foreigners in Lodz and Krakow. It had been a while since she had seen any Jews in Oldenburg. When they had all started to wear the yellow star she had noticed it immediately because it had reminded her of Manfred, who had suggested that this should be done everywhere in the Reich. However, the people with stars had soon disappeared from the streets. The man could have worn a star without her noticing or any other mark that identified him as a prisoner. He couldn't be German – that much was clear. She wished there were more nationalities in her camp so she could compare his accent to theirs.

When it was her turn next to go and visit Herr Kröplin all Ludwika could think about was the man and whether he was likely to cross her path again. What had he used the cart for? There were so many questions and no prospects for answers. She really didn't want to feel this way. She wanted to remain calm and focused to make it through this war – a romance would only complicate things.

A week went by and Ludwika didn't see him again. It was what she had hoped for and yet, every time she walked past the house where he had stopped his cart and didn't see him was a disappointment. She even had a quick look at the names on the letter boxes close to Kröplin's house. None of them indicated that a foreigner lived here.

Since she had seen him, Ludwika started to drop things, forget things and stare absentmindedly in empty space. Herr Kröplin was the only one to notice.

"What's up with you?" he asked. "You're behaving like a schoolgirl in love. If I didn't know you better I would almost presume that's what you are. Is everything alright?"

She was perplexed at such a personal question and just shook her head while continuing to tidy the room.

"I wonder how you can make such a mess when you claim to do nothing but lie there and stare at the ceiling," she replied eventually, trying to distract him.

He laughed. "That confirms it," he said. "Who is it? Someone from the camp?"

Ludwika's face flushed. Oh that cheeky man. She didn't respond to any of his many questions and teasing over the next few times she saw him. There was nothing to tell and she would not share that part of her. Talking would only make it real and she had to fight that impulse.

She should have been cross with him for making fun of her, but he seemed to be so pleased and full of excitement over her news, regardless of her denial. It was actually nice to see him this happy for once.

Herr Kröplin had a stove in the living room, and part of Ludwika's chores was to always keep enough coals for it in the room. As the levels were getting low she took a trip down to the basement to bring up some more. It was here that she bumped into the beautiful stranger and his cart, this time full with coals. How could she not have seen the black markings on the wood and on his clothes? She should have known what he delivered with it.

"There you are again," he said, clearly remembering her.

"Hello," she said, her voice cracking with nerves.

"I hoped I would see you again," he said.

She still couldn't make out his accent. It was easier to recognise an accent if someone spoke in your mother tongue. If the language was your second one, it was much more difficult.

"Let me go upstairs and get your money," she said and was about to turn away.

"I need you to open the coal shaft for me first," he said.

She opened the lock and then ran upstairs.

"It's the coal man," she said. "I need to pay him."

Herr Kröplin looked at her and burst into a laughing fit.

"It's him, isn't it?" he said and coughed. "Oh damn it, my head," he said and rubbed his eyes as if it were to help the pain. "You're in love with the coal man."

"I'm not in love with him," she said but her face felt redder than ever.

"If you say so," Her Kröplin said. "His name is Luca. I think he's a French prisoner. Marie likes him, too." He coughed some more. "I give you that, he is a handsome fellow."

He stood up and gave her the money for the coals.

"Take your time," he said. "You're only young once."

Ludwika ran down the stairs and watched as Luca shovelled the coal into the shaft on the floor outside the back wall of the house. She held out a large bucket.

"Is that for upstairs?" he asked.

She nodded, still unable to speak.

He began to fill it with coals.

"Thank you," she said.

"What's your name?" he asked. "My name is Luca."

"Ludwika."

"Polish?" he asked.

"Yes," she said.

"I'm Italian," he said. "Well, half Italian, half Dutch."

"Herr Kröplin said you were French."

"We're all the same to the Germans," Luca said with a broad grin. "French, Belgian, Greek – we're not German, that's all that counts to them."

"You wouldn't say that if you were in the Polish camps," she said. "Every year at Christmas we can see the difference. You get a tree and we got nothing. And you get paid more than we."

He smiled at her and put the shovel down.

"You're a feisty one, aren't you? I thought you couldn't open your mouth, but I was wrong."

She pressed her lips together tightly.

"Don't stop. I like it when you talk." He winked at her. "I would rather come back some time for the money so I can hear you talk some more."

She shook her head.

"No thank you. I better be going back upstairs. I've got chores to do."

"If you're from Poland you've got to be in Westerstrasse or at the Lindenhof. Which one is it?" he asked. "I bet you need coals there, too, soon."

She sighed.

"Please go Luca," she said. "We'll both get into trouble for it."

"No we won't," he said.

She marvelled at how persistent he was.

"You're not allowed to go with a German or a man from your own camp. I'm free game," he said.

"Ha ha," she said.

"Alright," he said. "I don't want to beg. How about this: there are two ways of locking the coal shaft door. The padlock can be either front or back. You see?" He showed it to her. "If you look closely, there is a little scratch here. Let's say if you put that part to the front after you lock the coal shaft, then it is your signal that you are ready to meet up with me. If not, then I know you really want me to leave you alone. I will come back regularly and check."

"Don't bother," she said, but without meaning to she leaned in to see where the mark on the lock was.

He grinned.

"Yes, have a good look," he said. "There it is," and he pointed at the scratch. "Make sure it is well to the back, or I'd be inclined to think you want to meet and I will come and ask you out."

She locked the coal shaft, putting the lock side with the scratch to the back and then she ran back to the door. Ludwika waved briefly before disappearing into the staircase. She closed the door and exhaled deeply, her heart beating fast.

She could hear him linger outside as she lifted the bucket and began the climb up the stairs to the old man's flat. Herr Kröplin had fallen asleep, so she left the bucket outside the living room door and busied herself in the kitchen, her emotions awhirl. If that Luca had such an effect on her she should be glad to see the back of him, she told herself. She'd been lucky to have stayed in Marie's good books and couldn't risk losing that now with a silly infatuation. Ludwika vowed that she wouldn't make the same mistake with trusting men again.

The next time she came to Herr Kröplin, however, she stole herself downstairs, took off the lock and then closed it so that it faced the other way and the scratch was facing the front and clearly visible. She knew she was playing with fire but she couldn't help it. It seemed that the only way she could get Luca out of her mind was to meet him. He couldn't possibly live up to her expectation. He was just a man like any other: Milosz, who got her pregnant; Manfred who had treated her like a commodity and Erich who had lied to her and sent her out of his sight. Why should Luca be any different? Polish, German or Italian – Ludwika was best advised to stay away from them all and look out for her own interests. If only it were that simple.

She slowly walked up the stairs to Herr Kröplin's flat and began the wait for Luca's visit.

Chapter 17

A few weeks passed during which she hadn't heard from Luca and she began to wonder if he had only being toying with her. She had made a real fool of herself. Even so, every trip to Herr Kröplin was exciting and full of possibility. When Ludwika got there and the patient didn't mention a visit from the coal man she was disappointed and went home with the resolve never again to raise her hopes about anything. The disappointment simply wasn't worth it.

And so it was with great surprise that she arrived one day and found Luca sitting in Herr Kröplin's kitchen, with flowers and a cinnamon pastry.

"Herr Kröplin told me you were particularly fond of the Franzbrötchen in Hamburg," he said. "I couldn't get one of those, but I got this on the black market. Isn't it amazing what you can get if you know the right people and pay the right price?"

She was speechless again.

"You have got to start talking to me one day," Luca said. "It's going to be tiresome if I need to ask Herr Kröplin every time I want to know something about you. I know that you can speak."

She sat down and bit into the roll.

"Thank you," she said. "It tastes delicious. I work in the kitchen of our camp, but I thought I'd never get to eat such a delicacy ever again."

"A miracle," he said, and laughed. "You can talk!"

"Try some," she said and offered him a piece.

"No," he said. "That's all for you."

When she had eaten all of it she looked directly at him.

"What is it that you want from me? You know we can't have a future."

"You're being overly pessimistic," he replied. "There is always a future, start believing in it."

"Is there?" she asked. "Go on and tell me about it."

"The future starts with a coffee and an ersatz Franzbrötchen at a friendly carpenter's kitchen. It continues with you telling me about your life and your dreams and with me telling you about mine."

"And then what happens?" she asked, feeling less reluctance than before. Luca made everything sound so easy. She liked that. Her defences had broken a long time ago and her resolve to lead a life of obedience and with her head down had been chipped away.

"Then we do this again, with the help of Herr Kröplin and over time you will fall helplessly in love with me and ask me to kiss you. I will say: 'No, I'm an honourable man who doesn't kiss strange women, regardless of how attractive they are and how much they beg.' Then you will say: 'I won't take no for an answer' and I will surrender. It will be the sweetest kiss of my life and I will be lost to you forever."

She laughed.

"You're a sweet-talking Casanova," she said. "How many women have you told such a story before?"

"Do you mean today or this week?" he asked and winked.

"You're impossible!"

"Nothing is impossible," he said. "One of these days I might even get a real Franzbrötchen for you."

"What about Herr Kröplin?" she asked and looked at the door to the living room. "I need to see how he is."

"He is fine and doesn't want to be disturbed by you, today. He's locked the door so we leave him alone and have an opportunity to talk," Luca said.

She got up and checked. The door was locked from the inside, she could see the key.

"I came here last week when the other woman was on duty," Luca explained. "Herr Kröplin was pleased to see me and asked her to send me up. We had a good old chat about you. He has a great sense of humour that man. Of course, he asked me first if I wouldn't prefer his daughter. He said she was in dire need of cheering up and he'd pay me handsomely. When I said I'd prefer you and would happily pay him for the privilege he gave up and suggested I come here today and surprise you. His daughter is out of town today and won't interfere with our rendezvous."

"Go on then," she said. "Tell me about your life and your dreams."

Ludwika decided to throw caution to the wind. She would enjoy this little oasis of happiness in her otherwise sterile and bleak world. She disagreed with Luca that any of this had a future, but she had deprived herself of joy and laughter for too long. She needed this.

"My father is a Dutch businessman who used to travel a lot throughout Europe," Luca began, putting a lot of drama and pathos into his words for comic effect. "He met my mother in Milan and fell in love immediately. She was not prepared to live in Holland so he followed her to Italy. They got married and moved to Rome where they had me. As you can see, I inherited their good lucks and charm, so much that they decided that they had perfected the art of making babies and produced no further children. I was an only child with a lot of pressure on me to keep up the family tradition of great beauty and successful business. My father sent me to his University in Amsterdam. Being Italian, I was surprised to find the Germans bothered about me when they invaded the country. Because my father and my surname are Dutch they rounded me up with other Dutch men to come and work here. It's not too bad, all things considered," he said. "I was getting bored with my business studies anyway."

She smiled at his cheerful attitude. She knew the truth had to be bleaker than this. He reminded her of her father, who had always tried to make the best of every situation and had never given up hope.

"Now what about you?" Luca asked.

She didn't want to counter his optimism with the tragedy of her own life and tell him of all the disappointments and hardships. Who could say if his story had been as easy and pain free as he made it out to be? She suddenly had an idea to 'spice' up her own history, too.

"When the Germans invaded," she said, mimicking his theatrical tone as much as she could, "they all were blinded by my beauty. A Bavarian officer took me to Hamburg so he could look at me and adore me. When he failed to bake me Franzbrötchen he was shot by the police and I took up residence in Berlin. A group of jealous German women there had me shot at and brought here, claiming that the few men who were still around no longer made eyes at them."

She could see he liked this, so she continued.

"The women in the Polish camp, sadly, also asked that I leave there at least every other day, so they don't feel so humbled and dwarfed by my natural charms and beauty; it seems we're both too popular for our own good."

"I'm lucky that Herr Kröplin has not made any claims on you, too," Luca said. "He is a decent fellow. In fact, there are quite a few decent people around. Never forget that."

"I'll try," she said, speaking more serious now. "My experiences have been a mixed bag."

She told him about Manfred, who had been the perfect gentleman one minute and patronising and demeaning the next.

"I still wonder what would have happened to me if he had lived," she said. "He was such a naïve man, yet his rapid rise within the army ranks and the nature of his work in the occupied territories mean that he couldn't have been all harmless: he was SS."

Luca nodded.

She then told him about Irmingard and Erich Danner, about the good and bad experiences in Hamburg and Berlin, about Eva, the events in the Grindelviertel and the Scheunenviertel. She left out the bit about her affair with Erich. That was a story to tell him another time, once she knew more about the real man behind the flirtatious entertainer.

Luca was a good listener and, despite his previous over-the-top demeanour, looked at her with caring, understanding eyes. She almost felt sorry for putting a damper on their time together with the dramas of her life.

"I can see you are a tough warrior princess underneath that pretty shell," he said when she was finished. "If you need someone to confide in or lean on, I'd be happy to do so. It must be tiresome being so strong all the time."

If only he knew how true that was. It had been a long time since she'd had someone to rely upon. The last person had been Erich and what a fragile and fake support that had turned out to be.

Luca looked at the clock.

"Unfortunately I need to go," he said. "One hour is the longest I can get away with before my colleagues are going to start asking questions. It will get easier with the spring coming."

"Thanks for listening, and for the treat," she said. "That was very kind of you."

"No, thank you," Luca said and kissed her hand. "Herr Kröplin offered to let us meet here again sometime. He'll let me know when there is an opportunity."

He paused and looked at her.

"Only if you want to, of course. Shall we use the lock at the coal shaft as signal again?"

She shook her head. There was no need for a signal. She had enjoyed herself and wanted to see him again in any case.

"No," she said. "I shall look forward to the next time you surprise me with a visit. As long as Herr Kröplin doesn't mind, I'd be honoured."

He was still holding her hand and used it to pull her closer to him. He stood right in front of her now, with the tiniest gap between them.

"Thank you," he whispered in her ear. His breath sending goose bumps across her skin. It frightened her and she tore herself away.

After Luca had left she began tidying the kitchen. Despite her fears of vulnerability and disappointment, Ludwika's heart was filled with joy and she felt as if she was walking on air. If nothing ever came of this, she would always remember it fondly.

Herr Kröplin unlocked the living room door and smiled at her mischievously. He was sensitive enough though not to spoil things with mocking. The living room had gone cold and she offered to put a fire on for him.

"The heat gets too much for my head," he said and handed her a blanket. "Take this."

She shook her head. She wasn't cold.

He looked pale and Ludwika worried that the carpenter had exhausted himself by walking down the stairs to let Luca into the building. What a fine man he was for doing this, only to make his housekeeper feel better. Without mentioning Luca, he asked her to switch on the radio broadcast for her and they both sat and listened to the differing claims from the German and the foreign news about the alleged triumphs and defeats on either side.

When it was time for Ludwika to go she shook his hand.

"Thank you so much Herr Kröplin. You have a good soul," she said.

"Call me Fritz," he said. "You have a very good soul, too. Never forget it and never let it get damaged."

All the way home she couldn't stop smiling. She was bursting with happiness underneath her winter coat. It didn't matter that her stockings had holes and let in some cold or that her shoes slid on the ice if she wasn't careful. What a big difference one hour with Luca had made to her life. Ludwika was grateful and content to wait until the next time she should see him. She knew it wouldn't be too soon, but the certainty that she would meet him again one day was enough to sustain her through whatever obstacles life would throw at her next. Her optimism was restored and she felt stronger than she had in a long time.

It took only a week before Luca came to see her at Fritz's kitchen again. Marie was overseeing another, bigger camp now which was much further from her father's house. That made it impossible for her to see him during the day, and knowing that he was well cared for by Ludwika, she limited her visits to late evenings or days when the other girl was on duty. This time, Luca had brought a portable gramophone and serenaded Ludwika with a record by the Swedish singer and film star Zarah Leander, who currently was very popular in Germany.

"You remind me a little of her," Luca said. "She is a great performer, whether it is melodrama or romance: she can be sentimental and cheerful."

"Let me listen," she said and put her fingers on his lips to silence him.

The first song that he played was called 'The Wind has Told me a Song' – a slow ballad about great love and happiness that would come Zarah's way, according to her friend, the wind. It combined longing and cheer and it seemed to Ludwika as if it had been written for her specifically. She craved a love as 'indescribably beautiful' as Zarah sang about. She could see Luca grin at how captivated she had become by the lyrics. She didn't care, it had been years since she had been able to listen to modern music and she loved it.

"How amazing," she said. "Play it again."

He did, all the while observing her with adoring eyes.

"Wait until you hear this next one," he said and put on 'Can Love be a Sin?', an upbeat song about love and its purpose in the world. It brought a smile to Ludwika's face. Falling for Luca might cause difficulties, but, as Zarah rightfully sang: what good would her life be without love?

"Play it again," she said.

The last song he put on for her was another upbeat number called 'His Name is Waldemar' and it spoke of an infatuation with someone totally unsuitable, yet irresistible. She knew why Luca had chosen this song.

"Thank you, Waldemar," she said to Luca, ruffling his thick hair. He told her about the singer and her career, how she had turned down a prestigious German award and left the country to go back to Sweden.

"She gave up a great career here," Luca said. "That woman had balls to say no to the award."

Ludwika couldn't believe it when Fritz interrupted their rendezvous to tell them that the hour was almost up.

"I hate to break up your party," he said, "but I don't want you to run into trouble. Speak some more next time," he said and returned to the living room, giving them a chance to have a few more minutes alone.

"I can't believe that was already an hour," she said.

"Time flies when you're having a good time," he said. "Thanks for the best hour I have had this year."

He kissed her hand and then packed the music away.

"I'll see you soon," he said and left.

She could not get the music out of her head and hummed all afternoon while cooking and cleaning and even on her way home. She noticed how the days had gotten longer, a sign that spring was coming. The world was no longer as bleak as it had been only a few weeks ago. The snow had melted away and was unlikely to come back until the fall. What a wonderful surprise this had been. Instead of making her talk about what she had left behind and all the sad stories that were to be shared, Luca had made a new memory and introduced her to such great music.

The women in the kitchen started to talk about her, carelessly enough for Ludwika to realise they had a good idea from where her happiness stemmed. Except they had no way of knowing who it was that made her so cheerful. She could only be grateful that Marie never spoke to them and wouldn't suspect that there was a man in Ludwika's life.

Although she never acknowledged the rumours and the gossip, Ludwika relaxed and became more open with her colleagues. They shared a joke, a cigarette and a song every now and again. The only person she trusted with her secret was Fritz, who already knew most that there was to know.

"I remember when I first met Marie's mother," he told her the next time she saw him. He sat at the kitchen table while she cooked him an omelette. "I lived for nothing else but seeing her. You may think you are the only ones having to play hide and seek but I had the same issues. When I first saw my Ilse, I was instantly infatuated. She was easily the most beautiful woman I had ever seen. Until this day nobody has ever even come close. Unfortunately, I was too young then to get married to her right away."

Ludwika listened eagerly to his story, watching him as he spoke. His eyes were sparkling, the love for his wife easily trumping the sadness of her loss.

"In the days before the Great War, going out with a girl was not a done thing," he continued with undeterred enthusiasm. "I was too young to propose to Ilse and at first, all I wanted was to be alone with her to talk. There were so few possibilities to do that. At barn dances and public festivities there were too many people around to declare your love. I had to ask friends to deliver notes on my behalf and wait for her reply – it really was ridiculous. . . as if the world had conspired to lay as many obstacles in our path as possible. Fortunately, human nature and love are resilient and will always find a way to bypass laws and rules. We arranged secret meetings in the forest or behind the church yard. I was not far off from becoming a certified carpenter when she got pregnant and we had to get married. The war broke out soon after and I had to leave Ilse and Marie alone. I only had ten more years with my Ilse after the French released me. She died of pneumonia. Such a beautiful and happy girl. You would have liked her."

"What a sad story," Ludwika said.

"It is sad," he agreed. "On the other hand, I remember how it felt and I often can still feel it. I think they broke my head but my heart is still intact, because I won't let it break."

"You make it sound so easy," she said.

"I had no choice," he said. "Marie was young and didn't need a crying father, did she? It was bad enough for her as it was. I'm sad about that which no longer is, but I don't have to stop being happy over all that was. I always carry that with me."

He waited until she turned around and looked at her.

"Remember that with Luca: don't let the worries about the future spoil the happiness you have with each other now. Life is too short. You need to enjoy it. Your existence is bleak enough as it is. I wish Marie would let her hair down once in a while and do something exciting or irrational. That woman is all work. Don't get to be like her, I beg you."

She took the frying pan from the stove and sat down.

"Why are you taking such an interest in me and Luca?" she asked.

He took a deep breath and exhaled slowly.

"Because I learn more about a person from what they don't talk about," he said. "The things you keep quiet about make me understand more than you think."

She marvelled at his sensitive nature.

"Your omelette is ready," she said, smiling, and served it on his plate.

"Thanks," he said and dug in.

It was some time before she saw Luca again. It was spring and people didn't need as many coals any more. He had promised that it would be easier to see her without the coal deliveries but now he was in demand to deliver other goods with his handcart, sometimes potatoes, sometimes wood logs and sometimes he spent entire days at the station helping unload trains. His work route would not bring him to this part of town at the times when she was around. Luca left messages and letters for her with Fritz, explaining his difficulties. By the time Luca got to the house each evening she had long left to obey the curfew for workers from the East.

The sentiment against foreigners in town was getting worse. Criminal convictions were made against a few foreign individuals and immediately harsh new laws were enacted against all of them. It was largely Western workers and prisoners who were caught breaking the laws, since they had more opportunities to do so than their eastern counterparts but the sentiments went against them all. In line with the racial ideology, the toughest policies were implemented against those from the east.

A French woman was imprisoned for stealing flowers from a graveyard, and several men were hanged for looting a bombed building. Fortunately for Ludwika, allied bombings were a rarity in

Oldenburg. So far, few raids had come its way and the destruction was minimal.

In all of his letters Luca, would include the lyrics for Zarah Leander songs. Ludwika soon knew them by heart. She couldn't wait to see him again and listen to the records. As if he had known how important music was to her, he left the gramophone with Fritz one evening.

"He feels bad for you," Fritz related the next day when he presented Ludwika with it. "He knows how much you love music and how deprived your life must feel without it. That curfew is such an unjust punishment for you. He hopes this will help remind you of him."

Although the music was not an adequate substitute for Luca, it was a great gift and brightened up her days.

In the same manner, the foreign radio broadcasts lightened her mood with news that the Reich was more and more on the defensive. Italy had come under heavy attack. Her joy was tinged with regret - fighting there couldn't be good news for Luca, whose family might suffer. At least her family was not in a battle zone. Nevertheless, Ludwika was loathe to think what they were suffering all the same.

When Luca finally got to the apartment again, in May 1943, the longing between the separated lovers was so great that they fell into each other's arms as soon as they had got in to the kitchen. Luca put a record on with music by Vivaldi and closed the kitchen door. He took her head into his hands and kissed her before starting to undress her. With so little time and so much craving for what was to come, Ludwika put up no resistance and the two soon rolled on the kitchen floor until the record came to a stop. Luca got up and put it on again, before returning to the floor and making love to her.

He was not as clumsy and quick as Milosz had been, nor was he as skilled and methodical as Erich. He was impulsive and forceful yet gentle, but it was her own passion that made her feel as if she was burning alive. In short, it was the best hour Ludwika had ever spent with a man. They finished just before the record stopped again.

"I have to go," Luca said, with sad eyes. "This time went by far too fast," he said, kissing her. They dressed quickly, only now fully coming to their senses. Fritz might have heard them. If he hadn't, he still would have a pretty good idea what they had just done. She felt ashamed and tried to make herself as presentable and relaxed as she could, but she doubted she would fool the old carpenter.

Luca rushed out the door, leaving her behind with ruffled hair and her mind awhirl. She played the record again, tidied up the mess they had made and began attending to the kitchen sink.

Fritz stayed in the living room, discreet and thoughtful. By the time Ludwika had cooked his lunch she had calmed down and felt ready to face him, even though he never said a word about what might have happened, and bombarded her with details about the war instead. Her life had changed. She now had moments in the present, as well as the future to look forward to.

Chapter 18

From then on, whenever they met, the two of them had a great time.

"I want to know more about you and tell you everything there is to know about me," he said and he would speak about the great city of Rome with its ancient history and magnificent buildings, his father's textile import business, his mother's fiery temper and how much she had hated it when Mussolini came to power. Hearing about his life was a wonderful escape from her fears and worries. By now she had heard so many terrible stories about life in occupied Poland from recent arrivals in the camp that she wouldn't allow herself to even think about what might have happened to her family.

The inmates were divided into those who continuously spoke about their dramas and those who never mentioned anything. She fell into the latter group and in particular didn't want to spoil the wonderful time with Luca by useless speculation. She was determined to stay strong and since her talk with Herr Gabler that meant looking forward only. She found it easy to distract Luca from finding out more about her family history by asking him plenty of questions about his. He was so passionate and loved talking that he easily got carried away until their time was up once again. His stories were so entertaining and time always flew by so quickly in their stolen moments together.

She saw it as a sensitive side to Luca that he stopped asking her more about her background. Just as Fritz had done, Luca probably understood, that she worried enough on her own and didn't want to allow those feelings to interfere with her day to day life.

In July, she realised that she was pregnant. It was a disaster that would throw up awkward questions and possibly get her into real trouble from those in charge. Ludwika couldn't bring herself even to say it out loud. The longer she could keep it a secret, the longer she could carry on as if nothing had ever happened.

The first person she told was Fritz.

"Oh dear," he said and smiled. "That brings back memories from my past. Why do we always think we can control nature?"

"What can I do?" she asked. "If Marie ever finds out about Luca then I won't be allowed to come here anymore and I will never see him again."

"You'll have to come clean about him," Fritz said. "If you don't, they will assume you were sleeping with a German man and punish you for that. What you did was not illegal per se. It is a loophole in the legislation. You may want to lie about where you two met, though, and where you did the deed," he said, laughing loudly. He coughed and held his head in agony.

"Are you sure about this?" she asked, but he couldn't answer. He sank back on his sofa and pressed his fists into his eyes.

Luca was not entirely pleased when she told him, but he did his best to reassure her.

"It has happened before," he said after a long silence. "Not me," he added with a wink, "but others have had children with Polish women."

When he saw her worried face he kissed her forehead and held her tight for a few seconds, then he continued, business-like:

"We can't marry under the racial laws. The little one will be made to stay with you in the camp." He sighed. "It's going to be tough for you two: a baby born in February when it is at its coldest."

She nodded.

"If anyone can do it, though it's you," he said and smiled adoringly at her. "And remember that this child is going to break hearts wherever it goes. Your looks combined with mine and my charm…"

He took her hand and looked into her eyes. "I will do whatever I can to help, however little that is."

"I know," she said. "I know."

Unfortunately, he had no idea how true that last statement would prove to be. In September, Italy signed a truce with the allies and the Germans lay siege to Rome. In retaliation for such treacherous action, the few Italian workers were re-classified as prisoners of war and locked away with the Russian prisoners of wars in the Drielake camp, condemned to work on road construction.

Although he had been kept with the Dutch prisoners before, Luca's heritage was known and so he suddenly disappeared. Ludwika was apprehensive about his long absence until Marie casually told her about the new measures against Italian men.

"Serves them right," Marie said. "When the tide is turning you don't just abandon your comrades. We started this thing together, we should see it through to the bitter end. Leaving us in the lurch like that – I have a good mind to make those bastards pay dearly for their disloyalty. Road construction is too good for them."

Ludwika felt awful. Poor Luca! He had done nothing but minded his own business. Would she ever see him again? And how could she tell Marie that Luca – one of those 'traitors' – was the father of her unborn child?

How could she even tell Marie that she was pregnant? Fritz had told her how keen his daughter was to have a baby and had been unlucky in that department. Marie was already a wreck whenever she spoke of her husband Herman. This would send her over the edge, for sure.

People started to comment on Ludwika's figure and it would only be a matter of time before the truth came out. Now that everyone was losing weight because of the poor rationing, Ludwika's putting some on brought suspicion. Pregnancy was not something people would have expected from her, but, given that she was in charge of the kitchen, accusations of theft and misappropriation were likely to come her way. She knew all too well how such cases were dealt with.

"You poor thing," Fritz said when she informed him of Luca's misfortune at the hands of the German administrators. "He may have fathered the child as a guest worker, but now that he is a prisoner his status has changed. That could create unnecessary complications for you."

He lay back on the sofa and stared at the ceiling. "Leave it with me," he suddenly said. "Don't tell Marie anything for now. I have an idea."

Ludwika was more than happy to grant him that favour. She was in no rush to face her boss.

A few days later Marie came to see Ludwika in the camp and took her to a quiet corner.

"My poor child," she said. "You mustn't be cross with him, but my father told me everything."

Ludwika looked confused but said nothing.

"I'm glad you told him," she said. "You do need a reliable witness for these things. Especially when there is no proof."

Ludwika didn't understand.

"Don't try to fool me," Marie said, her tone swaying between sympathy and authority. "Your secret is safe with me. I feel so sorry for you."

"What exactly did your father tell you?" Ludwika asked. She really wondered.

"About the rape," Marie said. "I know you don't want to talk about it but soon everyone will see that you are pregnant and then the questions and rumours will begin: Did she abuse her privileges to leave the camp to seduce an honest German man or did she break the rules within the camp? If father hadn't given such a detailed account of the state you were in after it happened I would have had to ask these questions of you myself. I've said it many times, there are far too many criminals let loose in Oldenburg. The fences and barbed wire should have been there years ago and all foreigners should have been detained. How some were allowed to walk freely is beyond me."

She stopped and looked embarrassed at Ludwika.

"Not you, of course. You know the type that I mean."

Ludwika knew the type.

"Now, I know it is awkward to go over this again. Father told me the details already, but tell me, do you remember anything at all about the man apart from the Russian accent?"

Ludwika shook her head.

"Of course not," Marie said and nodded, her face angry and hateful. "They all look alike those bloody Russians."

She patted Ludwika on the back.

"Don't you worry now. I'll file the reports for you, you only need to come with me once to the police station and sign the form. You've suffered enough."

Thanks to Fritz Kröplin's lie, no more awkward questions were asked and neither Luca nor Ludwika were punished for their love that had become a crime after all. Having been spared at least that worry, she began looking forward to having a child and focussed on the happy part that was to come. Being separated from her family, Ludwika loved being pregnant and becoming a mother again. Having to care for a new human being gave her a fresh lease of life. Unfortunately, there was nothing Ludwika could do but pray Luca was safe. She had to console herself with the fact that he was strong and likely to endure the hardship better than many others. She had to say goodbye to thoughts of them being together for now. She had coped without Luca before she'd met him, she would have to do so again, for the sake of the child in her belly.

Luca's gramophone was still with Fritz Kröplin.

Ludwika looked through the records and picked a new one that she had not heard before – 'Don't Cry Over Love', an upbeat song that told women that there were plenty of fish in the sea. In a particularly naughty verse, Zarah told a nondescript man that when she had given herself to him, she had thought of someone else. Even though that didn't fit Ludwika's situation, she was strangely comforted by the song and its lyrics and kept repeating to herself 'Don't cry over love'.

Soon she would have a baby to take care of and that helped her with the pain of the family she had left behind and might have lost for good.

Ludwika's kept herself busy, trying not to think of everything she had lost, and focused as much as she could on the daily routine. Marie always looked knowingly and full of sympathy at her. In Fritz's flat, there was now always extra food, to make up for the small portions in the camp.

She didn't realise how quickly Christmas 1943 came and it passed even quicker, un-celebrated and miserable as before. Ludwika's concern for her unborn baby distracted her at least somewhat from the gloom around her.

The birth surprised her – a few weeks early and in the middle of her dinner shift in February. The baby seemed to have an unexpected urge to come out and before a doctor could be found, Barbara Gierz – named after Luca's mother – was born on February 19. Thanks to the vast number of mothers around, everything went smoothly and mother and daughter were well.

"It's a shame she is so dark," Marie said when she laid eyes on the little one for the first time. "Else we could have given her away for adoption. Nobody will want a bastard child that looks like her."

Ludwika ignored the remark. Barbara was the most beautiful child on earth – of course, apart from her Irena at home. Marie relieved Ludwika from the kitchen work with the exception of an occasional spying and checking over the pantries. Ludwika still had to visit Fritz and cook for him, but that was but almost like seeing family now. Barbara proved to be a quiet child, and rarely cried, especially not when Fritz held her. He had as calming influence on the little girl as he had on its mother.

When the child was asleep, the two of them would listen to the foreign broadcasts once in a while and hear with joy that the Russians troops had reached Hungary and her beloved Poland. Hopes for peace negotiations and an end to the madness, however, were trashed by the German news programmes, which kept encouraging the German Volk to pull together and fight back at all costs.

"You know, I almost can't remember what he looked like, my Luca," Ludwika said. "Isn't it funny?"

It was the same with her family, but she didn't dare say that out loud. Their images seemed to fade into the distance sometimes and it frightened her to think she couldn't picture her loved ones, however hard she tried. She wondered what Irena would look like now.

Fritz nodded knowingly.

"I only met Luca for maybe 20 hours in my life," she said. "Still, I have his child."

"Life is funny," Fritz said. "Maybe one day he will be freed and you two can pick up where you left things. If not, you have the memories and this beautiful child. He made you happy then, and she makes you happy now. It's more than others have – free or not."

She agreed. Fritz Kröplin was a godsend. His patience and protection helped make this difficult time a pleasant and rewarding one.

When in June the Allied troops landed in Normandy it should have been another happy day for Ludwika. Unfortunately, it was one of the worst. Barbara had had a slight fever for a few days. Ludwika didn't think much of it. . . Irena had had those many times. She tried a few home remedies, such as sponging the baby and keeping it cool. Marie even got her some drops from a pharmacy: the childless overseer had taken an unexpected liking to the 'dark bastard'.

On the morning of the Allied invasion Ludwika spotted marks on Barbara's skin and alerted the overseers that the child was probably suffering from chickenpox. A Dutch doctor came to the camp and confirmed her suspicion. He recommended a partial quarantine by only allowing the construction workers out and anyone whose contribution to Oldenburg and the war effort was of an essential nature.

The orderlies divided the women's section in half with another curtain and declared one half the sick zone. When Marie heard about it she was worried about her father's ill health and arranged for his care to be supplied by a woman from a different camp. Ludwika, who had suffered from the disease as a child and was immune to it, was confined to working in the kitchen while her child was being tended to by one of the sick women.

Barbara was deteriorating rapidly and Ludwika, who had seen children with chickenpox before, suspected that something else was the matter. The child refused her breast and became unresponsive. A nurse from the local hospital had been sent to the camp. She thought that Ludwika was being overly dramatic and reassured her that Barbara would be fine.

"A child this young must feed," Ludwika insisted. "Something is wrong. Please have a doctor come and take a look."

"I would," the woman replied. "If they grew on trees I'd go and pick one for you right away. As it so happens, the ones we have, they've got better things to do."

Ludwika was stunned at the sudden venom.

"Please," she begged. "Barbara is so weak. Look at her."

"There isn't anything else that a doctor can do for your baby," the woman replied. "You've got to be patient and hope that the child is a fighter and gets over the disease. Usually they do."

Ludwika couldn't stop worrying and wished that she could catch the disease again so that she could be with her daughter during the day, too. Working long shifts in the kitchen without being able to look after her child was unbearable.

For a few days Barbara allowed her mother to feed her and seemed to improve, then, in the middle of the night, she again fell suddenly into an unresponsive state. The camp nurse refused to grant Ludwika access to emergency care and made her wait for the morning when the Dutch doctor was expected to make his visit. Ludwika held her daughter all night, trying not to cry, waiting for the morning and the doctor. She fell asleep on a bench in the sick zone before dawn, with Barbara held tightly in her arms. When she awoke she checked on her baby. Barbara was not moving, nor was she breathing. Ludwika couldn't find a pulse and called in panic for the nurse. The woman took a quick look, shook her head and confirmed that the little girl had died in the night.

"It's probably for the best," the nurse said. "A weak child like her, she would have died with the next disease if this one hadn't taken her."

Tears streamed down Ludwika's face as she held her dead baby close. Some women tried to console her, but Ludwika didn't even notice them. Instead, she rocked back and forth on the seat, scaring those who watched as she sang nursery rhymes to her dead child.

The doctor took the body with him.

"Where is she going to get buried?" Ludwika asked.

"I'll try to find out for you," he replied. His eyes looked compassionate and sad, but the tone of his voice betrayed his resignation and detachment. Ludwika understood that his hands were tied. She was under no illusion that her daughter would get her own grave or marking – if she got one at all. It didn't matter to her. Barbara was dead; there was nothing else to be done. No funeral would change that or make Ludwika feel better about the loss. The only thing left was to go on, but how much more loss could she bear?

Halina, the Polish girl who usually worked in the hotel and who had also been struck by the chickenpox, wrapped an arm around Ludwika.

"I've never seen anyone as strong and determined as you," she said. "You will get past this. You'll have plenty of children when you are older. You and I, we will come through all of this and be happy again."

Ludwika, too weak to speak, took hold of Halina's hand and squeezed it. It warmed her heart a little that Halina finally found it in her to open up to someone else. The two women had been the loners in the camp and maybe now they had found each other over the tragedy that had befallen Ludwika. The grieving mother was excused from her duties that day, but the next day the orderlies told her that she was back in charge of the kitchen.

More than ever, people avoided Ludwika, unsure how to behave around her. She didn't blame them. She had isolated herself deliberately and in some way she was pleased about that. Having people console her and talk about Barbara would only rub salt in her wounds. Halina seemed to know this and her compassionate looks helped more than any words could. Carrying on was the best thing Ludwika could do. Her life was nothing but loss and there was nothing she could do about it but to endure it. She mustn't cry over love, she sang to herself. Any love. . .

Chapter 19

Ludwika threw herself into work more than ever. The nights were not as easy and bad dreams and sleeplessness tormented her. Once the chickenpox outbreak had been contained, Marie let her know that she could continue to work for her father again. It was the first good news Ludwika had had in a long time. It was August and her first trip to see Fritz was a symbolic step for her out of the darkness. Beautiful sunshine warmed her skin and brightened her mind, together with the green of the trees and the parks.

Fritz Kröplin was waiting for her, his eyes sparkling with anticipation.

"I've missed you," he said, without mentioning the dead child. He always seemed to know what to say and what to omit.

"I've missed you, too," she said. Instead of talking, she busied herself in his apartment, seeking shelter in the re-establishment of her routine. After she had cooked him his favourite, an omelette with ham and cheese, they sat down together to listen to the foreign broadcasts.

"Aren't you eating anything?" he asked. "Your body must be weak."

"My stomach is funny," she said. "It must be all the grief that's suddenly hit me. An omelette would be too heavy. We're not used to that kind of food in the camp."

"All the more reason to share in mine," he said.

"Maybe next time," she said.

"I think you'll like what you are going to hear on the radio," he told her. "Your Poland is almost free. The Russians are not far from Warsaw already."

"The Russians took half of Poland when the Germans came. Maybe they'll keep it all for themselves now," she said. "It doesn't make Poland free, only rid of the Germans."

"Well, switch the radio on," Fritz said.

There was no news about Poland, though. The Russians seemed to have stopped short of Warsaw and instead continued their battles in the Baltic. The BBC reported Allied progress in Italy and France.

"It's always good to hear both sides of the story," Fritz said. "Let's hear how the German radio portrays the situation."

The newsreader for the Reich proudly reported that an uprising in Warsaw had successfully been smashed. Ludwika got up and switched the radio off.

"Enough sad news for today," she said and brought the gramophone in.

"You listen to that in the kitchen," Fritz said. "I've got another headache coming and need to lie down."

The music blocked out the pain of Poland, Warsaw, Irena, Luca and Barbara. "Don't cry for love," she sang along and Zarah's resolve gave Ludwika strength.

When she was done in the kitchen she switched the gramophone off and looked in on Fritz to see if he needed anything. She found him lying on the floor.

"Don't you think it's better to lie on the sofa?" she asked. In his agony Fritz often tried the strangest positions, searching for one that gave him less pain.

He didn't reply.

"Fritz," she said. "I could at least get you a pillow or a blanket to make you more comfortable. This can't be good for you."

She bent down to get his attention. Now she noticed a pool of sick by the sofa.

"Fritz?"

She gently slapped his cheeks. He was unconscious.

She jumped up and ran outside. The furniture shop had a telephone but at first the owner refused to let her use it. When she mentioned that she needed help for Fritz Kröplin they relented and called for help.

The ambulance arrived soon after and took him to the Peter-Friedrich-Ludwig Hospital. It was an intimidating, palatial-looking building that stretched out from either side of a neoclassical portico.

Ludwika had sat with Fritz in the ambulance in order to provide necessary information about him to the doctors. As soon as she had told them everything she knew about his operation, which was not much, and had given them Marie's details she was told to go. On her way out, she went to the bathroom. Her bowels were in upheaval and it took some time before she felt ready to leave. As soon as she got up she felt an excruciating pain in her stomach and felt nauseous. She sank to the floor outside the cubicles, crouched over, hugging her knees.

After a few minutes a nurse came in and when she saw Ludwika she stomped her foot noisily on the floor.

"Damn it. Not again," she shouted and bent down. "Come on, I'll bring you back to your room." She started to pull Ludwika from the floor. "The doctor will tell you when you're ready to leave."

Ludwika looked at the nurse with bewilderment.

"I'm not a patient here," Ludwika said. "I have an upset stomach, that's all."

"Of course you do," the nurse said with poorly disguised disregard. "What's your name?"

"Ludwika Gierz," she said. "I came with Fritz Kröplin."

She managed to get up and, with the support from the nurse, reached the reception desk where the nurse received confirmation that Ludwika was indeed a visitor.

"I was sure she was one of the girls from the second floor," she said to the receptionist. "You know. . . another runner," she added in a lower voice as if Ludwika couldn't hear her.

The receptionist gave a knowing nod.

"She has an odd colour," the receptionist said.

"I found her doubled over," the nurse said. "The second floor is just right for her."

Ludwika wondered what that meant but was too weak to refuse help. The nurse grabbed her elbow and led her up two flights of stairs to the 'Non-Arian' section. Ludwika was faint and barely made the climb. She needed the toilet a few more times while she waited for hours on a chair in the hallway to be examined by an unfriendly doctor. She was feverish and could hardly hear the man's questions. He took some blood and assigned her a bed in a communal room. It was all a haze to Ludwika, and only the next day when she woke up did she fully understand what had happened. The pain was still there and she felt hot and sweaty.

"You're not allowed to eat while the examination is in progress," a nurse told her. "Maybe you need an operation later. You need to keep an empty stomach for that."

Ludwika didn't care; she wasn't hungry, the thought of food made her sick. Her bed neighbour looked with pity at her.

"I hope they won't operate on you," she whispered. "They're performing hysterectomies on healthy women here. If they open you up, they take out everything else: I wish you luck."

Ludwika sank back on her bed, just wanting to be swallowed by the earth. No wonder the nurse had brought her up here. That hadn't been out of care, it had been out of malice. She had wondered why in the middle of the war a hospital bed would be made available to a Polish woman. What would they do to her? Had she not suffered enough?

She heard her father's voice, telling her to stop worrying and to believe in the future. She wondered if he'd said those words had he known what she would have to put up with. She drifted off to sleep and didn't wake until it was night. Ludwika was lucky not to have soiled herself. Now she needed to be quick. It was quiet and the room was dark. The door was slightly ajar and let a little light fall through from the corridor. It was enough for her to get up and find the bathroom.

When she was done, she returned to her sweat-soaked bed. Her eyes had adjusted to the darkness and Ludwika counted twelve beds – all full – in her ward. It was all she saw before sleep took hold and she was woken the next morning.

"Fraulein Gierz," the doctor said, "it appears that you have an inflamed pancreas."

"What does that mean?" she asked.

He looked at her and shrugged. "You'll stay here until we had time to make some tests. We need to keep you under close watch and find out what the underlying causes are."

He made a few notes in a folder and then moved on to the next bed.

She was left with too many questions. How serious was her condition? How long would she have to be here? Had someone told Marie where she was? How would they find out the underlying causes? After what her bed neighbour had mentioned about the sterilisation, she was mortified that all of this was an excuse to operate.

"Can you find out how Herr Kröplin is doing?" she asked one of the nurses. "He is a good friend and came here with me a few days ago."

"What's wrong with him?" the nurse asked.

"He once had a brain operation," Ludwika said. "I would like to visit him if he's still in the hospital."

"I'll see if I can find out," the nurse said, but for days she never came back with any news.

In the meantime Ludwika was rarely fed, usually only in the evenings. During the days she was frequently taken for further examinations, every time she was terrified it would end with an operation.

After a week full of fear-filled moments, Marie visited her.

"I've just been to see father," she said. "He sends his love."

"How is he?" Ludwika asked.

"You've got to get better soon," Marie said. "He's coming out of hospital next week."

"What was wrong with him?" Ludwika asked.

"They don't know for sure," Marie said. "Since the operation he has had some brain damage. I worried that the tumour had come back, but he is fine. Just one of those things, I guess."

"Thank God for that," Ludwika said.

"I need you on your feet again as quickly as possible; I don't want to hire another girl to look after him."

She gave Ludwika a probing look and then giggled. "Forgive me, you look ghastly. Your face looks as yellow as a Chinese woman. We don't call jaundice 'the yellow illness' for nothing. When do they think you can come out?"

"The doctors are still doing tests," she said. "I feel awful and the pain is very bad."

Marie stopped smiling.

"What a shame," she said. "Well, don't worry. You are so indestructible you'll make it through."

She touched Ludwika's hand quickly and got up.

"I've got to go now," she said. "Take good care of yourself and don't get used to lying on your bum. Father needs you."

She left without waiting for a reply.

Ludwika was stuck in the hospital for almost five weeks. Patients in her room came and went. Some had the feared operation and left the hospital sterile and crying. Ludwika was spared such a fate, although not the constant fear of it. She had lost more weight, but gradually she began to feel better. The physical recovery brought with it an emotional one. Ludwika looked forward to her release and to a return to a routine.

In October, she was discharged and returned to the camp. It was like coming home. Even though Halina was the only one who made some kind of a fuss over her, the familiarity of the place had long become one of the constant factors that sustained her. It was impersonal and cold at times, but she knew how life worked here and she had her secure place within it.

Fritz Kröplin was pleased to see her, but he looked worse than she had ever seen him. He, too, had lost weight and he was in constant pain. Pale and fragile, he moved with a walking stick and held on to a wall or a piece of furniture where he could.

"You look like a skeleton," he scolded her. "You need to eat."

He pointed at her bony hand.

Ludwika didn't care. She had been in Germany for four years now and had bigger worries than her weight.

Fritz sat down on the kitchen table and eventually she joined him to exchange their stories since they had last seen each other. She cooked and baked for him with enthusiasm and later they sat down to listen to the radio news.

"All of France has been freed by the Allies," Ludwika said. "Did you hear anything about Poland while I was away?" she asked. "They cannot still be waiting outside of Warsaw and doing nothing," she said. "Do you think that is a good thing?"

Fritz shrugged.

"I wish I knew," he said. "If Hitler would only negotiate with his enemies a lot of unnecessary fighting could be averted. I doubt he ever will, though."

"Of course not," Ludwika said. "You've heard the man on the radio. Hitler's convinced he can win the war. Better not think about it. You and I won't change anything."

It frightened her to imagine fighting in Poland. Were any of her family still alive after all these years? Irena would be ten soon. What did the future hold for her daughter? Would she ever see her again?

"You're right," Fritz said, interrupting her thoughts. "Put one of your records on for me, I've been missing that."

Part 3

Chapter 20

The last months of the war were surprisingly peaceful for Ludwika. She rejoiced in the liberation of Poland, although she was sceptical about the effects it would have on the country's future. The German radio accused the Russian soldiers of terrible crimes and she couldn't help fear that Polish people would also suffer at the hands of their liberators.

Marie's husband Herman was reported missing. The overseer took it reasonably well: stoic at first and then angry and determined to seek revenge. Her involvement in other camps took up most of her time now and she worked longer, only visiting Fritz on certain evenings, if at all. Ludwika saw her once a week to discuss the increasingly difficult supply and rationing issues for the Lindenhof inmates.

The Allied troops seemed to be stuck by the Rhine in the West and the Oder in the East for a very long time, but soon after these natural barriers had been overrun the war finally came to Oldenburg with increased air raids and the sound of battles nearby. The civilians, who had been incredibly shielded from the hardships of the war up until now, began to flee the city in droves. The coming end of the Third Reich was finally clear to all, even to those who continued the fighting.

Two weeks before the war would came to an end the doorbell rang in the middle of the afternoon. Fritz was in a deep sleep. Ludwika went down the stairs to open the door and found Luca standing outside. He quickly rushed past her and closed the door. Neither said a word as they ate each other up with their eyes, unable to believe that this was happening. He was thinner, but still cut a fine figure. They fell into each other's arms and made love there and then on the stairs, holding each other tightly for long after. She pulled herself away, re-arranged her hair and clothes and walked up the stairs, motioning him to follow. Fritz was still asleep, so she sat Luca down in the kitchen and made him some food.

"You lost some weight but you still look every bit as beautiful as I remembered you," he said. "I've been thinking about you every day and even more so every night."

She smiled.

"So what are you doing here?" she asked. "Isn't it dangerous?"

"Life is dangerous," he said and laughed.

"Did they release you?" she asked.

"No," he replied. "I escaped during the last air raid and hid in a coal cellar. There have been mad rumours that the Germans would shoot all of their prisoners. I wasn't going to hang around to find out at what must be the end of the war. I knew a couple of good hiding places but I needed food and I had to come here and see you, risk or not."

"I'm glad you did," she said and fed him from Fritz's larder. She knew he wouldn't mind.

Luca looked searchingly at her. "Where is our child?" he asked. "Is it a boy or a girl?"

Her heart broke when she looked in his excited eyes.

"I named her Barbara," she said, "after your mother."

"How splendid," he said. "What does she look like? Where is she? When can I see her?"

She shook her head.

"Barbara didn't make it, Luca." A tear rolled down her eyes as she watched him coming to understand the truth.

"She had chickenpox," she said, holding back the part about nobody taking her concerns seriously and the child dying in her arms. "She was a beautiful child, easy to please and would have made you proud."

She paused.

"I wish I had better news for you than this," she said.

"Me, too," he said and got up and took her in his arms. "I can only imagine what you went through. I wish I could have been there for you."

She leaned into him, grateful for his relentless spirit. In his arms she felt protected and safe, even if it could only last a few moments.

"I need to go," he said. "I mustn't endanger you or Herr Kröplin. If I'm found I'll be shot on sight as an escapee."

"You'd be safer here," Ludwika insisted. "You could hide in the cellar when Marie or the other girl come and then be with me when I'm here."

"No, I have a better hiding place, one that doesn't involve risks for anyone else. I can't take chances on other people's lives. This visit today was too much as it is. I need to go before anything could happen."

Her heart sank.

"When will we get to see each other again?" she asked.

"Soon, I hope."

He kissed her forehead, went down the stairs and left.

Ludwika checked on Fritz, who was sound asleep, then she sat in the kitchen listening to the gramophone and preparing his next meal. She left it on the kitchen table for when he awoke. She had to go back before curfew.

The nightly air raids were scary even though most bombers flew past the city to Bremen and Hamburg. The Lindenhof had only a small basement, which wasn't bomb proof, and didn't have enough space for all inmates either. To avoid hysteria and fighting amongst the prisoners, Marie had locked its doors. The whistling sound of the falling bombs and the explosions were bad enough, but the destruction and the dead bodies were worse. Ludwika had only seen bomb victims once up close on her morning walk to Fritz and she had doubled her steps and looked away. Usually the population of Oldenburg quickly covered the bodies up and limited the visibility of the impact of the air raids.

The days and nights seemed to drag. Every day that Luca didn't appear she feared that he might have been caught and executed. The foreign radio continuously demanded an immediate surrender and encouraged people to revolt against the leaders. The Reich answered these broadcasts with stories of unsuccessful attempts to bring down the government and the public hanging of the traitors. Ludwika wondered if it was worth risking one's life so late in the game.

At last, Canadian troops rolled into town, Germany surrendered unconditionally and the Führer was presumed dead. By the time a group of soldiers came into the Lindenhof camp to assess the situation their wardens had long left the city. The inmates had stayed in the camp together, worried to be mistaken for Germans by the Allies or falling victim to an act of vengeance by the defeated Germans. They all were frightened and intimidated at first when they saw men in uniform enter the building. The army took command with weapons drawn, but when it became clear that the soldiers were looking for Nazis in hiding and that the inmates were indeed now free, there was a huge cheer and relief. Ludwika and Halina fell into each other's arms with joy.

The soldiers spoke to everyone individually to establish their names and backgrounds and to find the people who could be trusted and those who might have been collaborators. The army chose a few trusted inmates as temporary camp leadership Ludwika was considered a suspect because of her 'friendship' with Marie and her privileges to leave the camp. Fortunately, and to her big surprise, many of the kitchen staff spoke up for her and testified how well Ludwika had treated everyone. The inspectors were eventually satisfied and let her stay. It didn't deter other inmates in the camp though from calling Ludwika names and bullying her when they could.

The most pressing questions on everyone's mind in the Lindenhof, however, were immediately about the fate of Poland and the Ukraine: What was the situation in those countries? When would it be possible to go back home? Was there a way to find out about one's family? When would a post service resume?

The soldiers reassured everyone that soon there would be answers to all of these questions and they asked the inmates to stay put until the conditions in all of Germany and the occupied and liberated countries had become clearer.

That brought with it the practical questions: How long would everyone have to remain here? Who would assume control and how would the camp be fed?

The liberation brought with it a whole new set of difficulties.

Ludwika wasted no time in seeing Fritz. Not just for his sake but also to see if he had heard from Luca. Maybe the Italian was already there, waiting. Walking wasn't fast enough; she had to run through the streets until she reached the house, opened the door and chased up the stairs. No sign of Luca. Instead, she found a deflated Fritz sitting in front of the radio.

"What's the matter?" she asked. She would have expected him to be happier than this. He, too, had longed for the end of the war. How could he be so miserable on such a glorious day?

"Marie has been arrested," he said. "Not that I should be surprised about it. She took that Nazi business far too serious. I doubt they'll release her anytime soon."

"Oh Fritz," she said, sitting next to him and taking his hand. "Marie will be fine," she said. "The people who arrested her are more civilised than the Nazis were. She's lucky she won't have to taste a cup of her own medicine, and she wasn't even as bad as others were."

"She'll have to pay for it one way or another," Fritz said gloomily. "After everything that has been happening, I doubt the courts will let any of them get off lightly; and rightfully so. To think my own daughter locked an air raid shelter. How can she not be punished for that? Only, when it's your own child, you don't want it to happen, even if it is deserved."

Ludwika didn't know what to say. She got up and began cooking. He joined her in the kitchen.

"I'll run out of groceries soon," he said. "Without Marie I'll be completely dependent on you. Will you be able to help me still? I can't pay you much more than Marie did, and that was a pittance, I know."

Ludwika smiled at him. "We will work something out," she said. "I've never regarded my time here as work, and have always thought of you as my family. Until the dust has settled and I can go back to Poland I will gladly look after you. Without you, I would have gone crazy."

The weeks that followed the camp's liberation were tough for Ludwika. The urging questions about Poland, loved ones and the future weren't answered, which caused a lot of anxiety and worry. On top of that, the day to day operation was not getting easier. The food supply for the camp was just as meagre as it had been in the last few months of the war. The only good thing was that everything was organised and protected by the occupying forces, who gave priority in food distribution to the victims of the Nazis.

"You shouldn't be getting any food," a woman shouted at Ludwika during dinner one night. "You shouldn't be here but outside with the Germans. You were one of them. You made your bed, now lie in it."

Ludwika ignored her, as she did with all other attacks and accusations. People suddenly had brought up Manfred's letter: support from a German Untersturmführer on her behalf, which many saw as treason and worse. She was astonished: how did they even know about that? Only Marie and the German camp officials could have known about Manfred. Had someone overheard them, or had Marie gossiped about her? It all made Ludwika's time in the camp much more difficult. Although she had never taken anything from anyone, many people treated her with contempt.

Luca had not re-appeared and she had to assume the worst. He should have been able to see Fritz by now if nothing had happened to him. Luca's continued absence made it most likely that he had been caught by either a bomb or the Nazi's in the last hours of the war. She couldn't think of any other reason why she hadn't heard from him. The thought was too much to bear. Was there no end to the tragedy and losses in her life?

As if things were not complicated enough, Ludwika also found that she was pregnant again. Naturally she was delighted, after leaving behind Irena and losing Barbara. Even if the father was missing and the timing and the circumstances were far from ideal. It generated a lot of questions, though: Would there be enough food for her and her baby? Would she be returning to Poland soon? Would she be able to travel while she was pregnant? She needed to find out about Luca before she could do that. For now, the inmates had just about enough for two meagre meals a day, but outside of the camp the supply was already becoming a big problem and there was fear that this would lead to shortened rations for the Lindenhof, too. The shop shelves were emptying and Fritz's money didn't buy her much anymore. The rationing system had collapsed and the black market flourished. Without the misappropriated food from its occupied territories Germany had not enough to feed its population, something Oldenburg's German citizens had not experienced during the war. Ludwika saved whatever she could from her miniscule portions in the camp and brought it to Fritz, who however refused to eat the food of a pregnant woman.

His health soon deteriorated and he was re-admitted to hospital.

The International organisations set up to restore order in Europe were compiling lists of the camp inmates to get an overview of the chaos in Europe. People were classified by type of their displacement: evacuees, war and political refugees, political prisoners and forced or voluntary workers. Ludwika and the inmates of the camp were categorised as forced workers and promised a return to their countries.

The Lindenhof had a radio that the inmates religiously listened to. News was also received from the Canadian officials who looked after the camps. Ludwika learned that many people in Europe were stranded in places they didn't belong.

Inmates could register their interest to return home as soon as possible, which many did, although when the authorities would start shifting people wasn't known. Some inmates didn't bother waiting and made their way home by foot, anxious to see their loved ones. Although they were warned that there was no free travel between the occupation zones, they were willing to take a chance. An equally large number preferred to wait until they had either reunited with missing members of their family or until the political situation in their home countries was better known. People were scared of communism and Stalin and didn't want to move from life under one dictator to life under another.

They were highly suspicious of the situation in Poland and spread rumours about the situation there. What was one to think of a Polish People's Republic? It reeked of Soviet puppeteers. On top of those general worries and about the gnawing uncertainty over Irena and her family, Ludwika couldn't be sure of her status should she return home. Was she not seen as a collaborator after leaving with Manfred and would suffer the consequences for this now? How bad would it be if the latter was the case? Was it safe or a foolish risk? Until she heard from her family she would not dare go back. She had registered a search for them with the Red Cross but had not heard anything so far. She knew this could take a long time. There were millions in the very same situation as her. Ever since living with other Polish prisoners she had heard stories of further waves of deportations of Polish people after she had left the country but usually in areas further east. Nobody had known anything about Przedborów or villages nearby.

Now the news reported how large chunks of formerly German territories had been given to Poland, Czechoslovakia and even some Baltic States, who had come under the Soviet umbrella. The Communist regimes and the Russian influence however deterred a growing number of people from returning to their home countries.

Some of the smaller camps were gradually dismantled and rumour had it that Ludwika and her colleagues would be transferred into a camp near the Dutch border which had more capacity.

"I need to stay here," she told the woman who had taken down all of her details. She was an elderly British lady who spoke excellent German.

"You may not have that choice," she said, looking up from her papers. "The brewery needs their premises back and we can't pay them when there is capacity in other camps."

"But I don't want to leave," Ludwika insisted.

"I know," the woman said. "Don't worry. For now I'm not talking about going back to Poland, only to a different camp."

"But here is where the father of my child will come looking for me," Ludwika explained, unsure if the Red Cross official believed her. She might have heard many similar stories already. How could Ludwika prove that hers was real?

"Have you registered a search for him?" the woman asked. "As long as you are entered into our lists he will be able to find you. It doesn't matter where you are."

Ludwika looked uncomfortable.

"I don't know his surname," she said. "He mentioned it a few times but it's Dutch and I can't spell it. DeWitt, DeVries… something like it. I don't remember."

"Does he know yours?" she asked.

"I don't know."

The woman raised an eyebrow. "I will try to keep you around here but I cannot promise you anything," she said. "Many of the Dutch and French prisoners have started their journeys back home already. I know, because we now have spaces in their camps. You Polish have a lot further to go and you can't stay on the street until your return is organised. We'll have to move you somewhere."

Ludwika realised the woman was right. She briefly considered living in Fritz's flat but then, how would she be fed and earn money?

In a minor karmic turn the mighty proud Oldenburg lost its status as a free state and was merged with the city of Bremen in a restructuring of Germany. The local population was deeply unhappy about it. Ludwika smirked a little when she visited Fritz in hospital and he told her what a humiliation that meant to the fallen oppressors.

She frequently went to his apartment to get away from the awkward atmosphere at the camp and to listen to the gramophone.

She was stunned when she found the flat suddenly occupied by a German family who had lost their home in a bombing. The authorities had declared it unlikely that Fritz would come out of the hospital soon and in exchange for his place in the hospital they had allocated his home temporarily to these homeless people.

Ludwika explained her complicated situation as good as she could and begged the family to give Luca her name and current address, should he ever appear.

"Whatever you do," she said before leaving the apartment, "please don't sell his gramophone and the records. They have a lot of sentimental value."

The German woman stared at her as if she was from a different planet and then nodded. Ludwika doubted her wishes would be respected and feared that Luca would also not get the message if he ever should return from wherever he was now.

The transfer to the new camp came without warning. One morning the Lindenhof inmates were summoned from their camp and led to the station. A freight train took them from Oldenburg station down south via Cloppenburg to Dalum near the Dutch border, where a group of former Nazi concentration camps had been adapted to house people displaced by the war. Almost all of their new inmates were Polish and so they were soon nicknamed the Polish camps.

Ludwika was disappointed that she didn't have the opportunity to tell Fritz or the people who lived in his flat where she was going. If Luca should ever come looking, he'd never find her now. She deeply distrusted the Red Cross officials and their lists. She knew only a handful of people who had been reunited, too few for the system to have credibility in her eyes. She had heard nothing of her family in Poland either. It was difficult to decide what to do: going home in the hope of reuniting with her family and risk of never seeing Luca again, or staying put while the authorities checked that she had a family to return to and hoping to find Luca? He didn't even know she was pregnant again. He was a survivor and she couldn't quite accept yet that he might be dead. She wanted to see Irena again but she had to think of her unborn child, too. She might get stuck in a communist

Poland for nothing, without finding her old family and depriving her unborn child of meeting its father. Whatever she did, people could get hurt.

Chapter 21

The accommodation in the new camp did not allow for much privacy. There were large rooms that held places for about forty people in each. The group barracks and communal bathrooms, however, were a step up for Ludwika and the other refugees. People volunteered to work in the kitchen or teach the children. Small black market trade began amongst the inmates almost immediately but beside the day to day operation the prevailing sentiment was that of insecurity, fear and boredom. Having been oppressed by wardens for so long, many found it hard to trust people in uniform and do as they were told, even if those orders came from their liberators.

The food was scarce and disgusting: a bowl of dark brown porridge made from oat husks. It looked like manure and tasted like dishwater. The lucky ones who got in line first also got a slice of black bread until it ran out. In the afternoon the food was more of the same.

Farmers from the area protested at the camp gates, complaining that chickens, ducks, geese, rabbits and goats were constantly disappearing from their land. They accused the inmates of stealing and demanded compensation.

Fortunately, over time, the food situation improved and such incidents were less frequent.

The political picture in Europe on the other hand remained chaotic, and with every news story came a wildfire of rumours and scare mongering.

"Przedborów?" she kept asking around, day after day, hoping that some of the many new people here knew something the Lindenhof inmates didn't. "Does anyone know about Przedborów?"

"Too far in the West," one woman at last replied. "All that area was made part of the Reich. Every single Pole was sent packing."

"When I left in 1940 my family still had their own farm," Ludwika said.

The woman looked suspiciously at her.

"That wouldn't have lasted for another five years," she said. "Not there. In the East, around Warsaw maybe. Przedborów – never."

Ludwika nodded. She had always feared that this might be the case.

"1940?" the woman continued. "You haven't seen anything if you had left by then. The Germans kept pushing us further to the East. If your family is still alive it won't be in Przedborów. I've not heard a single story about a Polish family being left in peace in the Reich."

"They could have returned to Przedborów by now," Ludwika said, trying to get her head round the situation, now that she spoke to someone who had some knowledge.

"Yes, if the Germans didn't burn the place down during the retreat from the Russians," the woman said. "God you're naïve. You would have heard by now if they had made it to Przedborów. That would be an easy case for the Red Cross. You're looking for a needle in a haystack, dear."

It fitted all too well with what she had heard before and the optimism that she had occasionally been able to sustain seemed ridiculous and naïve now. There was little hope that she would find her family unless she stayed put here and waited for the Red Cross to work its miracles.

At times Ludwika found it difficult to believe what she heard on the radio: Could the Russians really have begun to appropriate private and public property and establish communism in its occupied parts of Germany? Had all Germans really been expelled from Poland? Was it true that Breslau, the beautiful city she had seen on her journey to Hamburg, was part of the compensation and been returned to Poland in its entirety after several centuries? Sometimes she thought nothing could surprise her, and nothing would ever be stable as far as territories and politics were concerned.

Neither was there any stability in her life.

Now that she was showing, Ludwika was assigned a bed in a section reserved for expectant women and single mothers. She was back in her element, having children around her. Taking care of them helped deflect her mind from her own difficult situation and broke her out of her isolation. As before, children took an instant shine to her and Ludwika became the unofficial nanny of the barracks. Before a week was over all children knew several nursery rhymes in Polish, most notably the one about the goose, the fox and the hunter.

Christmas 1945 was the first time in years that Ludwika was part of a celebration. People didn't have much but they all chipped in to make it an event to remember. There was a huge Christmas tree that some of the men had cut down from the local forest, much to the protest of the Germans. People decorated it with coloured paper bows and ribbons. Some talented artists had folded up papers into figurines for a little nativity scene. There were some exchanges of gifts, even if it was only apples kept from the rations or similarly small tokens of affection.

At midnight on Christmas Eve they all sang hymns and people recited the Christmas story from memory.

Instead of cheering Ludwika up, the Polish traditions made her incredibly sad. It was almost impossible not to think of the people she was missing. Although everyone felt the same way, it didn't make things any easier for her. A few lucky people by now had heard from their relatives. With that further news about the state of the country spread.

Stalin had annexed the most eastern Polish territories, and so many inmates had no Polish home to return to, only a future in Russia, should they consider such a thing. Tales of indescribable devastation and destruction of entire villages everywhere deterred many from making the long journey into what was now Russia or into a communist Poland. Who was to guarantee that Stalin wouldn't take the rest of their country with the help of its Soviet-friendly government?

The stories that emerged from those letters and reports frightened Ludwika.

"Everyone in my village was shot," one woman lamented.

"My village has been burnt down," another one said.

From what she gathered, the Germans really had deported all Polish people from the annexed territories. There were no exceptions. It was disheartening and Ludwika's hopes of finding her family and Irena in the same place seemed nothing but delusional now. If they had been forced to move, they could be anywhere. She hoped the Red Cross and its lists would find them soon.

In January 1946, Ludwika gave birth to a son. The labour was uncomplicated and quick.

She couldn't remember what Luca's father had been called but it had been something sounding similar to Gerry, also the name of one of their Canadian camp managers. She decided to name the boy Jerzy, which was as close as she could get with a Polish name. Jerzy

Franz, the second name after her drowned brother. The boy was healthy and looked beautiful and Italian, like his father. The happiness over the birth soon put everything in her life into perspective. She would make sure he was all right and the joy over being a mother made all her other dark thoughts less prominent.

"He's very handsome," people said, and she had to agree. His face looked exactly like she'd imagine Luca's was as a baby. Those eyes were irresistible.

For the next few months life revolved around nothing but her golden boy and the other children in the camp. Jerzy was a lively child and very engaging. Being in the mother's section had its advantages. There was always someone around who understood and was willing to help.

Ludwika blocked out all political news and horror stories as best she could and consoled herself that the new Polish Republic was not a Soviet state yet. The Red Cross gradually reunited families or found information regarding their whereabouts. Surely, soon it would be her turn to receive news. Many people remained undeterred by the rumours about the uncertain life awaiting them in Poland, and when they boarded the transports back home Ludwika wished them luck and allowed herself to become infected by their optimism. Maybe the world would become a better place after all and everything would turn out fine.

Nobody was forced to leave the camp as yet, which was a big relief. Rumour had it that people from the Ukraine and Lithuania were less lucky. Stalin demanded that 'his citizens', as they were now, be returned and were given priority by the repatriation authorities. He hadn't made those demands about the Polish people, which was reassuring. Many people commented that the relations between the Allies in the West and Russia seemed strained but Ludwika tried not to let it worry her. With Jerzy in her arms it was easier to be positive. After years of strict German rules and sexual repression in the camps men and women began to mingle. Although still watched closely by the elders and subject to traditional and religious restrictions, many couples formed and weddings were announced.

Ludwika had admirers, too. It was funny, now, that she was free to do so, she wasn't interested in finding a man. She still hoped against all odds to meet Luca. One suitor was a teacher named Karol who was older than her. He often came to visit the mothers with the excuse of wanting to speak about the children's behaviour and their talents. She guessed him to be over 40. He was not bad looking but seemed a little bitter and too stiff for her liking. Luca had set the bar high with his charismatic nature.

Her other prominent admirer was Onufry, a broody builder from the Ukrainian border region, who led the effort to set up a playground for the children. He was quiet, but his silence seemed to hide something of interest. He had deep eyes, earthy hands and was about Ludwika's age. Small and stocky, there was something mildly intriguing about him.

However, neither man seemed quite right for her and she tried to avoid them to prevent any awkwardness. Onufry had never spoken to Ludwika, but he was not skilled at hiding his feelings and often stared at her just a little too long to go unnoticed. His affection was an open secret. Karol, the teacher, didn't hide his infatuation either but was more forthcoming and used excuses to get nearer to her. He kept asking Ludwika to give the children formal singing lessons in his class, which she refused every time.

"I don't think you can just reject them," Lena, one of the other mothers, said to her one day.

"I'm not rejecting either of them," Ludwika replied.

"Of course you do," Lena said and laughed. She was the same age and had started seeing one of the wardens, which was forbidden by the rules of the camp. "You're singing all the time, yet you won't sing for Karol? Of course that is a rejection. If anyone else asked, you would happily say yes."

"Maybe," Ludwika conceded. "I didn't mean to. With Jerzy being so young, it seems a little premature to be thinking of men."

"What about Onufry?" Lena continued regardless. "With a builder as a husband you will always have a roof over your head and he doesn't talk as much as the teacher."

"I've never even spoken to him," Ludwika said and laughed. Lena's persistence amused her.

"Then go and talk," she insisted. "You're not breaking any laws or doing anything outrageous by talking to him. If you don't, you'll never know what he's like, or if he's suitable for you."

"Thank you," Ludwika replied. "I'm just not ready yet."

"You mustn't waste opportunities like this," Lena insisted. "Whatever is holding you back, whatever you fear or hope – you need to get past it. Your son needs a father and you have two great offers. I wouldn't wait too long. There are plenty of women around here, also pretty. . . and without the baggage."

"How can you say that?" Ludwika asked, shocked at this directness.

"Listen," Lena said, more quietly. "I was raped. It was disgusting, more than I can express in words. But I can't punish my child for it, nor can I expect all men to be such pigs. My Alfie is different and he will take care of me and my girl."

Ludwika was in awe of such bravery.

Lena was risking a lot by going with Alfie. The occupation forces strictly interdicted fraternization by military personnel with civilians. Couples who became involved had to hide their relations and soldiers often were suddenly reassigned when their affairs were discovered, without time to say good bye. Some had wives and families to return to at home without telling their girlfriends.

On the other hand, Ludwika had to admit that waiting for Luca was starting to be silly. He should have found her easily by now if he was alive. She was on all lists, he knew more about her than she knew about him, and he was resourceful enough to find out from someone where she was or at least where was likely to be. He had to be dead; she just couldn't make herself admit it, yet.

"I'm not sure I want to go with a Polish man," Ludwika said after a short pause. "They may want to go back to Poland and I'm not sure that I can."

"You speak about it as if there was an option," Lena said. "Sooner or later we might all be sent back home. Better go with someone to support you than alone."

Ludwika thought about this for some time. The longer there was no word from the Red Cross, the more she had given up hope on finding her family. If she was forced back to Poland she might get the worst of both worlds: not finding her family and end up an outcast, branded a Nazi collaborator within a communist country. It couldn't get any worse.

"I'll just have to wait and see," she said in defiance to Lena. A man was not the answer to her problems.

"Suit yourself."

The dark thoughts about Luca's fate stuck with Ludwika and she gradually began to accept the idea that he would not return to her life. She became almost certain that it was her destiny to be alone in the world, without him or her family. In those circumstances, the new Poland was not going to be her future.

Lena must have spoken to Onufry on her behalf as a few days later the builder approached Ludwika at the playground and said without preamble: "I don't want to go back either."

"Why not?" she asked, without acknowledging the lack of introduction.

"I don't understand much about politics but one thing is clear to me: If a communist Germany is in the West and a communist Russia is in the East, Poland won't be a free land. Give it a few years and the Soviets will swallow the country hole."

"What are your plans then?" she asked. She liked the way he talked. He seemed grounded and sensible.

"I don't know," he said.

"No plan, then?" she said and laughed.

He smirked: "A strong man is always in demand after a war; with all the men that were killed there are bound to be many countries that will take us. I can't make a plan. I will wait for one of the countries in the world to realise that it needs labourers and I will be on the first train there when they finally see sense and invite us."

"That's what I call optimism," she said, smiling. She liked the way he was making everything sound so easy.

Onufry took Jerzy around the playground area. The little boy was only six months old and didn't benefit from the slide and the climbing ropes, but he was fascinated by the people and the excitement coming from the happy children nearby.

Onufry seemed to have taken a liking to him.

"He's well behaved," he said. "You're a good mother."

"He's all I have now," she said.

"Maybe," he said, "and maybe not."

Over the weeks that followed she grew fond of Onufry. She was not in love but, as Lena often pointed out, maybe that wasn't necessary; there was a hint of a temper about him but he seemed to have a good core. She definitely preferred him over Karol, the teacher.

When the post came Ludwika had long given up running towards it as many others did, seeking word from her family. The disappointment was not worth it so she was amazed when she received a letter late August: it was from Marie, of all people.

Dear Ludwika,

I hope this finds you well and that you're still in Dalum with the rest of the Lindenhof bunch when this letter reaches you. I expect you are running the kitchen in your new camp and cannot wait to go back home to Poland. I am sure you have fallen on your feet. Industrious and kind people like you always do.

I have been less fortunate than you and have been sentenced to three years in prison. I still don't know if Herman is alive and must begin to entertain the idea that he is dead.

I'm writing to you because I understand that you are not too far from Oldenburg. If it is at all possible for you, could you visit my father, or at least write to him in hospital? He has so often asked for you, yet it seems you have drawn a line under your past and what seemed to him like a friendship between you two.

Should you find it in your heart to see him it would mean the world to him, and to me. I know I have no right to ask you for anything. I'm beginning to understand the magnitude of my crimes and that of the Reich. Deep down I believe, however, that you and father were good friends and if you can find it in yourself to remember those moments and return to Oldenburg just once to show you care, I would appreciate it. God knows how long he's going to live.

He sends his regards.

Grateful for your consideration,

Best,

Marie

Ludwika was moved by the request and she, too, longed to see her good friend, Fritz, and immediately started to worry about him: Why had he been kept in hospital for so long? She showed the letter to Lena.

"I can ask my Alfie if he can organise a lift for you," Lena said. "They keep shuttling things between the camps. I'm sure if I ask nicely he will help you out."

"Thank you."

Two days later, thanks to Lena's connections to the camp management, an army truck took Ludwika on the 60km journey north. The driver didn't speak much German and she didn't speak English, so the trip was a quiet affair.

Fritz looked ashen and aged when she saw him in his hospital bed.

"They are keeping me because I have better food in here than I could get outside," he said and winked. "Medically, there is little they can do other than checking for new tumours and complications. I can't say I mind. Without you at home I would be lonely anyway. I got used to you too much."

She smiled, unsure that this was the entire truth.

"I had a baby boy," she said and grabbed hold of his hand. "His name is Jerzy. He has the same beautiful face as Luca and Barbara had," she said.

"Congratulations," Fritz said, struggling to smile. "You deserve it."

"I still have no news from my family in Poland," she said and told him about the multitude of rumours and depressing reports from her homeland.

He nodded sympathetically.

"Don't do anything rash," Fritz said. "Think of the little boy and what you can do for him."

"I know," she said. "If only I had Luca with us as the father to go with it, then I would have a family at last. It's about time I did," she said.

"Yes," he said. "I understand. I thought of you and him only the other day. I heard an Italian man swear next door. The nurses did something painful to him and he screamed the house down. I could have sworn he sounded like Luca. The things our minds do to us," he smiled. "Thank you so much for coming to visit me, though. I really do appreciate it and I'm glad to see you're as happy as the circumstances allow."

She told him more about Jerzy – at his progress and the mischief he could get himself into. They talked of the family now living in his house and what Marie might do whenever she was released.

A heavy coughing fit seized Fritz and he spat some blood. He tried to cover it with his hands but Ludwika had seen it. She wanted to tell the nurses, but he wouldn't let her.

"It's time I get back to sleep," he said. "You must have a long journey ahead of you. Thank you for coming, and I hope to see you again very soon."

She kissed him on the forehead and left. Fritz was in a bad way - they both knew it. Without saying it outright, Ludwika knew that this could be their final goodbye.

She stood helpless in the hospital corridor, the smell of disinfectant making her nauseous. What Fritz had said about the Italian man screaming had struck a chord, though, and she suddenly wondered if Luca maybe had been injured in the air raids and survived. Maybe he was right here in the hospital? Maybe he was too sick to write, or his pleas had fallen on deaf ears in Fritz's flat where that German family now lived. . .

Ludwika slowly opened the door to the room next to Fritz's and looked at the patients. Then she did the same with the other rooms on the corridor. No sign of Luca. When she reached the staircase she saw that there were more rooms on its other side. Ludwika opened the door nearest to the ward exit and there he was – Luca – in the bed right by the door. Ludwika's heart leapt.

"Luca!" she called out, far too loud to go unnoticed.

He looked at her with the same shining eyes she had always loved. They were sadder and he was more subdued. As she came closer she could see that he had lost part of his arm and part of his foot.

"Ludwika, my love," he said. "Where have you been?"

She smiled, unable to believe her eyes. He was alive!

"Listening to Zarah Leander of course," she said once she had recovered from the shock of his injuries. She was so happy, she didn't care. Ludwika was about to ask him about what had happened but stopped herself. She didn't want their reunion spoiled by talk of sad events. . . it didn't matter whether it was a shell or a mine or an accident. The last time she had seen him she had to tell him about Barbara's death. She wanted this meeting to be about nothing but their love for each other.

"You've become a father again," she said instead. "A little boy, he's six months old. I named him Jerzy Franz, after your father and my brother."

"Jerzy?" Luca said with put-on outrage. "My father isn't called Jerzy. His name is Geeraard De Witte. I'll tell him when we meet him and he will have the birth certificate ripped to pieces and make you change the name."

A nurse came in and reprimanded them for the noise they were making.

"Why don't you take a stroll outside?" she suggested. "That way you won't disturb the other patients."

"Of course," Luca said and got up.

He was surprisingly mobile. With the help of a crutch he could hop to the staircase. He handed the crutch to Ludwika and then he held on to the railing with his good arm and hopped downstairs where a wheelchair was waiting to be used by patients who wanted to go to the park.

"No," he said when she was getting it ready for him to use. "Another level down, to the basement."

She followed him, curious what he was up to this time. He waited for her at the bottom of the stairs and pointed at a series of doors. "See if one of them is unlocked," he ordered.

The first one was open.

"Go," he said and made his way towards her. It was a room used to dry towels. He closed the door quickly and used the crutch to block the door handle.

"Come here," he said. "I'm not going to let this opportunity slip through my fingers."

She did so willingly. He kissed her and used his one hand to explore her body. Ludwika helped him onto the floor and undressed him. He was still strong and athletic, despite his injuries and moved passionately and fast. When it was over she hit him playfully in the face.

"You better marry me this time," she said. "I'm bound to be pregnant again. Every time we do this I am."

Luca laughed, too and held her tight. "I'm the luckiest man alive," he said. "I thought I had lost you for good. I had someone sent to Fritz's flat. They said he had died and that you were back in Poland. When I get out of here I'll make sure I kill those bastards."

"All is well that ends well," she said. "I'd kill them for keeping the gramophone."

"Darling, my father has enough money to buy you more of those records when we get home to Rome," he said. "You will be able to listen to Zarah Leander all your life, if that's what you desire. And I hope we made a girl this time. We have one who looks like me, now we need one who looks like you."

Ludwika stared at his bandages, but then focused instead on his wonderful hazel eyes.

"I'll tell you about this some other time," Luca said, looking to his wounds. She nodded, too overcome to speak. She knew there would be plenty of time for that, now that they had found each other again.

"You need to visit Fritz," she said. "He's on the same hospital floor as you. Can you believe that?"

They got dressed and stole themselves out of the room before someone might find them.

The park was beautiful. There were small pavilions where patients could enjoy the landscaped garden, protected from the wind.

"A funny thing," she said. "Fritz thought he heard you swear at a nurse in Italian the other day. If it had not been for that throwaway comment I'd never have found you. I've been living in a camp for Polish displaced people by the Dutch border. This is my first visit to Oldenburg."

He laughed with her at the coincidence.

"At last a lucky star for us," he said. "It's a good sign that you are so close to Holland already."

She laughed and then told him everything she could think of about Jerzy, his mannerisms, his looks and his lively nature.

"He'll grow up to be just like you," she promised.

"I hope so," Luca said.

Time went by too quickly for them.

"If I had known you were here I wouldn't have agreed to go back so soon," she said.

"You'll come again," he said, "Won't you?"

"I hope so," she said. "This trip was a special favour from a friend."

"Fine. Now that I know where you are I can write to you, too."

"When will you come out of hospital?" she asked.

"I hope very soon," he said. "There are some small complications with the leg. It shouldn't be long before all is healed and I can get out and take you and Jerzy to Italy."

He looked at her and pulled a disgusted face.

"Jerzy? We've got to come up with a different name."

She rushed to the rendezvous point with Alfie's colleague. He seemed unhappy about her being so late but couldn't make himself understood beyond that. Ludwika didn't care. She was so happy and couldn't wait to tell someone the news. When she blurted out to Lena what had happened, however, her friend was less excited and more practical about it.

"Are you mad?" Lena said. "Your Italian cripple won't feed your child. Don't you think he would have found you if he'd wanted to? I think you're making a huge mistake. It's not too late. Break it off with him. Onufry is the way forward. Luca can't give you anything but false hopes."

She shook her head.

"No," she said.

"Don't be so stubborn," Lena insisted.

"Luca is all I'll ever need," Ludwika said. "He will find a way of putting food on our table."

"If you say so," Lena said and shrugged, but it wasn't the last time she brought the subject up.

"I'll need your help so I can see Luca again soon," Ludwika confessed. "I want to take Jerzy this time, so Luca can see his son."

"You've got a nerve," Lena said. "Alfie risked a lot for this. He can't be seen doing favours for us all the time."

"At least once," Ludwika pleaded. "Imagine you had a child and weren't allowed to see it."

"I'll try my best," Lena said, rolling her eyes dramatically. As if on cue Jerzy smiled at her when she said this and that made her laugh.

A week later, mother and child were on their way up to Oldenburg one more time. Jerzy slept all the way in the car. Ludwika was so excited about the prospect, she could hardly sit still.

The hospital receptionist looked disapproving of the child, but Jerzy was still tired and didn't make a sound.

"It's the first time Luca will see his son," Ludwika explained, hoping that would make a difference. "If there are any troubles we will leave immediately," she promised.

Unfortunately, Luca was not well. The wound in his stumped leg was giving him a lot of pain. He was feverish and his face was dripped with beads of sweat.

"My son," he almost shouted in exaggerated enthusiasm and waved mother and child to his bed. "Come here, quick."

He seemed to be in agony but he managed to play the part of the happy father. It was amazing how alike father and son were. Or maybe that was only in Ludwika's imagination.

A nurse came to see what all the noise was about. She nodded knowingly when she saw it was Luca.

"Our Italian tenor," she said. "He's enough to entertain the entire hospital."

Ludwika left Jerzy with his father and followed the nurse.

"Luca doesn't look well," she said. "Is he alright?"

The nurse looked awkwardly to the side and then shook her head.

"He keeps getting these infections," she said. "The wound has still not healed. He's already had blood poisoning once. He could well get it again."

"But he's got you to monitor him and help him," Ludwika said.

"Yes," the nurse replied. "He's got us. There's no need to worry."

Ludwika was relieved.

Back in the patient's room, father and son were having a great time, pulling faces and playing peek-a-boo. Luca seemed better already.

"He'll be a heart-breaker like his dad," Luca joked. "I know I'm a catch, but he's twice my calibre."

She took Jerzy back off the bed.

"The nurse said you have an infection," she said. "Maybe we should let you rest. You look dreadful."

"Seeing you two was all that the doctor ordered," he said. "The next thing that we need to do is go to that German family in Fritz's flat and get my gramophone and sell it. We need money to get to Holland or Italy. My family will take care of us, there."

"I'm sure the family have probably sold it already," Ludwika said. "They didn't seem very trustworthy."

"How much savings do you have?" he asked.

"Not enough for one train ticket, let alone three," she said. "Maybe Fritz can help."

"We will sort something out," Luca said, taking her hand.

Jerzy needed changing and by the time she had returned from doing that, Luca was fast asleep. He looked exhausted and so she told the nurse to say goodbye from her and went to see Fritz. He, too, was asleep.

"Herr Kröplin isn't well," the nurse on his ward said. "It's better if you leave him be."

Ludwika nodded and went outside to wait for her transport back.

Oldenburg was not a place she wanted to spend any more time in than she had to. Although she had been in love here, too many bad things had also happened in this town. She was more than ready to leave Germany behind. She only wished she could take Fritz with her. He didn't seem to belong here, either.

As she was waiting, Ludwika pictured her future. She knew she couldn't go back to a communist Poland and let Jerzy grow up in a country like that. She had heard enough about the kind of society that Stalin had created in Russia. Ludwika had experienced first-hand how forced labour and working for the greater good of a nation had felt. The Nazis and the Soviets had more in common than one would have thought. Thank God she had found Luca. Together they would move to Holland or Italy and as soon as they had found her, Irena could come and live with them. Maybe one day she could visit Stasia and her mother in Poland or they, too, could come and live with her. With Luca by her side the world was suddenly full of possibilities, and promise coloured her every thought. Ludwika knew that the money to make these plans happen would also come their way somehow.

Jerzy cried all the way home. The soldier who gave her a lift this time had not been happy to take her in the first place and made sure she knew it. It was a relief to get out of the car and back to the mothers' barracks.

After this trip Lena's boyfriend Alfie told her in no uncertain terms that Ludwika could not go to Oldenburg again anytime soon, and definitely not with the child. She understood. It was for the best anyway, she thought. Luca needed to recover. She would happily wait to see him when he was ready to leave the hospital. It was better not to use up all her favours with Alfie and Lena and be patient. All that mattered was that she and Luca had found each other and he had seen his son.

As she had almost expected, Ludwika missed her next period and was sure that she was expecting another child. She was delighted that Jerzy would have a sibling, although she couldn't believe how easily she fell pregnant. Almost every time she looked at a man it seemed to happen. At this rate there would be a whole bunch of them. Ludwika laughed at the thought – the more the merrier. How lucky her encounters with Erich had been more guarded and had not led to such consequences.

First, she must tell Luca the good news. In the absence of her coming to see him, writing was the next best thing and would surely help with his recovery. It wasn't a long letter. She wasn't good with words.

"You didn't waste any time, did you?" Lena remarked when she heard the news. "That certainly burnt your bridges with Onufry. Now someone else is going to snatch him up and you'll be stuck with the cripple, for better or for worse."

"Don't call Luca names," Ludwika said. "You should see him, then you wouldn't dream of doing that. He's a far cry from a man you need to pity. And I hope Onufry finds someone else. You're right: he does deserve someone special. It's just not going to be me."

And to prove it, Ludwika went to the play area the next day and had a long chat with the builder. She told him about the pregnancy and about her plans for the future, which needed only help from Mother Nature and a little bit of money.

"I'm happy for you," he said. "It's good for Jerzy to have his real father. Maybe you have a sister that will like me?"

The mention of a sister stung a little.

"When I get to see her I will tell her about you."

"I'll come to Oldenburg and sort out those parasites in Fritz's flat," Onufry offered. "I've never seen the city. It will be a day out for me."

"I couldn't let you do that," she said. "Thanks for the offer, though."

"No seriously," Onufry insisted, his face red as if he was really angry. "I mean it. You need to get your gramophone back; at least for the memories. Those people have no right to it."

"What if they've sold it on the black market for food?" Ludwika said, not wanting to get Onufry into trouble. He did seem to have a quick temper on him. "You couldn't blame them if it was to get food on their table."

"Then they are common thieves and will get what they deserve," he said, his hands forming into fists. "It's not a lawless society anymore. You can get justice."

"Thank you. It wouldn't be for a while anyway," she said. "Alfie said he couldn't let me use the army transport as private chauffeurs."

"I'll have a word with him," Onufry said. "He owes me a few favours, too."

And so, a week later Ludwika, Jerzy and Onufry went to Oldenburg together in the army truck. It was the same driver from the last time when Jerzy had cried all the way home. The man looked very unhappy with his lot and didn't speak to his passengers at all. Ludwika was very glad that Onufry was there. He sat next to him, shielding Ludwika from the miserable expression on the driver's face.

Nobody answered when they knocked at Fritz's door. Onufry took Ludwika's key, which she had kept, and let them into the deserted flat. The place brought back many memories for her and she almost started to cry. This beautiful oasis of peace and kindness was now someone else's home.

Onufry held Jerzy while she searched the rooms. She was relieved to see that the people who lived here had kept all of Franz's possessions neat and hadn't left their imprint yet. Ludwika should never have made assumptions about them anyway. She found the gramophone and the records in a corner of the bedroom when a man of about 50 walked in the door.

"What are you doing in my house," the man said. Onufry handed Jerzy back to Ludwika and grabbed the man by the collar.

"You said that the owner of the flat was dead and that Ludwika had gone back to Poland?" he shouted and shoved the man against the wall.

"I didn't… I mean…" the man stuttered.

"Maybe they were mistaken or misinformed," Ludwika tried to help the man out. She couldn't bear the violence and was scared for Jerzy, too.

"Rubbish," Onufry shouted and he threw the man to the floor.

"You lying scum," he said, kicking the man in the shin.

"It doesn't matter," Ludwika implored him. "Stop it. Everything is in order, we can go now."

Onufry took the gramophone and walked towards the door. "You better watch your back from now on," he threatened the man.

"What are we going to do with it now?" she asked.

"Alfie will find a place for it for you," Onufry said and smiled as if the scene in the flat was nothing.

They didn't have too much time before the truck was scheduled to return to their camp in Dalum.

"I'll wait outside," Onufry said at the hospital. "I don't want to be in the way."

"Don't be silly," she said. "You're not in the way. Luca will be glad to see the man who saved his treasured possession."

"Alright then," Onufry said and followed her inside.

The receptionist looked at them with puzzled eyes when they said who they were going to visit.

"I'm so sorry," she said. "Herr DeWitte passed away two days ago. Blood poisoning, it says here in the notes. We've sent a letter to his parents in Rome. How did you know him?"

Ludwika was too stunned to speak. It couldn't be true.

"This little fellow here is his son," Onufry said, "and this is his fiancée."

"The body is in our morgue in the basement. If you want to say your goodbyes…?" the receptionist suggested.

Ludwika shook her head. This could not be happening. Not again.

"I think it would be a good idea," Onufry suggested and took her down the stairs. She felt paralysed, but her feet followed him without her thinking. She felt numb and empty.

Outside the door marked 'Morgue' Onufry took Jerzy and the gramophone and let Ludwika go in by herself. The stench was overwhelming as soon as she opened the door. She made it inside but almost fainted. A hospital employee asked for the deceased's name and when she told him he took her to Luca's corpse, which was beneath a blanket on a bench in the corner. She wondered how the man could bear sitting in this room all day.

Luca looked different than she had remembered him. His facial expressions and his boundless energy had always been what made him so special. With his muscles relaxed and without that spark of mischief he frightened her. She had seen some bodies from the air raids, but none had ever scared her in the way Luca's did. She turned and ran towards the door, taking a moment to remind herself that Jerzy shouldn't see her upset. Ludwika opened the door and with the bravest of smiles that she could muster, said: "We better see how Fritz is doing."

She took Jerzy from Onufry and started walking up the stairs, humming. Sadly, Fritz was fast asleep and the nurse asked them to leave him be.

"Just as well," Ludwika said to Jerzy when they were outside. "Let's go home where we can play."

"And you can listen to your records," Onufry said. "You must have missed them."

"I did," she said. "I did."

On the journey home Jerzy fell asleep and nobody said a word. Only the noise of the engine and Ludwika's low humming filled the space. She hummed to keep herself calm. Onufry took her hand and she gratefully held on to it. Once they were at the camp she thanked him and rushed back to her barracks. Without explaining, she asked Lena to look after Jerzy for a while and then hid herself behind the barrack and sobbed her heart out. Not another loss! Not Luca! What would become of her now? She let herself go completely, let it all out: her grief, her pain, her everything.

After an hour she stopped, washed her face in the bathroom and went back inside to tell Lena.

"You should write to his parents," she suggested immediately. "They might want to take good care of the children. If they are as loaded as Luca said then your future is in Italy or Holland."

"I wish life was that simple," Ludwika said. "What about my family in Poland? And I couldn't just write to complete strangers and claim my children are their grandchildren.

"Why not?" Lena asked. "You said Jerzy looked like him. If it is true, then you have nothing to fear. The worst they can do is tell you to leave them alone."

"Maybe one day I will," she said. "Today I just want to sleep."

Alfie contacted the hospital on Ludwika's behalf and got the address of Luca's parents. Unfortunately, he also found out that the parents had not responded to any correspondence. With the body unclaimed, Luca had been buried in the Oldenburg Cemetery. Italy and Holland now seemed unlikely countries for her future. Ludwika wanted to get on the next train to Poland, but she feared more and more that there was nobody left for her there either.

Over the next few weeks, Onufry came frequently to see how she was doing. Ludwika was feeling this pregnancy more than the others: she was tired and slow. The grief was taking its toll and she found it more difficult to hide her sadness from her little boy. Lena and Onufry often took him out to the playground so Ludwika could rest and let her feelings out.

After Christmas, a rumour started that frightened many inmates. It was believed that Russia had laid claim to Polish citizens it regarded as part of the Soviet Union. Polish people from the eastern territories that were now part of the Soviet Union were regarded as Soviets in Stalin's logic. Since he demanded that his Soviet citizens be returned to their home countries, such as Lithuania and the Ukraine, this rumour seemed plausible. Lena, who came from that part of the world, was panicking.

"If Alfie won't marry me, I don't know what I'll do," she said. "The Nazis had one saying right: you're better off dead than Red. I wish nobody had started those goddamn missing people lists," she cursed. "Now they're only helping Stalin to claim us as his own."

"I don't think it will come to this," Ludwika said, but she wasn't too sure herself.

"Of course it will," Lena said. "Haven't you heard how many people from the Ukraine and Lithuania have been sent home already? The Western Allies have 'returned' them to their 'country of origin'," Lena said. "You should listen to the radio more often. They agreed to it in Yalta and it doesn't matter to them what the Russians are doing to these people. As if we all hadn't suffered enough. None of us should be forced to go anywhere against our will."

"I agree," Ludwika said. "But where are we going to go? We can't stay here in the camp forever."

Ludwika frowned. She worried for her children and the force of Lena's pessimism was contagious. Maybe the woman was right? Lena was not the only one to think like this. Panic had settled deep in the camp and petitions were written to the Allies to protect the Polish citizens. Many tried to flee to France and Holland.

Spurred on by this sudden spike of fear, Ludwika swallowed her pride and wrote a letter to Luca's parents that evening and had it translated by a woman who spoke a little Italian. She reluctantly sent it, with little hope of a reply. She felt like a beggar. . . small and unimportant, exactly as she sometimes felt here in the camp, too: waiting for politicians and countries to make up their minds and allow her an existence.

This would be Jerzy's first Christmas and Ludwika pulled herself out of her sadness to make it special for him and the other children. She taught them Christmas carols which they rehearsed in the weeks leading up to the event. Together, the children created one big Christmas calendar, which had a picture of Santa Clause on it. The atmosphere was joyous and for a brief few days everyone managed to forget their worries about the world outside. Onufry had carved a figurine out of wood for the little boy and a little angel for Ludwika. She was embarrassed that she had not got him anything, but he said he didn't mind.

There were many improvements over the festivities of last year. Two priests had been transferred from a different camp and they had established a small chapel on the grounds. For the Christmas service this was, however, too small and so the priests used the dining hall for the midnight Mass, which was crammed full with people. Onufry sat with Jerzy and Ludwika.

Soon after, in January 1947, it was Jerzy's first birthday and Onufry gave him another carved figurine. Outside, the children made a snow man for Jerzy and inside they played games with him and sang him a birthday song. It was easy for Ludwika to forget her worries over so much joy and play.

She had not heard from Luca's parents, nor had she heard from Marie or Fritz, and the Red Cross had not traced of her family in Poland.

"Stop looking elsewhere for your happiness," Lena reprimanded her. She was pregnant and, at last, married to her Alfie, since the rules over fraternisation between soldiers and civilians had been relaxed lately. She radiated happiness, now that she had her future as the wife of the Canadian soldier mapped out for her.

"Maybe you're right," Ludwika said. "It sounds like something my father would have said."

"Then be happy," Lena said and smiled.

At the Easter Service she sat next to Onufry again. She looked at him from the side. He was skilled and steady and, unlike everyone else she had met, he seemed reliable and trustworthy.

In the political arena, things finally started to shift. The Western Allies were looking for volunteer countries to take in the remainder of the displaced people who were unwilling to return to their homes. The first countries to open their borders were Belgium and the United Kingdom. Other countries soon followed suit. Some were looking for specific skills, or limited their offer to quality labourers.

In May, Ludwika had a baby girl after a fast delivery; she named her Halina Zophie.

Onufry came to see her in the maternity ward.

"I've been offered a visa for Britain," he said.

"I'm happy for you," she said.

"I think it is time we got engaged," he said as he held the newborn. "Your children need a family."

"I can't," she said.

"Why?" he asked. "You don't want to go back to Poland. Even if they find Irena, what kind of life would that be for Jerzy? No country offers places for single mothers, but if we get married before I leave you can follow in a year or two."

She sank back in her bed.

"The Red Cross will find you in England, if you're still worried about Irena. You can't stay here. I like you. . . you know what you get with me. Let me take you out of this limbo. Let's start a real life, away from fences and barracks. Come with me."

"I'll think about it," she said and took Halina back into her arms.

"Don't take too long," he said.

Lena was over the moon for her friend when she heard of the proposal. Heavily pregnant herself she radiated happiness and optimism.

"You're so lucky, I hope you know that," she said. "You picked one of the best ones in the camp. And he is good with your kids."

Ludwika agreed. Onufry was no Luca but he seemed a decent man who offered a single mother a steady home in a safe country. She wouldn't say no to that. Her dream of a family was finally coming true.

"Why are you being so nice to me?" Ludwika asked Onufry when she accepted his proposal at last.

"We all deserve help," Onufry said. "The war has already damaged me and made me an angry man. We need to do good things for each other to make up for all the bad things that have happened to us. Then the world can become a beautiful place with good people again."

Epilogue

Ludwika and Onufry married in February, just days before his departure to England. He left his new wife and children behind, only to claim their dependency on him at the first opportunity. Their application was successful and she and her children were granted entry to the United Kingdom, too, landing in Harwich on March 31, 1949.

For six years they lived in the Westwell's Displaced People's Camp in Neston, Wiltshire. Once in England, she continually tried to get in touch with her family in Poland but to no avail.

Then, in 1955, Ludwika and her family got a house of their own. With just a few suitcases of clothing, they moved into a small bungalow in Wiltshire. Onufry and Ludwika had three more children together: Christina, Andrew and Richard. He got a job in a meat-processing plant His short temper didn't always make life easy, nor did some of the locals, who resented the foreign migrants, but times were easier than before, and with the love of her family and the support of one understanding neighbour, things were looking up.

Money was tight, but Ludwika managed to make a cosy home for her five children, and never saw them go hungry. She loved her new home, and in the bungalow's small garden, she grew herbs, which she added to the tasty meals that she would create from the most basic ingredients. She loved the nearby city of Bath, which reminded her a little of the grandeur of Krakow and Lodz and she would frequently take her children on the bus to spend sunny afternoons in the parks there.

As the years wore on, the garden became her refuge – it was a place to grow life from the most unpromising of starts – rather like what she had done with her own family. One day in the summer of 1957, with the sound of the children's laughter floating about her, Ludwika sat amongst her herbs, inhaling their fragrance as she opened a long-awaited letter from Poland.

The Red Cross had located her sister Stasia in Warsaw, where she had registered to get married. Ludwika had immediately sat down and written a long letter to her, detailing her fortune during the war and asked for their news. She had included a separate letter to Irena, explaining with honesty her motives for leaving Poland and detailing her tormenting heartache over abandoning her daughter. The days since had been filled with excitement and hope but also with anxiety. At last, there was word from Stasia.

Dear Ludwika

My heart lifted with joy when I received your letter and learned that you are alive and so well. Here is a little about what happened to us:

We never had confirmation of what became of our father. He must have been killed early in the war by the Germans. The army could only confirm that there are no known survivors of his unit.

Soon after you left we were driven off the farm after all and went to live with mother's cousins near Warsaw. Poor mother died of malnutrition in 1944.

I got married this summer. Soon after you left I fell hard for Michal, the man Manfred brought to our home to help. We were engaged to be married but then he was killed during the Warsaw uprising. The war has decimated the number of eligible bachelors, so it took me a while to find someone new whom I really cared for. I hope one day you will be able to meet Tomasz.

Irena got married two years ago. She has a son already – you are a grandmother Ludwika!, She named him Michal. I have included a picture of her with a friend and Michal. Doesn't he look handsome?

It makes me sad to tell you that Irena is a stubborn woman and is not prepared to accept explanations behind your decision to leave her and go to Germany. I wish there was something I could say or do to make her see sense. She refused to even read your letter and threw it away. I hope maybe one day, when travelling is easier, you can come in person and speak to her. I am sure her heart will melt then. For now, know that she is a happy woman all the same.

Ludwika held the letter limply in her hand for a long time, the aching sobs of the past resurrecting themselves as she thought of her estranged daughter in Poland. She was overwhelmed with grief and guilt for what she had done. When the children were grown up, when she had saved enough money and once the political circumstances should allow, Ludwika vowed, as she sat in her English garden, that she would return to her homeland. She wished for nothing more than to die and be buried in Polish soil.

But then, as the pain became too much to bear a small hand held hers. Ludwika looked to see her daughter Christina's concerned eyes staring up at her.

'Are you alright mummy? Why are you crying?'

Ludwika stared into the innocent eyes and knew what must be done. . . what had always been done – she swallowed her pain. 'It's nothing my love: I'll tell you when you're older.'

It was a phrase she would use many times in the years ahead: one day, she would tell them about how she came by those scars on her legs and of her broken teeth, maybe one day, when the pain had eased.

That day never did come. In 1964, a year after Onufry's death from lung cancer, Ludwika suffered a brain haemorrhage and died suddenly, taking her family secrets to the grave with her. The older siblings became parents to the younger ones. It was a struggle, but one which they met, thanks to the legacy of love left to them by their brave mother.

What You Need To Know

Ludwika Gierz (pictured on the cover, picture on the right) was a real person. This novel is a fictionalised account of her story. She did live a life very similar to that described here in my book. I used all known facts and data to come as close to the real woman as possible:

Her parents were Agnieska and Franiciszek Gierz. She was born in Przedborów, Poland, had a daughter Irena, who was left behind when Ludwika was brought to Germany; and she did have a sister Stasia, who got married in Warsaw in 1957.

In 1942, Ludwika was living in the Ostarbeiter Camp Essig & Co, Westerstrasse in Oldenburg [I used the Lindenhof camp because there was more information about it]. Ludwika had a child named Barbara, who died of chicken pox.

Ludwika was in a hospital in 1944 with pancreatitis, where many foreign women were being forcefully sterilised during the war. She had two children in Germany: Jerzy Franz, born on January 26, 1946 in the Polish Displaced People's Camp in Dalum Lingen Elms, and Halina Zophie, born May 27, 1947 also in the camp.

Ludwika married Onufry Florko on February 12, 1948 in Dalum and followed him to the UK a little over a year later.

In the documents that her children found there was a reference to a Friedrich Kröplin, a carpenter in Oldenburg, although how he knew Ludwika and how his name ended up in her files is not known. People who were alive in those times and who still live at that address today did not recognise the picture of Ludwika nor could they think of a connection between her and Kröplin.

The real Kröplin did undergo a brain operation in 1938 and he had a daughter, but nothing is known of her other than that she has since died. My account of Marie is entirely fictional and does not reflect any rumours or truth about Kröplin's daughter.

Manfred Tischler, the Danner family and sadly, Luca, are all fictional characters.

The real Ludwika had gunshot wounds and several missing teeth. She made up stories for her children about how she came by her injuries and promised to tell them all about her time in Europe when they were old enough. Sadly, Ludwika passed away before the children reached that age. Contact to Stasia and Irena in Poland was lost after Ludwika died, due to the children's young age, something they regret very much to this day.

They are actively searching for their Polish relatives.

Many refugees, particularly the old and weaker ones, were forced to stay in the Displaced People's Camps for quite some time after the war. Many committed suicide in their despair, the survivors eventually were accepted into Germany and Austria as full citizens.

The former Nazi town of Oldenburg has since dramatically changed its colours and currently its strongest political group is the Green Party: it has an exemplary record of honouring the victims of its dark past.

If you know of any survivors of the Oldenburg Westerstrasse work camp or the Dalum Displaced People's Camps, please show them the book. If you are a survivor of any of these camps and recognise Ludwika from the photographs or from her story, or if you have any information with regards to her story, please get in touch.

Similarly, if you were in the Neston Displaced People's Camp for Polish people in Wiltshire or know anything about her family in Poland – an old picture of Irena is also on the cover - I would appreciate if you would contact me either via the contact form on:

www.christophfischerbooks.com

or via email to Ludwika's granddaughter

lisamortimore13@gmail.com

Ludwika's family would like to hear from you.

The End

Did you like the book?

Many thanks for reading my book. If you liked it then please leave a review on: Goodreads, your national Amazon or your favourite review site; it would mean a lot.

If you did like the book then read on and sample the first part of:

The Luck of the Weissensteiners

(Three Nations Trilogy: Book 1)

In the sleepy town of Bratislava in 1933 the daughter of a Jewish weaver falls for a bookseller from Berlin, Wilhelm Winkelmeier. Greta Weissensteiner seemingly settles in with her in-laws but the developments in Germany start to make waves in Europe and re-draw the visible and invisible borders. The political climate, the multi-cultural jigsaw puzzle of the disintegrating Czechoslovakian state and personal conflicts make relations between the couple and the families more and more complex. The story follows the families through the war with its predictable and also its unexpected turns and events and the equally hard times after. What makes The Luck of the Weissensteiners so extraordinary is the chance to consider the many different people who were never in concentration camps, never in the military, yet who nonetheless had their own indelible Holocaust experiences. This is a wide-ranging, historically accurate exploration of the connections between social status, personal integrity and, as the title says, luck.

Chapter 1: Bratislava 1933

Greta Weissensteiner was a passionate and compulsive reader who spent enormous amounts of her time and money in bookshops and libraries - too much time if you asked the rest of her family. She spoke several languages fluently and was able to read her favourite Russian and German authors in their original versions. For her literary needs she frequently went to 'Mohr & Kling', a particularly renowned bookshop in the Bratislava city centre run by two German men. Greta adored their exquisite selection of beautifully bound and illustrated books, even though she could never afford such luxurious items herself.

The public library stocked mainly reference books and held only a minor collection of dated or classic fiction. In there she rarely found any of her favourite writers which were the more modern romantics such as E.T.A. Hoffmann, Heinrich Heine and Friedrich Hoelderlin.

"All starting with an aitch, I've noticed," a Prussian looking junior sales assistant commented one day while he wrapped her latest purchases. "Is that a coincidence or are you working your way through the alphabet?"

His name was Wilhelm. He had spotted Greta from the moment she had first come into the bookshop and was fascinated by her. He could hardly take his eyes of her while she browsed through both selections of delicate rare prints and the new additions to the stock, and he was astonished at her dedication as a reader. Her questions demonstrated a sound knowledge of literature and her choices proved that she could tell the good from the bad. She also had a slight hint of mystery about her and a set of dark, deep and penetrating eyes that suggested an extensive inner life and a seriousness of character; in many other regular readers, it usually merely signified a melancholic mood and pessimism. However, Greta possessed no such negativity, just pure enthusiasm for the written word and a clear focus on whatever she was doing. Wilhelm loved and knew all about German literature and welcomed a local girl taking such an interest in the excellent hidden treasures that this bookshop held.

Frequently there would be girls or young women trying to

engage him in conversations about books, but many used this only as a pretext for flirting with the handsome new assistant. Those silly and unworthy creatures soon exposed how little they actually knew about literature which put him off. His time was too precious for shallow discussions and idle chit chat. He could tell that Greta was the exact opposite.

She did not seem to notice him at all, her focus was always on the books and when she asked him or the other assistants for information, she hardly ever even looked up at them. That, for the first time in his career, had created a desire in him to take the attention of a customer away from the literary treasures and bring her focus onto him. He was a good looking young man with strong facial features. Pleasant to the eye and well groomed, he was not used to having to work at being noticed. He thought it was ironic how her aloofness, the one quality missing in all the other woman who admired him, was the very thing that made him invisible to her.

In fact, his looks had not passed Greta by at all but she was a little put off by his confident manner, which didn't live up to her romantic ideals of a potential suitor. Yet there was something delicate and soft about him, hidden underneath his confidence, that she thought was very appealing.

His eyes were full of mischief as he spoke to her and his smile was disarmingly warm and friendly. Greta was taken off guard and was almost lost for words. Whenever she had seen him before, there had never been a simple pretext for speaking to him and being not the most confident 21 year old, Greta would never have thought that she would warrant a second look from him. Behind her rigid posture was more fear and anxiety than an outsider could have detected. When Wilhelm addressed her at the counter she only just managed to hold his provocative gaze and smiled back at him.

"The aitch is a coincidence," she quietly got out before composing herself and stating with a bit more confidence: "All of the modern romantic authors are my favourites, really. There are so many, it would be hard to choose amongst them. I also love Dostoevsky and Gogol - Russians and Romantics. If I had more money I would probably collect their complete works."

"You have an exquisite taste in books young lady," Wilhelm complemented. "I would recommend you have a look at Hegel and his work. He is also a German romanticist beginning with an aitch and his work is very remarkable – that is if you were ever stuck for more inspiration – which doesn't seem likely."

"Thank you. I will keep that in mind," Greta said gratefully. Of her few friends and family, only her older brother, Egon, loved reading as much as she did, but he was solely interested in history books and was not very knowledgeable when it came to fiction or contemporary literature. Her sister Wilma often read what Greta chose for her but she lacked the ability to analyse and discuss the works in a way that Greta would have found stimulating. The young book lover was on her own in her quest for intellectual exchange and so Wilhelm's recommendations and comments were very welcome indeed. She wondered if she would ever be in a position where she could tell the assistant in a shop like this something he didn't yet know about books.

"If you wanted to, I could always lend you one of my books," Wilhelm offered, looking around him to make sure no one was listening in on their little conversation. "You know, so you could keep expenses down – if money is a problem."

Greta was taken aback by his sudden forwardness.

"Wouldn't that get you into trouble with your boss?" she said evasively.

"Probably, but only if he found out," Wilhelm said with his mischievous look again.

"I would have to give you the books outside of work of course, not in here. Maybe I could meet you somewhere for a coffee or a drink?" he asked with a little wink.

"Thank you," she replied. "But I don't have a habit of meeting with complete strangers. I am sorry." She made for the door.

"Wait! Wait! Well, maybe I could just stop by your house and deliver a few books to you sometime? We would not have to meet or talk if you don't want to. I would just give them to you and then leave. I promise."

He was insistent this man and Greta felt charmed and singled out, but she wondered whether this handsome German was a genuine admirer of romantic literature and her, or whether he really was just a notorious flirt.

"Why would you do that for someone you do not even know? What would be in it for you?" she asked, instantly regretting that she had given him a chance to explain his feelings, which she guessed were not of the purest type.

"Because I can tell that you really like our books," he said, becoming a little more uncomfortable and shy himself. "We don't get many young women in here that appreciate our treasures as much as you do. I would like to help you with that!" Wilhelm surprised her with his noble answer and the more genuine and kind tone he was now using.

"Maybe," she replied. "I am going to read these books first. Can we arrange the delivery of your loan when I come here next?"

"Of course. When do you think that will be? Are you a fast reader?" he asked.

Greta had to laugh about the sudden panic she detected in his voice.

"I am, but I don't always get much time to read. My father runs a weaving and embroidery business and we are always busy. As a matter of fact, I should be going right now. He sent me on some other errands and only allowed me ten minutes in here. He will be cross with me when he finds out how much longer I have been here and how much money I am spending."

"There are only a few weavers in town. Maybe I know the place. Which one is your father?" Wilhelm had left the desk and was following her as she approached the door to leave. "Just so that I can come by sometime for those books, then you would not have to leave work."

He felt he was making a fool of himself but now that he had already gone this far, he did not want to let her go. Normally it was he who set the boundaries for admiring ladies; now that the roles were reversed, he did not like it much.

"I am not sure that would be a good idea," Greta said to his great disappointment.

"Why not?"

"I don't think my father would like it if strangers came to the house unexpectedly. When we are busy I don't even know if I could come out and talk to you when you get there," she told him.

"I will take the risk. So which weaver is your father? Please tell me!" he said with pleading eyes causing her to finally relent.

"We are the Weissensteiners on Gajova, in the dead end part of the road."

Pleased with the small progress he had just made, he tried to engage her in further conversation.

"What other writers do you like?"

Greta hesitated a little, and then she replied briefly while looking towards the street outside.

"Schnitzler, Chekhov, Pushkin, Hoffmannsthal and Joseph Roth; the list has no end," she laughed. "But I really need to go now."

"What is your first name?"

"Greta. And yours?"

"Wilhelm. Wilhelm Winkelmeier." He extended his hand and bowed slightly. "Nice to meet you."

"Nice to meet you too. Goodbye then, Wilhelm."

When he first showed up at her father's workshop a few days later Greta seemed almost cross with him and acted very abruptly. Much later she explained to him that she was only worried at the time that she would get into trouble with her father or her co-workers about the unannounced interference with her work life. As the daughter of the owner, she had usually no more rights than any of the other employees were permitted; they didn't like it when she got preferential treatment and her father, Jonah Weissensteiner, did not want to alienate his work force by allowing his children any more freedom or liberties. Weaving had become a fragile business and with the continuing growth of industrialization in the sector – more so in other countries than in Czechoslovakia - competition was fierce. The Weissensteiners owned a few semi-automatic looms, which were already substandard in France and Britain but productive enough for the kind of work they attracted.

The income of the family fortunately did not entirely depend on those looms and the production of fabrics. Previous generations of the family had acquired traditional embroidery skills in the Ukraine and ran this part of the company as an artistic side-line. Numerous commissions for hand woven 'made to order' work - usually for the local nobility - was the most lucrative branch of the business and Greta's father was lucky to have made a good name for himself. While he designed and spent endless hours on individual orders, his children and staff had to take shifts in overseeing the looms for the production of blankets and fabrics. Even though this was less demanding than other work, everyone disliked doing it because it was incredibly dull, which was why Jonah insisted that everyone took a fair share of these shifts. He knew that disgruntled employees meant lower quality and damage to his own reputation. When Wilhelm arrived to bring Greta the promised books, she had been on one of those boring shifts and had to make one of the other girls take over for her which earned her a hateful look.

Wilhelm had brought her two books to start with. Of course, it had been a lie that he had his own private book collection at home. He had left all of his books back in Berlin from where the Winkelmeier family recently had moved. He had none of her favourite German romantics at his family home on a farm just outside of the Bratislava city limits.

He owned up to his lie right away and admitted that to impress her he had taken the books from the shop store room and he would have to ask her to be careful with them so that he could put them back on the shelves before the next inventory. Greta laughed and promised she would treat them with the utmost care, but she had to go back to her duties now and so the meeting was over quickly.

He swore he would be back the following week to see how she had gotten on but she did not hear him as she rushed back into the house to relieve her angry and impatiently waiting colleague.

On his next visit, only five days later, she had already read the first two books.

“I couldn't help myself,” she told him. “I started before going to bed every night and I only meant to read a chapter or two, but I got so drawn into the books that hours passed before I realized how late it was and that I really had to go to sleep. Thank you Wilhelm, these were really a pleasure. Look, I made sure they are still clean and proper.”

Wilhelm was impressed that she had such a passion for books and that she had been able to keep her concentration up till late at night. It appeared that she was having to work very hard at her father's company and yet her passion was able to overcome her tiredness.

Originally he had meant to wait much longer before coming to see her again to give her sufficient time to read the books he had brought, but he was so eager to hear what she thought of the books that he could not help himself. Besides, with no friends in this foreign land, he really had nothing better to do. 'Mohr & Kling' was far from his home and he spent a large part of his day commuting on foot.

Frequently, he also worked right through lunch, completing orders and store paper work to impress the owners and secure his position. Usually he only had a little snack in one of the back rooms before being able to do a little reading of his own.

The owner, Herbert Kling, insisted that Wilhelm should go and stretch his legs and made him leave the shop for lunch at least a few times every week but Wilhelm was not grateful for the kindly meant gesture as it interfered with his precious reading time.

Hopeful that Greta had managed to finish at least one of the books he had brought with him the last time, Wilhelm had come with a few more treasures for her. He had managed to find her a book by Lessing. His own favourite, 'Nathan the Wise', had recently been banned because, as the German newspaper in Bratislava, Der Grenzbote, had quoted as the given reason, it 'practically put the Jewish faith on the same footing as Christianity'.

"It is such a shame that one possible interpretation of the book put it on the black list," Wilhelm complained. "You Slovaks are incredibly strict when it comes to religion."

"Do you think so?" she asked surprised.

"Oh yes, I do," came the instant reply.

"Who else do you like apart from Lessing?" Greta wanted to know.

"I do like the Enlightenment movement," he told her. "Do you know Schiller and Kant?"

"Yes, I do."

"Well, I have to say that although I am less worried about the religious implications of their argument, I share their belief in the greatness of the intelligent abilities of mankind. I like how Kant encourages people to make up their own mind and to take responsibility for their actions, rather than to look for already made up rules to live by," he said passionately.

"You are quite a philosopher I see." Greta observed.

"I guess I am. I like meaning in a book. Everything needs meaning!"

"What do you think about Romanticism then?" she asked. "That not always has a serious meaning."

"I also love passion which is in both the Sturm und Drang writings and the Romantic period," he consoled her. "It would be a mistake to limit oneself by reading just one particular type of genre over and over again. I hope that this is not what you are doing by reading so much of the Romantics? That would be an insult to your potential."

Greta thought that this was a very nice thing to say and a valid point to make about her reading habits. She had been rather one sided in her choices and so from now on she encouraged him to bring something she had asked for and also something he had chosen.

The next time he visited she was pleased to tell him that she had liked the book by Lessing he had brought and she regretted having to miss out on the banned book, which sounded so very interesting. Fortunately he had managed to get her some early works by Goethe which she devoured with speed and passion. Even though he could not supply her with some of the literature she was looking for – Jewish writers for example were more difficult to sell and were often not even in stock anyway - she said she was always open to his suggestions. He rejoiced in her willingness to read whatever author he recommended and could not wait for her to have read the books so he could bring her some more. He considered himself extremely lucky that no one in the book shop seemed to notice his loans.

Jonah Weissensteiner was very happy for Wilhelm to come to the workshop and supply his daughter with books. He had words with all the employees and promised them that they too could receive short visits like Greta and thanked them for their understanding. Jonah could be very persuasive when he chose to be and with the other workers on board, it was occasionally even possible for Wilhelm and Greta to have at least a little chat about the books before she had to return to her tasks. Jonah wanted Greta to find someone that liked her for herself and not only for her noticeably good looks. This young man had things in common with his daughter and treated her with respect, which was the most important quality he searched for in any potential son-in-law.

Wilhelm with his good looks could have his pick of the girls and his eyes were clearly set on Greta, which secretly made Jonah a very proud father.

"Does he not mind you being Jewish, that German book boy?" Jonah asked her one evening over dinner.

"I am not sure he even knows yet," Greta told him. "The way

he talks about the Jews, it doesn't seem to have any reference to me at all."

"How does he talk about the Jews?" Jonah said with raised eyebrows.

"He just mentions them in passing, like ... so and so is a Jew so we do not have his books in our shop. I don't think he has an opinion about it himself," Greta guessed.

"But the name Weissensteiner, that is a Jewish name! He must know," insisted Jonah. "I often wished we could have changed that. It would make life easier, wouldn't it?"

"It only sounds Jewish to you because you know that it is," disagreed Greta. "It could pass as a German name to a naïve young man, which I think Wilhelm just might be."

"In that case you should bring the matter up soon before this 'book lending' goes any further," Jonah lectured.

"He seems very smitten with you my darling daughter. It wouldn't hurt to get it out of the way before you waste any more of your time on him or any of his time on you, unless of course you were only in it for the books?"

"No I am not just in it for the books father," she admitted. "I like him. I think I really like him. He is very interesting. He thinks a lot."

"Oh he thinks a lot does he?" Jonah said, with a little sarcasm in his voice. "Then it is important that he learns to do something as well, thinking alone will only give him a headache."

"Do you like him father?" Greta asked, ignoring his previous statement.

"Does it matter if I like him? You must like the goy and make sure he does not mind your family," her father warned. "I'll like him enough if he makes you happy; even if he thinks all day until his head hurts. If a thinker you want, then a thinker you shall have. You have the pick of the men, my beautiful. Trust me. Make sure you choose a good man and that you do really like him."

"I do like him, father. He seems such a gentle man from what I can tell from our short meetings but I still need to get to know him better," she admitted.

"You take as long as you like to make up your mind. I hope you realise that he has already made up his mind about you. It is written all over his face how enchanted he is. He could accuse you of playing with him if you let him visit this often and your decision is not the one he hopes for. You must not lead him on. Be careful, you know, because I don't think we need to wait much longer for a proposal from this one."

"I am not so sure. There are plenty of girls who make eyes at him, maybe he just loves talking about books. That could be all he wants from me," Greta said more to herself than to her father.

"Yes, if you were a fifty-year-old librarian that probably would be all," Jonah said with a roaring laugh. "Why is he not content talking about his Goethe with the old men in his book shop then? I tell you why, they are not his type. Always remember that men of his young age mainly think with their loins. Once they have satisfied such needs, they may not be interested in your views on books anymore and go back to the shop to discuss literature there. An attractive girl like yourself always needs to choose wisely."

"I don't think he is like that, he is so serious," Greta defended.

"Yes he is serious, the Germans often are. Now let's hope his seriousness is good for something and makes him worthy of you," Jonah laughed.

Like in other regions of Czechoslovakia, there were a lot of ethnic Germans in Bratislava at this time. They often appeared like a closed circle, even though that was far from the truth. One part of these ethnic Germans were Austrians, many of whom had only recently arrived here and now found themselves stuck in the remains of what used to be a part of their glorious Habsburg Empire. Other Germans in the region were settlers from the German Empire who had moved there over the course of many centuries. Both groups moved in separate circles.

Wilhelm's Teutonic family roots had helped him to get his job at 'Mohr & Kling'. The Slovak population was generally friendly, if somewhat distant towards the Germans, but the communities did not mingle much.

Formerly known as Upper Hungary, the eastern provinces of Czechoslovakia also harboured large numbers of Hungarians who were less popular with the locals, were seen more of a threat and were considered as unwelcome aliens. By the time that the new state of Czechoslovakia had come into existence, many of them had already returned to Hungary to avoid an existence as a minority. After the Great War, international lobbying by Czechs and Slovaks in exile had persuaded the Allies to create this new state. The massive German population in the Czech border regions needed to be neutralized which was why Slovakia was separated from Hungary for the first time in centuries and added to the new state, where Germans and remaining Hungarians were now comfortably outnumbered by the combined total of Czech and Slovak citizens.

For the first time, the Slovaks had their own recognised region and their politicians were eager to use this historical moment and achieve more self-rule than they had been used to under Habsburger rule. Understandably the Slovakians longed to become an equal partner with the Czechs. In their view, the Germans were a harmless minority and not a serious threat to their cause. Political parties representing the German minorities were becoming more vocal of late, but this was mainly felt in the Czech part of the country, especially Prague or near the borders in the Sudetenland. Bratislava was little affected by these politics and remained the somewhat sleepy capital of a Slovakia that was quietly focused on its overdue independence.

The problem of anti-Semitism had never been exclusively associated with the Germans and was present in all regions of the state, but Bratislava had a large Jewish population that seemed widely tolerated. It was certainly not a foregone conclusion that Wilhelm would object to Greta's roots. After the Great War many Jewish refugees had fled the Russian pogroms and had swamped Central and Eastern Europe where they had received few welcomes.

The way Wilhelm had spoken about the Jewish intellectuals and writers had been both respectful and factual, and made Greta optimistic about a future with him. Still she kept delaying telling him more details about her family. The Weissensteiners were originally from the neighbouring Carpathian Ruthenia, part of the North Hungarian Oberland, that since the end of the war belonged to the Ukraine. There the family had conversed in Yiddish in their settlement, or shtetl, and in German in their home, but they also had learnt to speak Hungarian and Russian. Jonah Weissensteiner had spent large parts of his childhood in a Jewish shtetl, which existed separately to the Russian, Ukrainian or Polish communities and villages in the region. His family moved to Slovakia long before the Great War because there was not enough demand for weaving work and because it seemed wise to his father to be further away from Russia with its growing anti-Semitism and political instability.

As the only Jews in their new, rural setting the Weissensteiners were tolerated well enough. Jonah was a good craftsman and earned the respect of the villagers. He made sure to appear as unorthodox as possible. He celebrated only a few Jewish holidays, and unlike other Jews, he observed the Sunday and Catholic holidays. Jonah had picked up the local language in Slovakia very quickly. Greta and her siblings had already been born here and they were fluent in German, the Slovak dialect and learned Hungarian and Russian which helped with the business. The family observed the Sabbath because – as Jonah said - as long as he could afford it, he loved a day off.

Their diet was not kosher and they only sporadically went to a synagogue, which was too far away to attend the Sabbath service and not violate the travel restrictions. Some of the other Jews they had met at the congregation were outraged with the apparent lack of faith or discipline and accused the Weissensteiner family of opportunistic assimilation without acknowledging their own roots. Such disagreements were nothing new to Jonah and he had become an expert at avoiding answering any provocative questions. He knew that it was common in exile minorities to preserve their unity by sticking to the dogma because they felt they could not afford to deviate from it in hostile territories. Oberlander Jews were particularly notorious for their orthodox beliefs and many of them had pressured Jonah's father and his family to stick to their own kind and be part of their orthodox-leaning community.

Just like his father before him, Jonah refused to give in to such pressure on principle. For him, Judaism had always been a personal search to find the right way and whether it was a neighbour or a Rabbi, Jonah would always personally decide whether they were right or wrong.

After the war, Jonah had taken his family from the rural home in the Trnava province and had moved to Bratislava. Without the connections to the Hungarian trade across the border, he thought his business would be safer in a bigger city. Bratislava was not only the biggest city in the Slovak part of the new republic, it was also historically the only city - in what was then Hungary - that allowed Jews civil rights; everywhere else Jews were only tolerated or, at most, were given the right to practice their faith. Kaiser Joseph II had made protective statements for the Jews in Vienna and the Austro-Hungarian Empire; it was called the Edict of Toleration but executed law and order in the provinces had not always followed this liberal guidance.

Over the centuries Bratislava had become an island within widespread anti-Semitic sentiment and had attracted a large Jewish community from all over eastern Europe. Not trusting that deep rooted prejudice and hatred could be erased by modern laws, Jonah's main aim was to blend in when they got to the city and to not be noticed as Jews. Too close an association with the Jewish community might attract unwanted attention and damage his business, which was why he chose not to set up shop in the Jewish quarters of the city. In the 1921 census he avoided the issue by using a loophole; he did not declare his family as being of 'Jewish Nationality' but wrote that his mother tongue was German and so by the rules of the census form his nationality must be German.

Jonah was well informed about the political situation in Nazi Germany and its potential implications for Jews in Czechoslovakia. In his view it could only be advantageous for Greta to have a German boyfriend. The boycott of Jewish products was starting to make life difficult for Jews in Germany. If this started to spread over here, having a German passport and husband, especially one that did not seem to mind her heritage, could be good for the entire family.

Greta was a hopelessly romantic girl. Wilhelm knew this much from her book choices. When it came to girls he was admittedly less of a romantic at heart and more of a slave to his own raging and tormented hormones. He had convincingly played the enchanted lover to Greta, read her poetry and wrote passionate long love letters which he inserted in the books he kept giving her. Before long, he had managed to make her fall in love with him, yet his own feelings were still a little ambiguous.

Greta interested him as a person, that much was true. She was intelligent and wise but as important as her love for books was to him, he was becoming painfully aware that this had become an increasingly smaller part of her appeal. He respected her and found her ideas on literature very impressive but in his relationship with her his physical needs became soon the most important factor. So it turned out that he did not mind her Jewish heritage at all when she finally told him on his next visit to the workshop, following her father's orders to do so. She confessed that since the official census the family was officially known to the state as Lutheran Germans but there was always a danger that their lie might be uncovered.

To her relief Wilhelm was not in the least worried about any of this. When Greta commented how unusual it was to find a man who was so relaxed about the Jewish issue he curtly replied that he had once heard rumours that it was the Jews who had caused the crash at Wall Street but that meant nothing to him at all, especially since it was hardly Greta's doing what had happened over there.

Blissfully ignorant of most prejudices against the Jews he could not find anything wrong with his sweetheart. The closer and more 'intimate' the two of them grew, the less he wanted to hear about it. He knew that her family had not much money, so they had certainly nothing to do with the 'nasty Jewish financiers and bankers' that everyone so hated. She was simply the most attractive woman he had ever known, her eyes were seductive and her beauty taunting. All he wanted to talk about that afternoon was what it would feel like to be alone with her and spend a night with her. Nothing else mattered to him. At any other time she might have found his remarks rude or offensive but on that particular day she was too relieved to take offence and see the shallowness behind them.

He didn't have to wait very long for his 'curiosity' to be satisfied. Now that they knew he was kosher, her father encouraged her to progress with this relationship and she possessed none of the inhibitions other young women of her age were plagued with. Wilhelm bombarded her with compliments and declarations of eternal love and his hypnotic blue eyes made her melt in his arms. Before long they were kissing by the church wall after work. Soon kissing became only the first part of their amorous games and within a few months they consummated their passion, hiding in his family's farm barn on Sundays when everyone else in the house had gone to church. He claimed he had to go to work for an inventory which raised no suspicions whatsoever. Wilhelm was known as a keen worker and as he had not told anyone about Greta, his cover story was coherent with his usual dedication to the shop.

The Winkelmeiers were not even aware of her existence. Wilhelm did not want to become the laughing stock of his brothers, who were not very romantic and who would only talk dirtily about girls when they were in their own company. Wilhelm was far less romantic than Greta but compared to his brothers he was certainly a gentleman. Conversations amongst the siblings about his feelings were out of the question.

The length of his stay in Czechoslovakia had also never been decided, which made her being Jewish not a pressing matter. Wilhelm's family had come from Berlin to Bratislava in 1931 after the Great Depression. There were no jobs and no money for the men in the family in Berlin and so Wilhelm's father, Oskar, decided that the best place to survive would be with their relatives in the country where food was often more available in times of famine. Oskar had a cousin called Klaus Winkelmeier in Brno but Klaus and his family were struggling to survive and organized for Oskar, his wife Elizabeth and their children to live with another cousin, Benedikt, who owned a farm near Bratislava and who, assured Klaus, could easily accommodate and feed their Berlin relatives as long as they could help out on the farm.

Benedikt was an arrogant patriarch and anxious to preserve his status, from the very first day he treated the family as intruders. Initially, Oskar found that very trying but he managed to keep his head down and quickly began to enjoy the developing camaraderie between himself and Benedikt. Having been unemployed for a while, he appreciated the physical sensation of hard work and the way it made him feel like a real man again. He gradually earned Benedikt's respect for his strength and the effort he put into his work. Benedikt gradually started to trust him with bigger tasks and Oskar was always eager and proud to prove himself worthy.

Oskar's other two sons, Ludwig and Bernhard, were also a huge help to Benedikt, who had only two daughters and a teenage son, all of who could help with some of the lighter farm work but not with the really heavy loads. It was a relief for Benedikt not having to hire so many strangers for the season. You never knew how reliable these workers were and if any of them had long fingers or would try to get fresh with his daughters.

Benedikt's farm was in a good location and he was renting out some of his machinery to another farm which brought in additional income. Having family staying, for which he only had to provide food and accommodation, was very convenient. It also meant that

Benedikt's wife, Johanna, could stop wasting all of her time in the kitchen and do more of the regular housework like sewing and cleaning which she had lately neglected.

Oskar's wife Elizabeth was known for her expertise in the kitchen and took over those tasks. In addition, she taught Johanna's girls, Maria and Roswitha, a few tricks in that department that could come in handy when they were looking for husbands at some point in the future. The girls were still a few years away from the courting age but they had both inherited the good looks from their mother, who despite her sometimes harsh and bitter facial features was still able to turn admiring heads on the street.

Maria was the older of the two sisters and at seventeen probably the one Benedikt had to be protective over the most. She had completed her eight years of compulsory education at the German school in Bratislava and was now back at home helping full time on the farm. Her grades had been above average but Benedikt did not believe in educating her any further than necessary. She was beautiful enough to hope for a good marriage, especially with her links to a well-run farm and as the oldest child, he had naturally treated her with the harshest discipline so that she could be used as an example to the younger ones. The effect of this on Maria was that she had learnt to keep her mouth shut at all times and to always do as she was told. She spoke little, sat with her head down and appeared grateful for any attention she was given.

Any young farmer would be lucky to have such an obedient and hardworking wife, Benedikt often thought, and he felt incredibly proud of forming her character so successfully.

Maria however was far from being a happy girl even though she never complained. From early childhood, she had learned that this would get her nothing but a few slaps and humiliation from her parents. The rough treatment had beaten most of her personality out of her and unlike many of her friends at school, she felt completely useless and empty inside. Most of them were not the children of farmers but the offspring of rich landowners and skilled tradesmen. They never accepted this wallflower in their midst and ridiculed her for smelling of cows and horses. Even when she got good grades, the other students laughed about her outside the school building, screaming that she was empty in her head and that was why she could remember everything that they had been taught in the lessons so well.

In comparison, her younger sister Roswitha was outgoing, lively and always appeared to be happy, even though this too was not quite the case. At fifteen she had suffered two years less of the severe punishments than Maria and she had very quickly learned from her older sister's behavioural mistakes and become more compliant and submissive.

Roswitha was not as pretty as Maria and she was much slower at farm work and in school. She did however look much happier than Maria; she smiled more because she had realised that it was possible to charm people with a pleasant demeanour and they were more likely to give her attention if she seemed obliging. She enjoyed working as long as she was able to chat and socialize, unlike her sister who preferred to be left alone. Roswitha loved it best when the whole family was working in a field together and her happiest moments were the evenings when everyone was gathered around the wood stove in the living room and someone told tales or sang. She hated to be alone and when Wilhelm's family moved to the farm she was delighted to give up her room for the boys and to share with Maria.

Both girls were picture perfect blonde specimens of Aryan beauty, even though Roswitha's hair was much darker than Maria's. The sisters were not very close to each other which was due to Maria's almost permanent silence. Roswitha could talk for the two of them and would tell her sister everything there was to say about her life but she could not get through the quiet and blank exterior.

Maria was very grateful for the attention but somehow felt too timid, vacuous and uninterested to share much of her own life; she was often simply too unsure what would be expected of her and what might be an appropriate reply. Nothing ever happened to her anyway, so what could she tell that could compete with the elaborate stories of her sister?

Roswitha did not know how to read these silences. She carried on talking regardless and, in the absence of protests, hoped this to be fine but the one-sided nature of their conversation did not allow for much closeness between the two of them.

Now that both girls were back from school they were even less likely to have anything interesting happening to them. Their lives were dull and monotonous. A few excursions to the market with their mother were all they ever were treated to and even those trips were performed under time pressure and strict adult supervision.

The local country youth was mainly Slovak and the girls would have felt out of place trying to socialize with them. Benedikt warned them to stay away from the boys in the village. His daughters should try and find German husbands and he was concerned that the youth around here might persuade them otherwise. To meet fellow Germans they would have had to go into Bratislava, here in the rural areas there were only Slav peasants.

Their brother, Gunther, was the youngest of the three children and at the age of fourteen he was already regarded as a weakling in his parent's eyes, much better off at school than inefficiently wrestling with the heavy and physically demanding farm work that he was so clearly not cut out for. Gunther was intelligent and would probably make a much better living than his father one day; he was best advised to earn his money with his brain rather than with his two left hands and with the arrival of the Berlin relatives there was an opportunity for the boy to fulfil this dream without causing a labour shortage on the farm.

Gunter was actually much stronger than Benedikt gave him credit for but in the latter's macho male ideas of a boy of his age, he would always fall short of expectations and without fail would be made aware of these disappointments. This permanent criticism had robbed the lad of all his confidence and without a chance of ever catching up with his father's demands, he had long stopped even trying. It had never been spoken about but it was clear that Gunter would neither inherit the farm nor even ever work on it later in his life. Benedikt had used him as little as possible as help, worrying that he would constantly have to check anything Gunter had done to ensure that no mistakes had been made. With the arrival of the Berlin boys the heat was definitely off him. Oskar's sons, Ludwig and Bernhard, filled the role of farm hands effortlessly and far beyond Benedikt's already high standards. The farmer loved to instruct the two physically strong boys in the farm work and to see finally the results of his coaching in the way he wished his own son could have done; the fact that the Berlin boys were much older did not matter. In his view, Gunter was a failure of the highest order, always had been and that shame would stay with his father forever.

Benedikt also thought that Wilhelm was a bit of a weakling and probably not much use at the farm. His mother, Elizabeth, had suggested right away that he should maybe find work in a library or a bookshop as he was so fond of reading and with the help of some people at the German club, Wilhelm was soon set up at the bookshop and even managed slightly to supplement the farm income with his salary. Wilhelm was away from the farm for most of the day and was hardly ever even noticed. That suited Benedikt very well; Wilhelm was the only handsome son of his cousin and he did not want his daughters to get any wrong ideas. Wilhelm was not ever likely to run the farm either, so the less the girls saw of him the better.

Despite their different backgrounds, the two Winkelmeier families bonded surprisingly well. Johanna was a very cold woman and not comfortable as the female leader of the clan but Elizabeth took on the role as the warm and giving heart of house and kitchen to whom the girls came with questions and their problems. For the first time in its history, the house started to have a friendly feel to it. Elizabeth hated shouting and arguing and she always tried to bring people back together rather than stirring things up like Johanna was used to doing.

The attention starved Roswitha loved that there was a person on the farm that made time for her and seemed to like her without any conditions attached. The more introvert Maria on the other hand was just relieved that she no longer had to help her mother in the kitchen. Although Benedikt had ordered the two girls to learn everything that they could from the new domestic boss, Elizabeth was not interested in pressurizing anyone into something they did not want to do and so she let Maria quietly steal herself back to the fields, where the girl could be as isolated as she wanted to be and so suffer less from the social pressures on the farm. Gunter was also extremely pleased about the new developments on the farm, mainly because of the superior cooking. All three children were content with the new situation and Benedikt's wife Johanna was relieved too that a competent woman had taken all these unwanted tasks off her hands. She did not form a strong bond with Elizabeth but was polite and thankful to her – much more than Benedikt would have expected from his otherwise cold and closed wife.

Oskar and his boys obeyed the laws of the ruling patriarch and accepted his role as teacher and leader without the slightest hint of questioning his authority, which pleased Benedikt no end. Everyone seemed happy.

After only a few times of her and Wilhelm meeting in the barn, Greta became pregnant and the young Prussian – despite his feelings towards her still being a little unsure - decided to do the right thing by her and proposed. Now that fate or bad luck had tied him to the bibliophile woman he became aware of the reasons behind his earlier hesitations.

Greta was more of a muse and a fantasy lover to him than a woman he would have chosen to marry. Too many practicalities were speaking against it and he did not even know if she could cook and be a good wife. It was his code of honour that forbade him walking away from her now. They got married in a civil ceremony in 1934 with little Karl already showing through her wedding dress.

Wilhelm's family was not particularly pleased with this marriage either but felt it only right that no Winkelmeier child should ever be brought up a bastard. When Wilhelm told the family about her background, Oskar had raised the issue of having a Jewish wife in these difficult times but Elizabeth made him see that the damage was already done and that there was no other Christian way out of this situation. A Christian solution was not necessarily something that would have mattered to Benedikt, but he was fond of the idea of grandchildren and the continuation of the family. The sooner this process began, the more he would be able to personally pass on and mould the next generation; a thought that was dear to someone who was so self-loving and arrogant, and so he gave his blessing. Besides, the bride was not an official Jew and her presence would destroy any ideas his daughters might have about the handsome young book seller.

After the wedding, Greta and Wilhelm lived together in a small room on the farm and soon after the birth of their son, when she was not nursing little Karl, Greta was called upon to help on the farm. Having been brought up so liberally by her father, she initially found it difficult to adjust to the new harsh climate where Benedict dictated what would be done and where she had the lowest part in the female pecking order. Working in the fields would have taken her too far away from Karl, so for most of the day she was made to cook and clean. Greta hardly managed to read, so exhausted was she in the evenings. She had to take orders from both Johanna and Elizabeth and while the latter was gentle and caring, the former could not have given a damn about the 'Jewish whore' who had trapped 'her' beloved handsome Berlin boy into marriage.

Wilhelm got promoted to assistant buyer at his book shop, a favour to the family out of respect for his new role as young father. He came home even later every day and then still had to read or work till late at night. Jonah had offered for them to live with him in Bratislava at the workshop, but Johanna and Elizabeth both were heavily opposed to the young family living with Jews. For the sake of peace and with one eye on the political situation in Germany, the Weissensteiners agreed that the farm would be a much safer place for the little boy to grow up.

Greta was able to see her sister and family at most once a week. When everyone else went to church on Sunday mornings, she was allowed to walk into town with the little one. Elizabeth and Oskar were not very religious but succumbed to the continuous social pressure from Benedikt and Johanna, who said that village life revolved entirely around church attendance. If you wanted to be part of the community, or at least find buyers for your goods, you had to stay friendly and always show your face at church. The rural population was incredibly devoted to Catholicism and it was best to go at least to be seen regardless of your actual beliefs, which in the case of the Winkelmeiers were Lutheran.

Hardly any of the locals knew them more than by name and no one ever came to visit apart from those farmers that borrowed or rented Benedikt's equipment, but keeping up appearances could never harm. Elizabeth and Oskar gave in to this logic and made their children go regularly to mass as well, but they didn't quite dare to ask Greta to come to church too.

Only Johanna tried to persuade Greta to convert. She found an unlikely ally in this campaign in Jonah Weissensteiner, the father of the bride. He felt that a family should be all of one faith and go to church or the temple in unison. When Wilhelm pointed out that the Winkelmeiers were actually not even Catholic but Lutherans, he shrugged and said why could they not convert, after all they were already going to the services, it should not make any difference to them.

Lutherans at that time were particularly unpopular in Slovakia because the politicians in Prague appeared to favour them. There was already a lot of ill feeling towards the government because it consisted mainly of members of the dominant Czech half of the country and the resentment was transferred to the innocent Protestants.

Johanna caught on to Jonah's idea and suggested immediately that her family should all convert together. It would ingratiate them deeply in to the local community and one could always do with some allies among the neighbours.

Greta refused to convert, saying that she felt it wrong to commit herself to a church she did not believe in, but since she was not a very committed Jewess either she declared herself happy to attend some of the church services. Since those occurred at the one time a week that Greta had been allowed to visit her family in Bratislava, she asked to be excused from at least a few services so she would be able to carry on with the visits to the workshop.

Johanna noticed how weak Greta sounded when she voiced this request and it seemed a good opportunity to try and bargain further with the young mother. Would Greta be prepared to have Karl baptised - after all it would do wonders for his future if he was raised in the predominant faith of the region? Greta said she would leave that up to Wilhelm. If he felt strongly enough to support Johanna's suggestions then she would happily go along with it. Secretly she was sure Wilhelm would never agree to such a silly idea and such an obvious sucking up to the local church members. However, to her surprise Wilhelm was very enthusiastic with the plan. His superior at the book shop, Herbert Kling, came from the Catholic Bavaria and had often commented on him not having had a church wedding. Wilhelm had laughed it off with much appreciated rude comments about the bride not being able to wear white at the wedding and refusing to walk down the aisle in a different coloured dress, but it was made clear to him that if he converted to Catholicism and baptised his son Karl, it would be appreciated and his career prospects would be much stronger.

To everyone's surprise the local priest seemed the first real hurdle. He was not particularly happy for any of them to convert and was certainly not prepared to baptise them without a series of harsh conditions. Father Bernhard Haslinger was of the old guard and demanded that they should all attend regular catechism lessons for several months during which he would test their current knowledge of the Bible and then teach them in detail the differences between the two branches of Christianity. He also scolded them for having gone to Catholic Church so frequently when in fact they were not of the right faith. In his book that was as blasphemous as eating meat on a Friday.

Benedikt found it hard to keep his anger in check and to let the priest carry on with his sermon, but Johanna and Elizabeth made up for his offensive body language by throwing admiring glances at the priest, playing up to his own grand vision of himself as the wise and charitable saviour of these poor souls before him.

Wilhelm and his father Oscar kept quiet and when put on the spot, they showed their lack of knowledge without any attempts to hide it or even make excuses for it. Father Haslinger was enraged whenever he saw the depths of their ignorance and ordered them to do homework. He knew that it was the women who were behind this whole conversion idea and if the men were ready to take on the new faith, he wanted to make sure they had to work for it. It shouldn't be made easy for anyone to convert and receive the reward of salvation. Baptism was a privilege and its right should be earned.

When the date of their baptism was near, Johanna mentioned little Karl to the priest and asked him if - after his father Wilhelm had become a Catholic – it would be possible to baptise Karl too? Father Haslinger thought about this for a while and then he said he would only do so if Karl's mother was a Catholic too.

Johanna immediately saw where this was going and in a desperate attempt to hide from the priest that Greta was a Jew she said, yes, the mother was kind of a Catholic, but she had only been baptised, had not been raised in the faith after that and had not received her confirmation. Elizabeth stared in disbelief at such speedy lying but Oskar punched her gently in the side to signal that she had to go along with it.

"I will personally see to it that she receives the sacrament if she is willing to. I can't have a little Catholic boy raised by a non-believer. It would not be in God's will," Father Haslinger stated with seriousness in his eyes and turned to leave.

Johanna rolled her eyes behind his back and then addressed him with as much humbleness that she could muster without laughing. "You are too kind. Of course you are right. I will speak to the mother."

Greta was shocked when she heard the proposal by Johanna.

"You want me to pretend I am baptised so I can learn about Catholicism and convert, just so that my son can be baptised as well? That is a lot of lying and effort for something so unimportant. Will your God not punish you for all this deceit of a priest?" she said.

"It must be better in his eyes than remaining Protestant or Jewish," Johanna replied.

"Do you really think that it will make such a difference in the community? No one is interested in Germans, regardless of their religion," Greta guessed.

"I think it will make a big difference with the locals. It is not too much of an effort. We have all just taken that stupid course, so don't worry about the studying. We all can help you with the preparation. After that you only need to go to church once in a while, just like before," Johanna assured her. "Who knows when we might need the help of our neighbours. It can't be wrong to make more friends and get the locals to see us as peers and fellow church goers and not just as rich German land owners. The Catholics love seeing someone come onto the right path with them. We'd have the Father as an ally which is good and the congregation hangs on his every word."

Soon Greta gave in and went to the lessons, even though it meant she had to give up even more of her precious little spare time allotted to reading. Father Haslinger was less strict with her than he had been with the others. He was quite aware that Greta was not doing this for herself but for her son and he admired nothing more than a selfless mother. Unlike in his other lessons, he was incredibly patient and gave her much less homework than he had done with the other Winkelmeiers. He was content as long as she could recite some prayers and knew the main parts of the Catholic Church service and, of course, how to confess her sins. In his eyes, this woman had singlehandedly shown more dedication and Christian spirit than her whole family.

"Greta, the only thing I would dearly ask you to do now is to get married in a Catholic Church service. It pains me to see you living in sin in the eyes of God. Everyone in the village assumed you were married in a different church in town, but now that I know you only went to the registry office, I don't feel this is right. Once you are both Catholic you should seek the right blessing for your union. I can do it secretly so you won't have the shame of being exposed. You know that in the eyes of your God it needs to be done."

"You will need to speak to my husband and his family. If they are happy with it then so am I." Greta said, quietly accepting her fate.

"That is very good of you. What about your own family? Why did they never carry on with their faith?" the priest asked.

"My father converted to Catholicism for my mother. When she died of the Spanish flu he was very upset and neglected his duties," she said, reciting her well-rehearsed lie. "He was very modern in his thinking."

"What a shame," Father Haslinger responded. "Especially when in the midst of pain and sorrow one should look up to Him for guidance and find faith, not lose it."

A few months later Greta went through the absurd charade of being confirmed one day and getting married the next, all in secret, and lacking all the formal foundations as well as all the ones of true faith. When she had her mandatory confession before both sacraments, she had to omit so much of her lying and other sins that she thought she should have been struck down by lightning if this Catholic God really cared that much.

Father Haslinger congratulated her with tears of joy in his eyes and welcomed the whole Winkelmeier family into the Catholic community. The whole affair had one big advantage, Father Haslinger gave Karl and Greta an official accreditation as non-Jews, adding their names into the church's lists of the faithful, something that was always handy in these days of potentially renewed pogroms.

However, Greta soon had a rude awakening when she found herself continuously pressured into going to church. This happened more or less every Sunday - despite the sworn promises that she would still be able to regularly see her family during that time. In their longing to become integrated into the community, Johanna and Elizabeth both insisted that the whole family displayed the strength of their faith and their belonging to the church. Nothing would make that point stronger than if they could all show up together every Sunday without fail. Johanna especially argued further that the locals had to know about young Karl and start to see him as one of their local church community. If the stigma of being a half Jew could be put to rest at all then it could probably only be achieved by showing him at church time after time. In trade for this concession, Greta was granted the right to see her family on some Saturdays which her father often still managed to spend in the Jewish tradition of not working or travelling.

Wilma was always incredibly happy to see her and the two sisters spent the days exchanging gossip. Greta told her about the Winkelmeiers and how their new belonging to the Catholic Church had probably made them more of a laughing stock amongst the local community than the respected citizens they had intended to become. Wilma laughed when she saw Greta impersonating her new family and their behaviour during mass, the over acted facial expressions, the loud singing of hymns and the passionate and exaggerated head nodding during the sermon. Admittedly, some of the other church members needed to express their faith with equal intensity and exhibitionism, but surely everyone else had to find this as ridiculous as Greta and her sister did.

Wilma told her about the news at the weaver workshop where business had picked up again. A former Hungarian countess had taken up residency in a large manor house outside of Bratislava and had ordered two massive hand-woven wall carpets, including one depicting her family history and another that displayed a variety of Bible figures. Jewish people were not supposed to be involved in the manufacture of symbols of the Christian faith as far as the Church and local law were concerned, so there was a little bit of a risk involved, but it was too much of an opportunity to turn down. The project meant that all three remaining Weissensteiners would have to weave continuously on these two commissioned works and leave the hired help to oversee the looms all by themselves. For the next few months the family would earn a lot and Jonah was positive that the display of his work in such a reputable home would bring in more custom, which was why they had to work doubly hard to make sure they delivered immaculate carpets to the best of their ability.

The Countess fancied herself as the sponsor of traditional and modern art alike and frequently came to the workshop to instruct Jonah with her latest ideas and last minute changes to the agreed designs. Despite being a tough business woman during negotiations, she also became a kind and a warm hearted friend, and she adored Greta and her little boy Karl. She took a strong personal interest in the entire family without ever letting anyone come too close. There was never a mentioning of a husband or a Count and the ageing woman exuded a strong air of in-approachability on the subject matter and so no one ever asked her about it. Her status and riches were intimidating and helped her to keep a distance whenever she wanted.

One of the young girls in Jonah's employ had asked for a raise during that period as the work would be so boring. Jonah was outraged at her cheek, but the girl was sure that it would not be possible for Jonah to find a sufficiently qualified or trained replacement for her on such short notice now that the big order had been placed. Jonah had agreed to the raise but he had immediately written to some of his fellow tradesmen seeking to replace the cheeky and greedy woman. The Countess also supplied him with a few addresses of craftsmen she thought might be able to help him out.

The rich aristocrat loved to join Greta and Wilma when they talked about the books they had read or wanted to read and she frequently made recommendations. Sadly, Wilhelm only brought books home for himself these days and only occasionally did he keep them at home long enough for Greta to have enough time to read them too. Wilma was, by nature often too restless to sit down and read a book but if she did read, it was always something her sister had chosen. Occasionally the Countess brought books from her own large library for the two sisters to read, emphasising how important it was for young ladies to have a sound knowledge of literature and the arts. When they were on their own, Greta and Wilma were often rather unladylike. They started a silly competition between them about who would grow the longest hair. Greta had a slight advantage as her hair was less thick and therefore easier to look after. Wilma's hair curled slightly and never seemed as long as Greta's because of its structure. They even got their brother Egon to use a piece of knitting wool and measure each woman's hair; when pulled, Wilma's hair was longer than it seemed but she never caught quite up with Greta all the same.

While Jonah played with his grandson and tried to teach him to talk, the women braided their hair and tried out different hair styles. Egon usually read a book by the window or in the winter on a bench by the oven. He didn't make much fuss about his sister or his nephew. He loved his sisters in his own way but he wished he had a brother with whom he could share his more scientific interests or with whom he could have pursued more manly pastimes. His sisters were a disappointment in these areas and, in his opinion, they fussed too much about everything. They usually talked too much as well.

At school Egon had found it difficult to socialize. When the family moved to Bratislava, all three children had been admitted to the German school. Greta had found it easiest to make new friends there because of her good looks. She also had only two years left at school when they moved and found the girls her age surprisingly mature and reasonable compared to some of the girls at her school in the countryside. Wilma, only a year younger than her sister, found friends through association with Greta. Her class mates knew that she had the protection of her older sister's friends and left her alone - even during her last year when Greta had already left the school. Egon on the other hand was the youngest and had to spend four long years at the school. He was not a great athlete and unfortunately in his age group, that had been the only way to earn the respect of his class mates. He was considered odd and had it not been for his excellent grasp of science and his willingness to let other boys copy his homework, he would have probably ended up having a much harder time. There was an unspoken truce between him and his class mates that allowed him to exist quietly without being picked on, but to strike up a proper friendship with anyone was not on the cards.

While they still lived out in the province, Egon had developed a strong bond with a Jewish boy named Daniel and after his mother had died in 1918 of the Spanish flu, had spent a lot of time with Daniel's family. Egon had been impressed by the philosophical approach which Daniel and his family had to death. This was only the beginning of further spiritual inspiration Egon received from his friend and gradually Egon had developed a surprisingly strong sense of being Jewish. He felt he could never tell his grief stricken father or sisters about it, who seemed to be coping fine without religious guidance. On Jonah's instructions, Egon attended the Protestant religious education classes at the German school - just like his sisters - and he was immediately intimidated by the obvious anti-Jewish teachings and sentiments in these classes. He was mortified that he should be found out and this further added to his difficulty in making friends.

When Jonah and his parents had lived in the shtetl in the

Ukraine, they always used to light the Sabbath candles, a habit that the weaver had carried on, more out of a sense of tradition rather than out of actual belief, when he had moved into the Trnava province. The Weissensteiner family had moved there before the big waves of Jewish immigration and were accepted as just another Ukrainian family. When the big mass exodus of Jews expelled from the Russians happened, many of those who arrived in Slovakia were orthodox and very noticeable; the anti-Semitic sentiment began to grow.

Wanting a better life for his family and not being discriminated against as he had seen happening to the new arrivals in Trnava, Jonah decided to hide his already only lukewarm faith completely when he arrived in Bratislava. Since he and his family were coming from a Slovak province and not from Russia directly, they were never questioned when they called themselves Protestants and with their language being assimilated too, they found themselves easily separated from the Jewish community. As they were not living in a Jewish quarter, Jonah had to abandon some of the traditions like lightning the Sabbath candles - very much to Egon's regret. The Jewish community however did notice them all the same. Especially in the early days of the workshops on Gajova, Orthodox Jews would visit and try to persuade Jonah and his family to come to the synagogue regularly. Jonah always treated them kindly and with generous hospitality, but stood firm on his decision not to practice his faith. He knew how dangerous it was to offend the very faithful of any religion and so he offered donations to the Jewish community to maintain friendly relations, explaining that he just did not feel comfortable in any religious community. Of course, this did not buy him the respect of the Rabbis, but the donations lessened the frequency and intensity of their visits, which was important to Jonah and his plans to remain religiously anonymous. It was suspicious enough that they made the girls in their employ work most Saturdays on their own with only minimal supervision from the Weissensteiner family, but so far the plan had worked and their secret was safe.

Jonah was particularly pleased about Greta's conversion to Catholicism and the prospects this would bring to his grandson Karl. If this was what society demanded from his child and grandson to treat them with the respect they deserved, then lying was a minor price to pay. To Jonah, the only thing that counted was your inner life and that, no one could control. He wished his other children would do the same. Wilma and Egon were very lethargic and seemed to have no interest in either a good or an exciting life. If only they would be interested in the other sex or at least go out from time to time and experience things. It seemed they would be staying at home with him for quite some time to come. Greta however was his pride and joy, and his hope. She could not come home often enough to satisfy Jonah's longing for her.

Whenever Greta came back home from such visits to her family in Bratislava, Johanna couldn't help herself and immediately found as many tasks for her to do as she could, just to show that the time away from the farm was like missed working hours that needed to be made up for. Johanna hoped this would discourage Greta from going away as often as she did, but the young mother possessed an abundance of patience and never showed any signs of rebellion against these orders. Elizabeth however, had more understanding and always managed secretly to save some food for Greta and Karl, knowing full well that there wouldn't have been much food to be had at the Weissensteiner house, especially ever since that mad and disorganised sister Wilma had become the one responsible for the domestic duties.

While Greta was being fed in the kitchen, Roswitha was always keen to play with little Karl and to carry him around. She cherished these moments during which she could be in charge of the little child.

In exchange for a smile and a little warmth, Maria was also happy to help out and she would assist Greta with those tasks that Johanna had compiled for her on her return. Since the start of these arrangements, Johanna had unwittingly created a team of deceivers in the four women and instead of punishing Greta for leaving, she had given her an opportunity to grow closer to the women of the farm. A real circle of friends had developed from which Johanna herself was excluded.

Johanna however persisted in her campaign to keep Greta from leaving the farm so often and started to suggest that it should be the Weissensteiners who should make the journey from now on – if they wanted to see so much of their Greta. The Winkelmeiers could not afford to spare her for such long periods of time anymore and, as far as Johanna was concerned, it just was not natural for a married woman to spend so much of her time with her old family. Elizabeth tried to intervene on Greta's behalf but Johanna was adamant, even though it was an obvious exaggeration. Benedikt could not care less and in order to be left alone he decided in favour of his wife's demands. From here on, the Weissensteiners would have to travel on the Sabbath to the farm or they would not get to see their beloved Greta…

Praise for The Luck of the Weissensteiners: "… powerful, engaging, you cannot remain untouched…" "Fischer deftly weaves his tapestry of history and fiction, with a grace…"

Amazon: http://smarturl.it/Weissensteiners
Goodreads: http://bit.ly/12Rnup8
Facebook: http://on.fb.me/1bua395
B&N: http://ow.ly/Btvas
Book-Likes: http://ow.ly/J4X2q
Rifflebooks: http://ow.ly/J4WY0
Trailer: http://studio.stupeflix.com/v/OtmyZh4Dmc

More Books by Christoph Fischer:

Sebastian
(Three Nations Trilogy: Book 2)

Sebastian is the story of a young man who has his leg amputated before World War I. When his father is drafted to the war it falls on to him to run the family grocery store in Vienna, to grow into his responsibilities, bear loss and uncertainty and hopefully find love. Sebastian Schreiber, his extended family, their friends and the store employees experience the 'golden days' of pre-war Vienna, the times of the war and the end of the Monarchy while trying to make a living and to preserve what they hold dear. Fischer convincingly describes life in Vienna during the war, how it affected the people in an otherwise safe and prosperous location, the beginning of the end for the Monarchy, the arrival of modern thoughts and trends, the Viennese class system and the end of an era. As in the first part of the trilogy, 'The Luck of The Weissensteiners' we are confronted again with themes of identity, Nationality and borders. The step back in time made from Book 1 and the change of location from Slovakia to Austria enables the reader to see the parallels and the differences deliberately out of the sequential order. This helps to see one not as the consequence of the other, but to experience them as the momentary reality as it must have felt for the people at the time.

Praise for Sebastian: "I fell in love with Sebastian…a truly inspiring read for anyone!!!!" – "This is a MUST read, INTELLIGENT, SENSITIVE, ENGAGING, PERFECT."

Amazon: http://smarturl.it/TNTSeb
Goodreads: http://ow.ly/pthHZ
Facebook: http://ow.ly/pthNy
B&N: http://ow.ly/Btvbw
Book-Likes: http://ow.ly/J4X8M
Rifflebooks: http://ow.ly/J4Xgv
Trailer: http://studio.stupeflix.com/v/95jvSpHf5a/

The Black Eagle Inn
(Three Nations Trilogy: Book 3)

The Black Eagle Inn is an old established restaurant and farm business in the sleepy Bavarian countryside outside of Heimkirchen. Childless Anna Hinterberger has fought hard to make it her own and keep it running through WWII. Religion and rivalry divide her family as one of her nephews, Markus has got her heart and another nephew, Lukas has got her ear. Her husband Herbert is still missing and for the wider family life in post-war Germany also has some unexpected challenges in store.

Once again Fischer tells a family saga with war in the far background and weaves the political and religious into the personal. Being the third in the Three Nations Trilogy this book offers another perspective on war, its impact on people and the themes of nations and identity.

Amazon: http://smarturl.it/TBEI
Goodreads: http://ow.ly/pAX8G
Facebook: http://ow.ly/pAX3y
Book-Likes: http://ow.ly/J4Xpp
Rifflebooks: http://ow.ly/J4XqX
Trailer: http://studio.stupeflix.com/v/mB2JZUuBaI/

In Search of a Revolution

In 1918 young Zacharias Nielsen boards a ship in Copenhagen to join the Red Guards in the Finnish Civil War. Encouraged by an idolised teacher with communist leanings, he follows the call for help from his Nordic Comrades, despite his privileged background.

His best friend, Ansgar, has opposing political ideals to Zacharias but, for his own personal reasons, finds himself soon stuck in the Scandinavian North with Zacharias and Raisa, a Finnish nurse who helps them in their new life.

Through the years that follow the brotherly war the trio see the political landscape in Finland and Europe change as Communists and Fascists try to make their mark and attempt to change the world order.

Our heroes must find their own personal and ideological place in these turbulent times as friendship, honour, idealism and love triangles bring out some personal truths.

The book spans almost thirty years of history and the various Finnish conflicts: Civil War, Winter War, Continuation War and the Lapland War. Watch the political and personal self-discovery of characters in search of their own revolution.

Amazon: http://ow.ly/MKNeu
Facebook: http://ow.ly/MKNf1
Goodreads: http://ow.ly/MKNfG
Book-Likes: http://ow.ly/MKNm5
Rifflebooks: http://ow.ly/MKNgc

Time to Let Go

Time to Let Go is a contemporary family drama set in Britain. Following a traumatic incident at work stewardess Hanna Korhonen decides to take a break from work and leaves her home in London to stay with her elderly parents in rural England. There she finds that neither can she run away from her problems, nor does her family provide the easy getaway place that she has hoped for. Her mother suffers from Alzheimer's disease and, while being confronted with the consequences of her issues at work, she and her entire family are forced to reassess their lives.

The book takes a close look at family dynamics and at human nature in a time of a crisis. Their challenges, individual and shared, take the Korhonens on a journey of self-discovery and redemption.

Amazon: http://smarturl.it/TTLG
Goodreads: http://ow.ly/BtKs7
Facebook: http://ow.ly/BtKtQ
Book-Likes: http://ow.ly/J4Xu0
Rifflebooks: http://ow.ly/J4XvR

Conditions
(Conditions Series: 1)

When Charles and Tony's mother dies the estranged brothers must struggle to pick up the pieces, particularly so given that one of them is mentally challenged and the other bitter about his place within the family.

The conflict is drawn out over materialistic issues, but there are other underlying problems which go to the heart of what it means to be part of a family which, in one way or another, has cast one aside.

Prejudice, misconceptions and the human condition in all forms feature in this contemporary drama revolving around a group of people who attend the subsequent funeral at the British South Coast.

Meet flamboyant gardener Charles, loner Simon, selfless psychic Elaine, narcissistic body-builder Edgar, Martha and her version of unconditional love and many others as they try to deal with the event and its aftermath.

Amazon: http://smarturl.it/CONDITIONSCFF
Goodreads: http://ow.ly/
Facebook: http://ow.ly/C0ZqX
Book-Likes http://ow.ly/J4Xzj
Rifflebooks: http://ow.ly/J4XBl

The Healer

When advertising executive Erica Whittaker is diagnosed with terminal cancer, western medicine fails her. The only hope left for her to survive is controversial healer Arpan. She locates the man whose touch could heal her but finds he has retired from the limelight and refuses to treat her. Erica, consumed by stage four pancreatic cancer, is desperate and desperate people are no longer logical nor are they willing to take no for an answer. Arpan has retired for good reasons, casting more than the shadow of a doubt over his abilities. So begins a journey that will challenge them both as the past threatens to catch up with him as much as with her. Can he really heal her? Can she trust him with her life? And will they both achieve what they set out to do before running out of time?

Amazon: http://ow.ly/J4Wt6
Facebook: http://ow.ly/J4Wun
Goodreads: http://ow.ly/J4Ww4
Book-likes: http://ow.ly/J4WxU
Rifflebooks: http://ow.ly/J4WzY

The Gamblers

Ben is an insecure accountant obsessed with statistics, gambling and beating the odds. When he wins sixty-four million in the lottery he finds himself challenged by the possibilities that his new wealth brings.

He soon falls under the influence of charismatic Russian gambler Mirco, whom he meets on a holiday in New York. He also falls in love with a stewardess, Wendy, but now that Ben's rich he finds it hard to trust anyone. As both relationships become more dubious, Ben needs to make some difficult decisions and figure out who's really his friend and who's just in it for the money.

Amazon: http://ow.ly/S5tJC
Facebook: http://ow.ly/S5tcQ
Goodreads: http://ow.ly/S5tmE
Booklikes: http://ow.ly/S5sU9
Rifflebooks.com http://ow.ly/S5t2W
Createspace: http://ow.ly/S5txM

Conditioned
(Conditions Series: 2)

CONDITIONED dives back into the world of gardener Charles, his friends and the state of his mental health - one year on. We meet loner Simon and his battle with the outside world, co-dependent Martha and her abusive husband Clive, neurotic poet Catherine on the verge of getting married, Tony, who finds his strange brother Charles a challenge, psychic Elaine looking for a new direction in life and quirky widow Sarah Roseberg who has a go at sorting out all of their problems.

CONDITIONS aimed to sensitise readers and make them think about tolerance and acceptance.

CONDITIONED wants readers to look beyond their attitude towards Conditions and examine what we all do and what we can do to overcome our challenges. The sequel is another snapshot of this circle of friends. Some will have improved their lives, others will not.

Amazon: http://ow.ly/UoUaL
Facebook: http://ow.ly/V4V7o
Goodreads http://ow.ly/V4UOT
Booklikes http://ow.ly/V4Vft
Rifflebooks.com https://read.rifflebooks.com/books/503357

Thanks and Further Reading

A big thank you to my sister Susanne Weigl, who went beyond all calls of duty to find out more information about Ludwika in Germany and make connections. It was her idea that I write the story.

Thanks to Bernice L. Roque for her valuable advice; Kurt Buck vom DIZ Emslandlager in der Gedenkstätte Esterwegen and David G from the National Archive in Kew.

Thanks also to my wonderful beta readers: Nancy Loderick, Joyce Whetherby and Susanne Weigl for their amazing feedback. Special thanks to Lorna Lee whose beta reading was as invested and involved as if it was her own project.

Thanks to David Lawlor for his excellent suggestions and his dedicated editing. Thanks to Daz Smith for yet another smashing cover design.

Thanks again to Ludwika's family who generously shared information and helped me to establish as much truth as possible. Thanks for your trust and the kind permission to use Ludwika's real name and data for the story. I hope this will help to make contact with more of your Polish relatives or people from the camps who know more about your mother's life.

Here is a list of books that I have found helpful:

Vasily Grossman: A Writer At War: Vasily Grossman with the Red Army 1941 – 1945

Max Hastings: All Hell Let Loose – The World at War 1939 – 1945

William I Hitchcock: Liberation – The Bitter Road to Freedom, Europe 1944-1945

Gitel Hopfeld: At the Mercy Of Strangers – Survival in Nazi-Occupied Poland

Ian Kershaw: The End: Germany 1944-1945

Keith Lowe: Savage Continent: Europe in the Aftermath of World War II

Ben Shephard: The Long Road Home: The Aftermath of the Second World War

Timothy Snyder: Bloodlands: Europe Between Hitler and Stalin

Dan Stone: The Liberation of the Camps: The End of the Holocaust and its Aftermath

Frederick Taylor: Exorcising Hitler: The Occupation and Denazification of Germany

A Short Biography

Christoph Fischer was born in Germany, near the Austrian border, as the son of a Sudeten-German father and a Bavarian mother. Not a full local in the eyes and ears of his peers he developed an ambiguous sense of belonging and home in Bavaria. He moved to Hamburg in pursuit of his studies and to lead a life of literary indulgence. After a few years he moved on to the UK where he now lives in a small town in West Wales. He and his partner now have only two Labradoodles to complete their family.

Christoph worked for the British Film Institute, in Libraries, Museums and for an airline. 'The Luck of The Weissensteiners' was published in November 2012; 'Sebastian' in May 2013 and The Black Eagle Inn in October 2013; 'Time to Let Go', his first contemporary work was published in May 2014; 'Conditions' in October 2014 and its follow up 'Conditioned' in October 2015. His medical thriller 'The Healer' was released in January 2015; 'In Search of a Revolution' in March 2015, and his thriller 'The Gamblers' in June 2015. He has written several other novels which are in the later stages of editing and finalisation.

Twitter:
https://twitter.com/CFFBooks
Pinterest:
http://www.pinterest.com/christophffisch/
Google +:
https://plus.google.com/u/0/106213860775307052243
LinkedIn:
https://www.linkedin.com/profile/view?id=241333846
Blog:
http://writerchristophfischer.wordpress.com
Website:
www.christophfischerbooks.com
Facebook:
www.facebook.com/WriterChristophFischer
Goodreads:
https://www.goodreads.com/book/show/23662030-the-healer
Amazon:
http://ow.ly/BtveY

Made in the USA
San Bernardino, CA
19 January 2016